THE PRODIGAL ONES

The One Who Rocked Away

JOANNA ALONZO

No part of this publication may be reproduced, distributed, or transmitted in any form or by any means, including copying, recording, or other electronic or mechanical methods, without the prior written permission of the author, except in the case of brief quotations embodied in critical reviews and certain other noncommercial uses permitted by copyright law.

This is a work of fiction. Names, characters, businesses, places, events and incidents are either the products of the author's imagination or used in a fictitious manner. Unless otherwise specified, any resemblance to actual persons, living or dead, or actual events are purely coincidental.

Copyright © 2018, 2020 Joanna Alonzo
All rights reserved.
ISBN: 9786219636476

Published by: Hineni Publishing
Editor: Anna E. Meyer
Cover Designer: Joanna Alonzo

CONTENTS

THE ONE WHO NEEDS TO THANK SOME PEOPLE

Thanks to this book's editor, Anna, for her kindness and generosity, as well as her continuous encouragement.

Thanks to my family for bearing with me throughout this process.

Thanks to this book's beta readers, Liwen, Anna, Elizabeth, Darlene, Tiffany, Jennifer, Peggy, and Hope for their invaluable feedback.

Thanks to Tamcat for his expertise on his expensive hobby.

Thanks to the Author of Life for enabling me to write. May each word be incense.

△.F.T.L.

To those with broken hearts,
their souls lost in midnight,
their eyes fixed on the stars.

I pray you find the courage and
strength to love and dream again.

THE ONE
WHO ROCKED
AWAY

This is a story
About making music,
And touching the supernatural.
About creating art,
And embracing the radical.
About taking risks,
And rejecting the typical.
About choosing love,
And forgiving the prodigal.

This is the story of childhood
            sweethearts,
      Nolan and Serene,
Who painted and played
      glimpses of heaven,
Lost themselves in
      all the fame and wonder,
And found themselves
      still longing to be together.

PRESENT DAY

CIRCA LATE 2000'S

one

THE ONE
WHO FOUND
A NEW RED

Losing Serene Sinclair was the best thing that happened to *Red & Ice* — at least that's what Nolan Stone's manager, Ramona, kept saying.

"You're the star of this duo, anyway," she said after finding out Serene had gone AWOL. "Serene's talented and gorgeous, but she's not for this industry. You, on the other hand—" Ramona eyed him from head-to-toe, then back. "How far are you willing to go to succeed at this, Stone?"

Desperate for something — anything — to distract him from Serene's absence, Nolan could only shrug in response. "How far do you want me to go?"

Ramona grinned. "Just you wait, Nolan Stone. Work hard at this, do what I tell you to do, and I promise you: you'll become a world-famous star."

From that point on, everything happened in lightning speed, and in it all, Ramona proved herself to be no liar. Within a few weeks of Serene leaving their tour and dumping Nolan, Ramona spun the entire thing to emphasize how Serene, his childhood sweetheart and former partner, had deeply wronged Nolan by leaving.

The broken-hearted rock star gave Ramona's PR Team an amazing angle to work with. By the strength of that premise alone, in a matter of days, Ramona secured a contract for a reality show on a major TV network: *The New Red*. They designed the show to capitalize on Nolan's broken heart, his qualms about faith, church culture, and Christianity, and his search for a girl able to replace Serene's spot in their musical duo, *Red & Ice*, perhaps even in his heart.

In a span of three weeks, they traveled from state to state, auditioning redheads, until they found Diana Rake in a small town in the middle of nowhere. She joined a group of twelve women hand-picked by Nolan — or at least that's what the network wanted the audience to believe. They shot the TV show soon after. Only months after Serene left *Red & Ice*, the network aired *The New Red*. The audience voted who they thought "The New Red" should be.

Nolan had held no doubt from the beginning Diana would win. In fact, they had conditioned the show to favor her. He and she started writing songs together even before the show aired.

Then came the evening when finally, the rest of the world would know: *Red & Ice* had found a new Red. The question on everyone's minds was whether Nolan Stone had found his new Red as well. The smile he pasted on his face as he stood backstage waiting to be presented by the TV show's host would convince the world he had moved on. He would use all the charisma and confidence he could muster to make sure of that, but Diana Rake — beautiful and talented as she was — could never be Serene Sinclair.

"Ladies and gentlemen, on their grand debut as the all-new and improved *Red & Ice*, Nolan Stone and Diana Rake!"

The audience's applause exploded across the studio as Nolan and Diana walked to the center of the stage. The main lights dimmed, allowing LEDs and neons to create an atmosphere accentuating the music.

"Break a leg." Nolan grinned at Diana as he picked up his electric guitar, Magenta, the same *Les*

Paul Serene had given him the same day she had rejected his wedding proposal.

"Be careful what you wish for, rock star." She smirked as she took her place behind the drum set. "You don't want me outshining you."

Nolan chuckled. "Arrogance." He strummed the first chord and positioned his mouth in front of the microphone.

Diana hit the cymbals.

Nolan sang the first song they had composed together: *Broken Thunder.*

The studio audience drank in every minute of the performance. The animated expressions on their faces as they responded to what Nolan and Diana were giving energized him in a way nothing else could. From the audience reaction alone, there was no questioning what a hit the new *Red & Ice* was. Their fans adored the new Red to Nolan's Ice. How could they not? They had voted for her. With the veiled manipulations of Nolan's label, they had chosen Diana to be their *New Red.*

The cascade of wild, red curls on Diana's head bounced and flew as she skillfully played the drums. Nolan drew a breath at how hot she looked. As he belted out his final note, he winked at her. She blushed.

His fingers skillfully maneuvered the strings of his guitar to arrive at a thunderous climax while Diana's cymbals gave the music the support it needed. There was no denying it. She was a lot better at this than Serene ever was, yet deep inside, despite how amazing the new Red was, Nolan couldn't stop pining for the old Red. The show made for a frenzied distraction from that painful reality.

The wild applause — the love coming from all these strangers — rocked Nolan into wave upon wave of exhilarated bliss as he gestured toward his new partner. Diana quickly made her way to him, stood by his side, and held his hand. They both bowed.

The part Nolan dreaded most followed.

The winding down.

Music always faded away into the silence, leaving Nolan behind, depleted and grappling with the aftermath. His jaw tightened as Diana squeezed his hand. Nolan let go of her and used the back of one hand to wipe the sweat from his brow, while he laid the other hand on the small of her back so they could take a seat on the couches at the center of the TV studio.

The show's host interviewed them after a short break, allowing them to recuperate after performing in front of a live studio audience.

"Your chemistry is off-the-charts!" The host took on this delighted expression on his face the moment the show came back on. "I mean, we all saw that in the show, but seeing you together in person, whew!" He fanned his face with his hand.

Nolan and Diana exchanged glances and laughed.

"It's him," Diana said. "Nolan is such a talented artist. He makes everything seem so easy, and with him, it is. Or at least it's a lot easier. He lightens everyone's load just by being himself."

"Play up the flirting, Nolan. She's giving you a lot to work with. Reciprocate." Ramona's voice in his ear piece almost made him jolt out of the couch.

Nolan cleared his throat and tried not to show discomfort on national TV. "Diana is being incredibly kind. She's a professional through and through, but she's more than that. Other than being talented, she's an amazing human being. I'm privileged to work with her."

"Doesn't hurt that she also looks the part, does it?" the host asked.

"That goes without saying. She's beautiful." Nolan addressed the audience. "Don't you think she's beautiful?!"

The audience yelled and applauded to signal their agreement.

The rest of the interview went on without a hitch, but not without Ramona's voice instructing both what to do.

By the time Nolan walked off stage, he wasn't even sure if Diana was into him or if the young progeny was like him: just following Ramona's instructions.

Nolan returned to the dressing room reserved for him and was about to get changed when Diana burst inside his room.

"I'm sorry," she said. "I know this is inappropriate, but Nolan, you can't keep leading me on like this. In the show and out of it, I've made it clear over and over again how into you I am. Why aren't we together?"

Before he could say anything, she marched up to him, threw her hands around him, and kissed him full on the mouth.

She awakened all his senses physically. His pulse raced. His mind whirled. But all it took was one glimpse of his guitar to remember Serene, and everything halted.

He pulled away from Diana.

She gasped.

Nolan shook his head. "I'm sorry. I'm still not over her. You don't deserve to be some rebound."

"I can help you forget her," she said as she sauntered toward him.

"That's just the thing, Diana. I'm not sure I want to forget."

She stopped her approach and narrowed her eyes at him. "All right then. I'll give you time, but trust me when I say this isn't over. You'll see, rock star. We're perfect for each other."

Nolan's lips curled. He could tell how easy it was to get her to do anything he asked. All he needed to do was play along and take what she was already offering. Still, somehow, he couldn't bring himself to act on his desires. He reasoned to himself that it was because of Serene, but when he laid his head to rest that night, he felt an intangible tug in his heart. What if it wasn't Serene? What if it was all those years of going to Sunday School and attending youth group and leading worship? What if it was God?

Whatever the reason, one thing Nolan knew to be true was that the world might have found a new Red, but he certainly hadn't. For a long time, it seemed to him that Serene would forever be the only Red in his life.

Until one day, he realized that he might no longer be the only Ice in hers.

- THREE MONTHS LATER -

Nolan gripped the steering wheel as he drove to his old neighborhood to celebrate Christmas with his family. It felt like a lifetime ago since the first time they had driven through these streets, with Nova shrinking in shame because of how their clunky, old car, Neutron, kept backfiring.

This time, Nolan arrived in a state-of-the-art, luxury Hummer and a stunning rock star in the passenger seat.

Diana wrinkled her nose. "You live here?"

"Hey. Don't judge. Your hometown was no better."

"Let's leave the past behind us, shall we?"

"Unfortunately for me, I can't quite do that, because Ma is stuck in the past. No matter how much I promise her a better house in a more upscale neighborhood, she insists this is her home. I can't make her leave."

"Do you think she'll like me?"

Nolan smirked as he threw a glance at her revealing midriff and ripped jeans. "Dressed that way? She'll hate you. My mother's name is Clara. We have this culture in the Philippines called *Maria Clara*. It's all about being demure and conservative, about playing hard-to-get. Diana, you're the exact opposite of that."

"Then why would you bring me here? Your older sister doesn't like me either."

"What? Nova likes you just fine."

"Oh please. Remember when she and her husband attended our concert? Both were so judgey."

"Not true. Nova even complimented your looks and your talent."

"Shade. All that was just shade. I know girls. Your sister hates me."

"Oh, come on. You're so cynical." Nolan pulled over in their familiar driveway. He grinned at the open garage where he still found Neutron parked inside. Waves of nostalgia crashed over him.

"What have I gotten myself into?" Diana scowled. "And what is that?"

"That's our old car, Neutron."

"Is it like a thing in your family? Naming inanimate objects? Your guitar is Magenta, and this new SUV is Demi..."

"It's Ma. She named almost everything when we were growing up. I picked it up. Speaking of my mother—"

Clara Stone tucked a strand of her wavy, dark hair behind her ear as she rushed out of the front door and jogged down the porch steps. Nolan got out of the Hummer to hug his mother, twirling her around the small path crossing their front yard.

"Son!" she exclaimed.

"Ma!"

"You look so handsome! *Gwapo*[1]."

"That's because you're still so *maganda*[2], Ma. Have you been taking good care of yourself?"

"I try, *iho*[3]. I get a lot of help from our church, you know. Especially the Sinclairs next door. And who is this lovely young woman?"

"You remember Diana?"

"The name suits you, *iha*[4]. I wish you'd put more clothes on though. Why are you dressed this way? Come inside. We don't want you catching a cold."

---

1 gwa·po /gwah-poh/ adjective; handsome; good-looking [male]

2 ma·gan·da /mah-gahn-dah/ adjective; beautfiul; good-looking [female]

3 i·ho /ee-hoh/ noun; son; appellation by elder to boy or younger man.

4 i·ha /ee-hah/ noun; daughter; appellation by elder to girl or younger woman.

Nolan dragged himself behind them. As much as he tried to keep himself from doing so, he glanced at the house next door. Was she there?

"Are you looking for Serene?"

Nolan turned around to find his older sister, Nova, getting out of a black family van. He tilted his head to the side and smiled. "If it isn't Super Nova herself." He spread his arms to coax her into a hug. "You're huge!"

She obliged and wrapped her arms around his waist. Or at least tried to. The large bump on her stomach made it difficult to hug him. "That's an awful thing to say to a pregnant woman."

"I know, but seriously, Nova. You look amazing for someone who has two humans inside her."

She blushed.

"I agree," her husband, Caleb, said as he approached.

"You must be so excited to meet your twins." Nolan shook his brother-in-law's hand. "I know I am. Can't wait to be their cool rock star uncle and spoil them rotten."

"I wouldn't call you cool, but—" Nova's words drifted into the crisp air.

"Hey, Nolan."

Shivers climbed from the base of his spine to the nape of his neck. He turned around and sure enough, there she was. Serene Sinclair. The love of his life. At least she used to be. He drew his breath at the familiar, yet foreign, sight of her — the freckles on her cheeks, her green eyes, and pink lips.

"You cut your hair," he said, noticing the straight, shoulder-length layers. "I've never seen it like that. It looks good on you."

"I thought I'd try something new." She shrugged. "How are you?"

"Serene!" a male voice disrupted the exchange before Nolan could respond.

A lanky guy with tousled brown hair, black-rimmed glasses, and a lopsided grin ran from the Sinclairs' front porch to Serene. "Your dad's looking for—" He noticed the company she was with. "Oh.

Hey. I'm Drew." His eyes widened at the sight of Nolan. "I can't believe it. You're Nolan Stone! Big fan."

Serene shot a glance at him. A twisted smile appeared on her lips. "You're a fan?"

"I am! I have been from the moment that first viral video of *Rocking Serene* appeared online." His hand ran the length of her spine and stopped at the small of her back.

Nolan flinched.

Serene's eyes flickered as she bit her lip. "Drew and I are great friends. He's my agent."

Nolan's brow quirked up. "Your agent?"

"He drove all the way here to see my art."

"She's incredibly talented," Drew said.

Nolan's stomach turned. "Talented enough for you to drive to see her during the holidays?" He couldn't mask the edge from his voice.

"My family isn't big on celebrating Christmas," Drew explained.

"Christmas is a huge deal to the Filipino side of our family," Nova interrupted. She passed Nolan to embrace Serene. "Girl, you look lovely."

"Nova! You're so... pregnant!"

The rest of the conversation went over Nolan's head. All he could focus on was this man whose hand kept finding Serene's back, and she didn't seem to be the slightest bit bothered by his touch.

Only when Diana showed up, wearing a cardigan to cover herself up, and linked her arms with his did he snap out of his building ire.

"Who are your friends, Nolan?" she asked before fixing her eyes on Nolan's ex. "You must be Serene. I'm the new Red."

Nova's face scrunched up in disgust, but Diana didn't seem fazed by it at all. Her smile was wide and her gaze dead set on Serene.

A twisted part of Nolan found delight in the way Serene's face fell at the sight of Diana. It was for only a moment. Just a flicker.

Proving to still be the classy human being she had always been, Serene recovered and smiled back at Diana. "You're even more beautiful in person. It's nice to meet you." She extended her hand to Diana, who stared at it for a second.

She glanced at Nolan. "Your mother is asking why you're still not inside."

Nolan didn't know what possessed him to do it, but he placed his arm over Diana's shoulder and pulled her close. He kissed her on the temple and then turned to the woman whose presence still managed to make his heart miss several beats. "I have to go. It was nice to see you again, Serene."

He ignored how his older sister harrumphed at him as she planted a hand on her waist. He walked back to the house with Diana wrapped in his arms, her body pressed against his. The moment masked his jealousy and hurt with a false sense of triumph that lasted only until his head hit the pillow that night. He wondered if Drew could be more than just a friend to Serene. Did he hurt her by pretending to be with Diana as much as she had hurt him when she had abandoned him? Why was it that no matter how much he had tried to get over Serene, he still wasn't over her?

Nolan didn't think it through. All he wanted was to stop hurting, and the only way he knew to do that was to knock on the guest room's door and take advantage of what Diana had been offering since he met her.

Forget this Maria Clara nonsense, he thought as he sank into Diana's bed. *I'll do whatever it takes to get over Serene.*

What bothered Serene more? That Nolan's arm had been around Diana or that Drew had known her as the original Red and had never once mentioned it?

"Are you two sure you don't need any help?" Mama Aida lingered by the table as Serene and Drew cleaned up.

"Mama, you didn't let us help with preparing dinner. The least you can do is allow us to clean up." Serene stomped her foot on the hardwood floor to emphasize that she wasn't changing her mind. "Join Dad and Jeremy. Watch that movie with them."

"Okay then." Mama Aida sighed with resignation. "Thank you."

The moment Mama Aida left, Serene tensed. She focused on cleaning up and tried her best to avoid eye contact with the friend she had been trying to ignore.

"Serene? Is something wrong?" Drew asked.

"Hmm?" Serene stacked the dinner plates on the table. "Why would you think that?"

"Well, you haven't spoken to me or looked me in the eye since we bumped into Nolan Stone." He froze. "I still can't wrap my mind around the fact he still lives next door to you. He's freaking Nolan Stone!"

Serene winced and dropped the forks onto the pile of plates. Its clang made him jolt. "His mom lives next door to my parents. Nolan most likely lives in some mansion somewhere. Did you know?"

"Know what? Where he lives?"

"No. Did you know I used to be Red? Is that why you agreed to check out my art? Because I was once Red from *Red & Ice*?"

Drew stopped moving. He took a deep breath before he stacked glasses. "Of course I knew. You and Nolan were online sensations. Serene," he said, "I loved the original videos that shot you both to fame. I never understood why you broke up with him and quit the gig, but—" he shrugged "—it happens. Fairly typical for show business. I was aware of all of that, but I'm here because I love your work. That is why I came. Not because of *Red & Ice*. I never mentioned it before, because your public break-up didn't seem like something we needed to discuss."

"My actual break-up with him wasn't public." She shook her head. Flashes of Nolan turning his back on her at the church parking lot revisited her. "He turned it public with that reality show." Serene got choked up. "I can't believe talking about this is still getting to me. I'm so over him!"

Drew flinched. "Are you?"

"I hope I am."

"Doesn't look like it. You should have seen your face — crestfallen and all — when you saw him walk away with Diana. I don't think they're together, by the way. I would even wager he was deliberately trying to make you jealous."

Serene creased her brows and raised her eyes to meet Drew's. "Never pegged you to be such a fanboy."

"I hide it well, but I was pretty stoked when I first met you. Celebrity and all, but—" he shrugged "—meh. You're not that special." He chuckled.

"Hey." Serene deadpanned. She carried the plates and utensils to the dishwasher.

"For all it's worth, you had so much more chemistry with him than Diana."

"We were quite in love back then."

"Not anymore?"

Serene sighed. "Achieving his dream changed him. He's no longer the boy I fell head-over-heels in love with, but it still hurts to see him, so I guess I'm not as over him as I want to be. But in love? No. Not anymore."

"If you say so." Drew helped her load the dishwasher in silence.

Once they finished, he nudged her on the shoulder. "We're good, right? You'll still help convince Laila to go on a date with me?"

Serene rolled her eyes. "Yeah. We're good."

"Great then."

Serene sighed. "Want to go watch that movie with the family?"

"Yes, please."

The rest of the night went by as any normal night at the Sinclair residence would. After the pleasant family evening, Serene expected to go to bed and sleep in peace. However, just as her eyes drooped and her consciousness gave way to dreams, a tap on her bedroom window woke her up.

Tap.

She furrowed her brows.

Tap. Tap.

Was someone knocking on her window? She got out of bed and dragged her feet to the window. She opened it and gasped when a stone flew less than an inch past her ear.

"Oops. Sorrryyy…" Nolan drawled. He snickered before stumbling on the grass of their front lawn. "Didn't mean to hit you with a stone. Well, almost." He snickered again, then something akin to fury sharpened his gaze. "Why did you open your window so suddenly? You should have warned me or something."

"Nolan." Serene hissed. "What are you doing here? Are you drunk?"

"What if I am?" He made a face. "Is that Drew guy your new boyfriend? It's not good to lie."

"I told you, Nolan. He isn't. Can we discuss this some other time? I don't want to wake my parents up."

"Come down here then so I don't have to yell."

"No."

"Serene! Come down! Pleeease. You have to."

Serene flinched. "Fine, fine." Had it been anyone other than Nolan, she never would have descended the stairs and stepped into the front lawn, but this was Nolan. Her best friend. Her childhood sweetheart. She had no reason to assume he would ever do anything to hurt her. She was wrong.

The moment she was within reach, Nolan grabbed her arm and pulled her close. Focused on her face, he spoke. "Swear you're not with him."

She winced at the stench of alcohol on his breath. "Why would it even matter to you if I am?"

"Because I always thought we would be together, Serene. Not you and him." He hiccuped. "But you left, and you broke my heart, Red. You shattered my heart."

She tried to fight back the tears, but they came anyway. "I'm sorry."

"You should be, because if you hadn't left, maybe I wouldn't be such a sinner now, and I wouldn't have to go to hell or something."

"Nolan." Serene blew out some air. "I have no clue what you're talking about. I've hurt you. That is something I can admit and apologize to you for. I'm sorry for the way I handled everything, but you can't blame me for the choices you make. Whatever you did, that's not on me."

"I slept with Diana. I saw you with Drew, and it hurt so bad, I slept with Diana." His eyes cleared and a wry chuckle escaped his lips. "It felt good and horrible at the same time. That's the problem with growing up in church. It's like the Bible is hard-wired into your brain. It's true what we kept saying back then: *the Word does not return void.* Ha!" He threw his arms in the air, stumbled backwards, and fell on the ground. A string of colorful cussing followed.

Serene stared at his limp form slouched over on the grass. He tried to get up but fell back down. The weight of his confession fell on her chest. She wiped away her tears but more came. How had it come to this? "Nolan, please go home."

"You don't even care, do you? You don't care that I'm going to hell."

"Nolan, you know as well as I do how to return to God. The choice is yours to make. If your goal was to hurt me tonight, then consider it done. You broke my heart too, Nolan Stone, and you'll keep breaking it as long as you keep going on this path. I'll be praying for you, but I can't return to you just to—"

He cussed to interrupt her. "You really are something, Serene. A bit full of yourself, don't you think? What on earth gave you the idea I would ever want you back?"

Serene stepped back and swallowed hard. She nodded and wiped her tears away. "Okay. Point taken. Just please go."

He tried to stand up but failed at it. Afraid that her parents might wake up to see him passed out on their front lawn, Serene helped him up and dragged him to his mother's house next door. When she was about to knock to wake someone up, he stopped her.

"Don't," he said. "I don't want Ma to see me this way."

Serene nodded and helped him sit on a bench on their porch. "Will you be able to hold yourself up?"

He grunted in response.

She straightened. "Goodbye, Nolan. I am sorry for the pain I've caused you."

"I hope you get hurt the same way you hurt me, Serene."

All she could do was force a smile before she walked away. Only when she reached her bedroom did she realize she was no longer crying. She got on her knees beside her bed and whispered a prayer to God. "I surrender him and all the hurt I feel to You. Help me love You more than I ever loved him."

Serene never spoke to anyone about that night, but it was one of the most memorable nights of her life, because before she drifted from wakefulness to dreams, assurance came over her. For the first time in a long time, she had confidence that she loved God more than she loved Nolan Stone.

two

THE ONE
WHO MISSED
THE ONE

Nothing filled. Nothing satisfied.

As he stood on the red carpet of his first Grammy Awards night, with cameras flashing and a reporter's microphone shoved in front of his face, Nolan couldn't shake the sense of surreal dissatisfaction he had inside.

He blamed it on the awareness that the wrong redhead was in his arms.

He had no idea where the right one was, but as he flashed a smile for the cameras, her fiery hair and the kind features of her freckled face circled his mind.

"What was that again?" Nolan gestured toward the fanfare surrounding him at the red carpet event. "It's crazy out here. I didn't get what you said." He winked at a fan waving at him behind the reporter.

Beside him, Diana Rake leaned her head on his shoulder, the top of her wild red curls brushing his jawline.

Unfazed, the reporter repeated the question Nolan had pretended not to hear. "I said *Red & Ice* gets cozier every time we see you. Can we expect wedding bells in the future?"

Nolan tried not to scoff as his mind raced to process the question. Wedding? Who said anything about a wedding? What was wrong with this guy?

He and Diana were barely dating. "Uhhh—" he scratched his head and laughed "—hmm."

The admiration in Diana's green eyes as she looked up at him made his heart ache. She wound her arms tighter around his waist. He dropped his arm from her shoulder to his side as he cleared his throat.

"Diana and I are still getting to know each other," he said.

"You've been costars for almost two years now. A lot of fans are shipping you hard!"

"We feel the love," Diana said, "but Nolan and I are trying not to get pressured by all of it. We're taking our time."

Nolan smiled in agreement. Diana was a natural at dealing with the press. He could almost imagine the entertainment videos analyzing their body language. Were the *Red & Ice* duo together for real? Or was it all just a show to ramp up press for their tour? Even Nolan didn't know for sure.

"I need a drink," he whispered in Diana's ear when the reporter finally ended the interview.

"Let's go then," she said.

They kept their heads down and rushed quietly out of the red carpet and to their waiting limo.

"Let me get you what you want." Diana poured two glasses of champagne for both of them as soon as they settled themselves inside. "We may not have won tonight but the fact that we got nominated is still worth celebrating."

"Did you see Ramona after?" He browsed the crowd past the tinted window in search of their manager. At that point, not winning the Grammy was the last thing on his mind. "I wanted to properly thank her, but it was insane back there. We completely lost her."

"It's fine." She handed him a glass of champagne. "We'll see her at the after-party, so don't worry about it."

"After-party?" Nolan scoffed as he swirled his glass of champagne. "I'm zonked, Diana. There's no way you can drag me to that after-party."

Her face fell. "You're joking! Nolan, everyone will be there."

"Well, I won't. I'm going home, so I can rest and prepare for the tour. Get back to the music. It's the only thing that's been keeping me sane these past weeks."

Diana pouted. "Nolan, come on. It's my first time being in one of these things. Don't you want to experience this to the fullest?"

"It really isn't that big of a deal, Diana. For one thing, you'll be in a lot more of these things. Also, if you really want to be there so badly, you can go without me."

"They're expecting us both to be there. What would they think if I go without you? It doesn't send a good message."

Nolan shifted on his seat. What message were they trying to send exactly? "Diana, no one there will be thinking about us. If you go alone and they ask you why, tell them the truth. Tell them I prefer to rest, because we have a tour coming up. That's it."

"Yes, but—" Her lips quivered as she crossed her arms over her chest and leaned back on her seat, her glass of champagne held steady in her fingers. "I can't believe you're doing this to me. What will the press think?"

Nolan gulped his champagne down and gritted his teeth. Who cared what the press thought? Serene never cared about any of that. He looked outside the window. The familiar ache in his chest grew, spreading all the way to his gut and to his head, causing a sickening lightness that reminded him of the constant emptiness he had ever since Serene walked out of his life. He had wanted to experience his first Grammy Awards Night with her.

Diana purred and snuggled closer to him. He winced. Her lips pressed against his jawline, trailing on to his lips. "Come on, Nolan. Please? Come with me. I'll make sure to make it worth your time tonight." Her body language made it clear what her intentions were.

He broke away from her kiss.

She gasped.

"Sorry, Diana. Not tonight. I'll make it up to you, I promise." On any other night, he would've given in, but not that night. Not when during one of the biggest milestones of his career, all he could think about was how much he wished the redhead he wanted could be there.

To his surprise, a tear ran down her cheek as she moved to the other end of the seat and looked out the window. The limo slowly milled through some sort of jam preventing them from getting to the street.

He ignored the drop of conscience that had nagged at him ever since he first slept with Diana and every time after. He didn't want her the way she wanted him to, and he tried to appease himself by the fact that he had made his feelings — or lack of it — clear to her, but she still chose to throw herself at him anyway. "What is taking so long?" He said through gritted teeth. He pressed a button that rolled the partition down, so he could talk to the driver. "What's going on?"

"Probably an accident or something. We're almost out. Off to the after-party?"

"We can drop Diana off there, and then you can drive me home."

"No," Diana said. "I'm going home with him."

"I thought you said—"

She didn't look at him. "I want to be with you."

Nolan tried not to groan as he rolled his eyes at the driver who was looking at them from the rear-view mirror. "Let's go home."

Her cold treatment relieved him. He welcomed the quiet and focused on the view outside.

Unfortunately, Diana was not one who could handle him ignoring her. It didn't take long before she caved and scooted back beside him. She linked her arms with his and laid her head on his shoulders.

The closer Diana got to him, the more Nolan missed Serene.

Later that night, long after Diana had gone to sleep, Nolan dragged himself to his bedroom after an hour of quality time with his guitar and several shots of whiskey. He paused at the door upon catching a glimpse of the redhead on his bed. He leaned on the door frame as guilt once again twisted his gut. Diana could never be the one he wanted. No. His heart belonged to someone else, and Nolan doubted he could ever get it back. He had already given it to another redhead a long time ago.

An intense impulse to call her enveloped him — an impulse crushed by the mental image of her the last time he had seen her. At peace. Happy. What if she had already found someone else? What could he possibly offer her when she had already once rejected everything he lived for? He shook his head. He must move on.

Nolan climbed to his bed. Diana shifted and turned to her side. She blinked her eyes open and purred when she saw him beside her. She pulled him close and kissed him. This time, he didn't resist. He plunged right back into the alluring arms of folly. It swallowed him whole as he disappeared into momentary bouts of pleasure.

The pleasure shifted into a restless sleep made up of painted dreams of a black-haired boy flying to the moon. There, he found a red-haired girl who painted his heart blue and ran away. He chased after her but failed to reach her.

The next morning, Nolan pulled himself out of an empty bed, half-asleep, half-awake. The niggling voice of conscience brought about by his midnight tryst with Diana pounded his head before the recollection of his dream induced dear childhood memories with the woman he loved and lost. His heart broke yet again from the longing he had for her. He picked up his phone, found her number, and pressed the call button. The phone icon shook as the phone screen registered ringing. One ring. Two. Three. He must talk to Serene to tell her she made a mistake.

"Breakfast is ready!" Diana yelled from the kitchen.

Nolan snapped fully awake. The name on his phone screen incited a shudder: My Red. He ended the call. Nolan pushed all thoughts of her aside and tried to live his life, trying not to dwell too much on the reality that whatever he did, no matter what success he reached, no matter who he was with, nothing filled. Nothing satisfied.

The finished work of art in front of Serene brought about a sense of accomplishment and satisfaction that painted the wide smile on her face. Purples, blues, and blacks made up a string of thorny musical notes rising through wisps of icy blue air to a blood red lily, a flower that didn't exist in the natural but blossomed to life in her mind. The piece formed mental images of bruises and scars — innocence lost — and of blood shed — redemption offered. She tapped the edge of her palette with the handle of her paintbrush as she studied her own work. A cool breeze wafted past the window of her bedroom and caressed her skin, heightening the pleasure of having done something and having done it well. The final piece for her first art show was complete.

"Thank You, God," she mouthed as she shut her eyes, aware of her own story of redemption and how much God had preserved and promoted her. The acoustic music coming through her earphones deepened the emotions coursing from her to her art. Glimpses of someone loved and lost flashed through her brain. In a lot of ways, Nolan had made her first art show possible, but how could she ever inform him of that without risking hurt for both of them?

The pain on his face the last time she had seen him gripped her chest. Serene doubted Nolan would ever want to see her or talk to her again. *"You shattered my heart,"* he had accused her, and she knew it to be true. He had blamed her for a lot of things, but for that one thing, he had been right. She had shattered his heart. Not knowing what to do, Serene did the only thing she could do to thank him and bless him. She prayed for Nolan.

Lord, wherever he is, whatever he is doing, may he find peace, joy, and love. I want him to have that. After everything I put him through, he deserves to find happiness. I hope he finds it in You.

A deep longing filled her, a yearning for Nolan's presence, but Serene ended her prayer with an amen and shook her head to reject the feeling. Just nostalgia. All of it.

The music died down as the song ended. Her player shifted to the next song, and the momentary silence allowed her to hear her vibrating phone. She had left it on her bedside table earlier, away from her, so she could concentrate on finishing her work.

Serene pulled down her headphones and rushed to her phone, expecting a call from her agent, Drew, or from her roommate, Laila. Instead, the name on her screen caught her completely off guard.

Nolan Stone.

Frozen, she stood there and stared. Her mind traveled through endless possibilities as she figured out whether to answer the call. Finally deciding, she was about to accept the call when the vibrating stopped.

Regret and relief washed over her, accompanied by sharp curiosity. Why would he call? Should she call back? What if something was wrong?

The questions came one after the other, answerable if she would only call him back and ask. However, the very fact that all her senses seemed to awaken just at the thought of talking to him made Serene back away. She was over Nolan. She had to be. For his own sake and hers.

Serene replaced the headset over her ears as she put her art supplies away. She had to call Drew later to let him know she had just put in the final touches on the painting and that it would be ready for the art show. She gave herself a mental pat on the back for finishing way ahead of schedule. Her heart leapt at the notion of sending an invitation to her parents and brother for her first art show. They would be so proud of her. So would Nolan. Serene stopped herself.

I'm over him.

Serene sighed.

Lord, help me get over him.

With one missed phone call, Nolan had once again captivated her heart and mind. The music in her ear only exacerbated how much she missed him, because as much as she tried not to think about it, she couldn't finish a painting without listening to the musical stylings of Nolan Stone.

three

THE ONE
WHO NEEDED
A FAVOR

"Wait." Laila gripped the arms of her cushy velvet chair. "Nolan freaking Stone called you, and you didn't answer him?"

Serene replaced her bubble tea on top of the hardwood table between them. She shrugged. "I was going to answer, but he ended the call."

"Because you took forever to answer…" Laila drawled. "And you could've called back! Or at least texted him to ask why he called. Why didn't you?"

"I don't know. What could I possibly say to him? What if it was a wrong dial, and he didn't even mean to call?"

Laila waved her forefinger in the air. "What I want to know is why he still has your number. After your epic breakup, I would think he would've gotten rid of it. What if he's still not over you?"

At that, Serene had to laugh. "Oh, please. My brother just sent me a video of a Diana Rake interview. She confirmed that she and Nolan are a thing now. Trust me, Laila. Nolan isn't even thinking about me."

Laila made a face. "He called you."

Before Serene could respond, Drew Oliver's lanky form appeared through the coffee shop's door. He scanned the room, caught sight of her, and nodded at her. She smiled and waved. He gestured toward the counter as an indication that he was about to make an order first.

"Sure," she mouthed.

Laila twisted her torso to catch a glimpse of him. She blushed.

"You still haven't told me about your date with Drew," Serene said, grateful for a chance to divert the topic away from her ex.

Laila didn't bite. "That's because you can't admit mostly to yourself why you refuse to call Nolan back."

"Drop it, Laila." Serene said it gently as she leaned back on the leather couch. "Please."

"Fine, but we're picking this back up some other time."

"Pick what up?" Drew slid on the couch beside Serene. He winked at Laila, who couldn't keep the smile from her face at the sight of him.

"Nolan Stone called Serene."

"Laila!" Serene threw a hand in the air.

Drew's mouth dropped open. "No way."

Serene sat up straight on the couch and angled herself to face Drew. "It means nothing."

"It means a lot. He didn't seem very happy with you that Christmas we spent at your parents' home. What did he say?"

"He dropped the call before I could answer," Serene said. "As I said, it's nothing."

The barista at the counter yelled out: "Drew! Cappuccino!"

Drew cast a pointed look at Serene before rushing to get his drink.

"What are you doing?" Serene mouthed at Laila.

Upon his return, Drew set the drink on the table, turned to his side to face Serene, took a deep breath, and said, "You have to call him back. I didn't even know you had his number."

"What? Why?" Serene frowned. This was getting ridiculous. "You don't understand, Drew. He doesn't want me in his life."

"Then why would he call you?" Laila asked.

"True." Drew agreed. "But more than that, Serene, trust me when I say this: we need him for your art show."

At that, deep-seated indignation rose within her. "I can't believe I'm hearing this." Serene shook her head. "Drew, we talked about this. I agreed to name the art show *One Red Hue* for promotional purposes, but you promised me that the focus would not be that I was once part of Red & Ice. I'm not Red anymore. Nolan should have nothing to do with the art show."

"Yes. I said that, but your pieces speak for themselves, Serene. Nolan has everything to do with this show. All your paintings have some element of him in them!"

"That's not true."

"Your last painting is of musical notes connected to a red flower. How does that not have *Red & Ice* painted all over it?" Drew smirked. "Pun intended." He took a sip from his coffee.

"There's no ice in that painting. Nolan shouldn't have to be there. It's not a *Red & Ice* concert. His music may be a part of the art, but it's not a part of the show. Accept it. I can't believe how much you're pushing this."

"Only because it's what I came here to discuss with you in the first place. I showed some of your work to one of the show's sponsors, and they practically begged me to convince you to get Nolan to show up. Not to play music or anything. The focus is on the art, but the chances of people showing up will skyrocket if they know that the second half of *Red & Ice* will make an appearance." Drew's expression changed from firmness to sympathy. "I'm aware that you and Nolan didn't exactly part ways on good terms, so I told them I'll see what I can do, but maybe him calling you is a sign, Serene. If it helps, you don't even have to make the call. Just give me the number. I'll do everything. After all, we already met, and—"

"No." Serene shook her head. "If anyone's calling Nolan, it'll be me."

"So you'll call him?" The pitch of Drew's voice rose to show expectation.

"I haven't decided yet." She swallowed hard. She picked up her drink and gulped down the last of it. Her thoughts drifted toward Nolan and away from her friends. Much as she tried to deny it, the unexpected call from him had been at the forefront of her mind. Maybe it was time for both of them to heal. He was in a new relationship now, and as much as it pained her to think of him with someone else, was it time for them to mend fences? What would he say? How would he react? Her phone sat on the hardwood coffee table, right beside her untouched muffin. There was only one way to find out.

Later that night, in the privacy of her bedroom, she stared at the ceiling, her phone clutched by both hands against her chest. Did she really need Nolan to make the art show successful? Was she incapable of reaching success without him in the picture? Did the show have to be about him and not the art? No. His presence would help, but the show's success didn't hinge on it. Serene nodded. Her chest rose and fell. She bit her lip as her eyes moistened. Truth be told, Serene would give anything to hear Nolan say her name again. With eyes closed and her shoulders trembling, Serene sat up on the edge of her bed and made the call.

Here goes nothing.

The name on the screen — *My Red* — first registered a spark of curiosity in Nolan, but it only took a few seconds before he fully realized who was calling, and all his reflexes went on red alert. His shoulders squared, his spine straightened, and his sensibilities snapped. He picked the phone up from the coffee table, but didn't answer immediately. Why was she calling? What could she possibly say to him?

Eyes fixed on his screen, he leaned back on the black leather couch inside his dressing room. Only a few seconds before his phone had started buzzing, he had been debating whether to gulp down another shot of whiskey. Intoxicated by a different substance, he checked his breath and finger-combed his hair. Realizing what he was doing, he gritted his teeth and shut his eyes. *She won't see or smell you, you idiot.* After breathing in and out to gather the courage, he answered the phone.

"Serene?" His voice barely came out.

"Hi, Nolan."

It was really her. "Hey."

"How are you?"

She cared, because? "The usual. On tour. Tired."

"You never seemed to get tired before."

At that, he seethed. What did she want? "I don't mean to be rude, Serene, but why are you calling? I'm sure it's not just to take a trip down memory lane." Pride and shame whirled within him at how cold he sounded towards her.

"Sorry."

The pause that followed felt like an eternity to Nolan. *Mercy, Serene. Say something.*

"This is out-of-the-blue," she said.

Upon hearing her speak, he held back an audible sigh.

"I just—" She took several deep breaths. "I need a favor."

He leaned his head back on the top of the couch's backrest. "What is it?"

"I'm having my first art show soon. It's called *One Red Hue*. Do you remember Drew?"

The name alone made Nolan want to hit something. Drew. That lanky guy with her the last time he had seen her. Why was he still in her life? "What about him?"

"He's my agent. He said it would make a huge difference if you show up for the art show. Just a confirmed appearance would bring more people in. Would it be possible for you to be there? I'm aware I don't have the right to ask anything of you, but it would mean a lot to me."

Nolan could barely comprehend what she had just said, much more how he felt about it. He couldn't form words as he tried to process through the indignation, pain, and utter delight brought about by her request.

When he didn't respond, she broke the silence. "For all it's worth, you inspired this show. Everyone who sees the paintings recognizes your influence in every single one of them."

A short pause followed, then with a broken voice, she replied, "I understand. I appreciate the honesty, Nolan. Thanks for accepting my call."

"It's good to hear from you. Sorry I can't give you this one."

"No, no... I told Drew it was a long shot. Take care of yourself, okay? I miss you."

He wanted to tell her how much he missed her too, but all he said was, "Right. Congratulations on your show, Serene."

"Thanks. Bye, Nolan."

"Bye."

He hung up. She missed him. That's what she said. Those three words alone left him with a range of emotions he didn't know he even had for her. How did she still have this much power over him? Eyes on the ceiling, he let out a guttural yell, the sound pain-laced and furious, yet so full of longing for something he once had and cherished, but somehow rocked out of his life.

The door swung open and his manager, Ramona, stepped in to check on him. "Why are you yelling?"

"Nothing." Nolan shook his head. He reached for the bottle of whiskey, but before he could, Ramona rushed forward and grabbed it.

She gave him a stern tsk-tsk as she shook her head. "Last time, you were a drop of alcohol away from being legally drunk on stage. I won't have that this time."

"Stop trying to be my mother, Ramona." Nolan rose to his feet and tried to reach for the bottle, but one look from Ramona told him he would not win this one.

"Believe me," she said, "the last thing I want is

to be your mother. Get a hold of yourself, Stone, and sit down. There's something we need to talk about." Ramona tucked the bottle beneath her arm and sat on the love seat across from the sofa where he plopped himself down. "Have you seen Diana's interview this morning?"

"That was today?" Nolan grimaced. "I forgot. What about it?"

Ramona took out her phone and showed him a video clip of Diana's interview on a nationwide morning talk show.

"So, Diana," the host said, "what's the scoop on you and Nolan Stone? Rumors are you're definitely his new Red now — on stage and off."

Diana blushed. "Well, we're definitely exploring the possibility of a future together," she said confidently.

Nolan gripped the phone so hard, he wondered if it would snap. He couldn't believe his ears. She continued to gush about her relationship with him, how serious it was getting. One photo she had posted on social media — a selfie she snapped as she kissed him on the cheek — flashed on the screen.

Nolan squirmed. What was she talking about?

He wanted to break up with her right then, but how? They weren't even dating. How did one end a relationship that didn't even exist? Had it ever been this complicated when he had been with Serene? How had that relationship ended?

Nolan winced.

He couldn't just disappear into the night and run away from his own tour, could he?

Why not? He grimaced. That was what Serene had done. Now, here he was. Stuck with Diana.

With a groan, he stopped the video and returned the phone to Ramona.

Back straight, eyes burning a hole through him, Ramona crossed her legs, straightened her skirt, and raised one brow. "So?"

Nolan didn't break eye contact with her. "What?"

"When were you going to tell me you and Diana

are official?"

"Never." He cussed beneath his breath. "I need a drink for this."

"Nolan, I don't like this. The label will ask me about this, and I need to know what's going on. What if what—"

Nolan let out a long groan. "Chill, Ramona. I say never, because Diana and I are not official, and we will never be. Nothing is going on between us. Sure, we hook up sometimes. Okay, maybe more than we should, but I've made it clear to her I'm not ready for anything serious."

"Then why did she—"

"I don't know."

"We agreed you and Diana are a showmance. Make sure you two are still on the same page when it comes to that. We can't have a repeat of what happened between you and Serene, where it's so serious, we almost lost you when you lost her."

The sound of Serene's name on Ramona's lips made him flinch. It sounded so strange, yet so familiar. He glanced at his whiskey, the bottle still trapped in Ramona's arm. Desire twisted his chest. "Diana is nothing like Serene, and you know it."

"Perception is everything, and you know it. To your fans, Diana might as well be Serene, if not more. Fix this, Stone."

"Fix what? What do you want me to do, Ramona? Fix Diana? Why don't you be the one to talk to her and get her to stop lying on TV?"

"Oh, believe me, I will. But, Nolan, stop fooling around with her if you're not into her. You either commit to a relationship with her and make sure you marry her and make her forever your Red. Or, you make sure Diana never pulls a stunt like this again." Ramona stood up and straightened her pencil skirt. "Make sure it's clear to her that she may be the new Red of *Red & Ice*, but she's not yours. We can't afford to lose another Red, Nolan. If you lose Diana, it'll be the end of *Red & Ice*."

"Do me a favor, Ramona." He stepped forward just as she turned to leave.

"What?" She didn't even bother to face him.

"Break up with her for me?"

She laughed. "You wish. Deal with your own mess, Stone."

"Can't blame me for trying."

"Clean yourself up. Hair and makeup will be here in an hour."

"Can I have my drink back?"

"After the show." Ramona walked toward the door.

"You're annoying."

"So are you."

Nolan ran his hand through his hair when a sudden urge hit him. "Ramona!" He rushed to the door before his manager could shut it.

Ramona turned her head to face him. "Hmm?"

"Give me a minute." He checked the date of Serene's art show online and gave the date to Ramona, without mentioning why it was relevant. "We have nothing scheduled on that day?"

"We'll be on the road."

Nolan nodded. "Got it."

"Why?"

He shrugged. "Nothing." He shut the door behind Ramona, his mind racing. Despite everything she put him through, Serene never would've pulled a stunt like Diana had. That much he had to give her. She wasn't the manipulative kind — always so sincere, so caring, so— Nolan gritted his teeth. So much for getting over her.

He dragged himself to the bar and took out his hidden stash of whiskey. He took a shot glass and played with it between his fingers. Could he handle seeing Serene again? Probably not. Should he go to her first art show? He really shouldn't, but as much as he tried to drown it out with whiskey, the truth was that Nolan would give anything to see Serene paint again.

four

THE ONE WHO COULDN'T SAY NO

Society pages headlined *One Red Hue*, the first art show of Serene Sinclair, once known as the Red half of the break-out musical duo, *Red & Ice*. Rumors circulated that she had invited Nolan Stone, the Ice half of the duo, to appear, but he had declined to go.

News spread that he couldn't even be bothered to show up to support Serene, and it brought public sympathy her way. The buzz made her first art show one of the most anticipated events in the modern art industry. The pressure caused by all the hype had almost been too much for Serene to handle, so when she saw her family enter the venue, the weight on her shoulders felt a lot easier to carry.

"Dad!"

Samuel Sinclair wrapped his arms around her. "This is amazing. I'm so proud of you, sweetheart."

"So very proud," Mama Aida reiterated before planting a kiss on Serene's cheek.

"Mama..." Serene hugged her mother.

Her teenage brother, Jeremy, snapped a photo with his state-of-the-art camera — her gift to him last Christmas.

"I'm making good use of it tonight," he said. "Congratulations, gingerbrain. Proud of you." He pulled her in an embrace. His best friend, Max, hung back behind him, waiting to give her a hug. "I hope you don't mind that I brought an assistant."

"Hey, Max." Serene smiled and pulled him in for a hug. "I can't believe you're taller than me now. You're the same age as Jeremy, right?"

"Yup." Max nodded. "Sixteen soon."

"I'm glad you came."

"Wouldn't have missed it for anything, Serene."

"I'm actually not sure if you guys are allowed to take photos of the event," Serene explained. "Could you please clear that with Drew while I show Dad and Mama to the refreshments table?"

Jeremy shrugged. "Sure." He looked around and caught sight of Drew. He nudged Max, and they were off.

Serene turned her attention back to her parents. They didn't even make it to the refreshments table before Drew approached with a handsome gentleman in tow.

"Pastor Sam." Drew shook hands with her father. "Mama Aida." He hugged her mother. "I'm so glad to see you both again. You must be so proud of Serene."

"Of course." Her dad nodded.

Drew gestured toward the gentleman next to him. "I'd like to introduce you all to Ethan Caine. He's a businessman, a philanthropist, and a patron of the arts. This is tonight's artist, Serene Sinclair, and her parents, Pastor Sam and Aida Sinclair."

"It's a pleasure to meet you." Ethan shook hands with her parents before holding her hand in his firm grip. His grip lingered, and so did his gaze. Something about him was familiar to her. "Miss Sinclair, I'm sure your parents are proud."

"Very much." Mama Aida nodded.

"Why don't we leave you two to get acquainted?" Drew said. "I'm sure Pastor Sam and Mama Aida would like some refreshments."

Serene wanted to go with them, but one glare from Drew told her that the man in front of her was someone she had to pay attention to, so she waved them off and smiled at Ethan.

"It delights me to discover that the artist is as beautiful — if not more beautiful — than her art," he said.

"You're being too kind, Mr. Caine."

"Please. Call me Ethan."

"Ethan." Serene nodded, still trying to recall where she had seen him before.

"It's not too kind to speak the truth. You are quite lovely."

"You don't look so bad yourself," she reciprocated, while admitting to herself she found him attractive. The gray on a few strands of his hair and the wrinkles that showed up on the corners of his eyes every time he smiled showed he was older than her. Still, something about him drew her in, made her feel comfortable and safe. "Please tell me more about yourself."

He shook his head. "Believe me. I'm boring compared to you. Former rock star, now a budding artist about to take the art world by storm. These paintings are breath-taking."

Former rock star. She cringed. At twenty-three, a musical has-been wasn't exactly what she wanted to be known for. "Is there a particular piece you're drawn to?"

From the way he looked at her, Serene feared he would divert the conversation back to her, so she sighed with relief when he pointed out one piece as his favorite. One red cowboy hat worn by a random person in a crowd of black and white. The painting's one red hue.

"There's something lonely about it," Ethan explained. "But there's also a sense of hope. Like there's always this one detail about anybody that could make them stand out in a crowd. We're all obscure, but there's always something that makes us stand out."

Serene listened and took every word in. She said nothing in response.

"Was that what you were going for?" he asked. "Did I get it right?"

Serene flashed him a smile and shrugged. "Does it matter? Isn't art subject to the interpretation of whoever is beholding it?"

"Maybe so, but the creator's voice is always important to listen to."

Serene narrowed her eyes at him. "I could swear I've seen you before. Have we met?"

"I would've remembered meeting you, Miss Sinclair."

"Please call me Serene."

"Serene." His facial features softened; his gaze on her remained keen. "The name suits you."

"You're so familiar. What is it you do again?"

"I own several businesses, but I'm known for inheriting my father's publishing company. Caine Corp."

"Wait. You're that Caine?"

"Guilty as charged."

"Caleb and Nova Grant work for one of your imprints. Do you know them?"

"Yes. I've worked closely with Caleb for a long time. He's one of our most trusted and valuable employees. He invited me to your father's church once."

"I think I know where I've seen you. You were at their wedding! Nolan pointed you out to let me know you're Nova and Caleb's..." her voice trailed off. Just mentioning Nolan made her feel guilty and hurt.

Ethan grinned and said, "Yes. I was there. I can't believe I didn't see you. At that time though, I wasn't aware of your music just yet. How are you acquainted with Caleb and Nova?"

"We went to the same church. Nova was like an older sister to me. She's Nolan's older sister."

Ethan seemed taken aback. "I had no idea."

Serene shrugged. "If we weren't on your radar then, there's no reason you would've remembered either Nolan or me."

Ethan opened his mouth to respond, but someone cleared his throat behind her.

"Excuse me," Serene said to Ethan before turning to find Jeremy raising his brow at her. "What?" she asked.

He removed the camera strap from his neck, so he could show her something on the screen: an image of a man in a black hoodie, leaning back on his chair inside a restaurant. Nolan.

"Don't look," Jeremy whispered in her ear. "The restaurant is right across the street. Nolan's there, and I've seen at least two people leave the gallery, cross the street, and chat with him."

Serene fought every urge she had to glance toward the direction Jeremy mentioned. She lost the fight, stole a glance, and immediately locked eyes with the man who had once been everything to her.

"Is that Nolan Stone?" Ethan asked in a voice loud enough for the people near them to hear.

Suddenly, everyone was looking out the window. Serene's heart dropped. *Nolan, please don't run.*

One moment, Nolan seethed over how much time Serene was spending with this one man, who was so old, he was sure he could be her father or at the very least, her suave, corporate-type uncle. The next moment, Serene's gaze locked with his, and all other gazes followed. Electrifying thrill and momentary panic coursed through his entire system. Now what? Frozen in his seat, Nolan's mind raced to figure out what to do. He could either make a run for it or cross the street and steal the show. He couldn't imagine her being happy about the latter, so he decided on the former option. Run.

After tossing a hundred-dollar bill on the table as a tip for the server, Nolan was ready to bolt. However, the moment he reached the door, the sight of Serene crossing the street made him stop.

Her emerald green gown hugged her curves in just the right way. Its hem swayed over the road that shimmered from a slight drizzle earlier that day. One knee buckled beneath him as she glided like an ethereal being floating toward him.

He feared she was coming to slap him on the face, so he blew out a sigh of relief when all he got from her once she reached him was one trimmed brow lifted at him in question.

To answer, Nolan lifted his right shoulder. "I bid on a painting," he said as if that would explain everything. "I loved the painting of the guitar with a red capo. Magenta deserves to be in the spotlight like that."

Her silence caused tension to crackle between them.

"Come on, Serene. Say something. Did you really think I'd miss your first art show?"

Her lower lip quivered and her shoulders sagged.

For a moment, he feared she would cry. He wouldn't have known how to handle that, so he exhaled with relief when she regained composure and straightened her shoulders.

"What makes you think the guitar is Magenta? The only color on that painting is the red capo."

He smirked. "I would recognize Magenta anywhere. Besides, you named the piece itself Magenta."

"I didn't name the pieces. My agent did."

"Magenta is Magenta. That your agent even knows about her says a lot."

"All your fans know about Magenta."

"Oh yeah." His brow quirked up. "Your agent is a fan. For the record, I think you're way out of his league."

"Nolan, he's not—" She bit her lip and narrowed her eyes at him. She opened her mouth to say something, but silence filled the air.

He drank in the sight of her. He didn't bother to tell her how stunning he thought she was. She was aware, he didn't doubt it. "Congratulations, Serene. I'm sure this means a lot to you."

"You said you wouldn't come."

"I lied."

"It means a lot that you're here. Your girlfriend is okay with you being here?"

Nolan threw his head back in surprise. Was she referring to Diana? The nagging voice of conscience returned. "I don't have one."

"Oh." Her brows met. Her lips parted and confusion momentarily tensed the soft angles of her face before her eyes moistened with what appeared to be hurt. Serene then shook her head. Her expression cleared, and her gaze lightened. It seemed whatever was bothering her had flown away through the sheer force of her head-shaking.

Fascinated by the multitude of stories the mere changes in her facial expression brought about in his imagination, Nolan stood mesmerized by her. What was running through her mind? Once upon a time, she was less of a mystery to him, but the time and distance spent away from each other gave Serene a sense of mystique that allured him.

"You should come in," she said, her voice soft and throaty. "I've been told more than once that the paintings are clearly inspired by my time with you."

The sentiment both irked him and pleased him. He smirked. "I'm not done eating my pizza."

"Doesn't seem to be very good pizza if you're already bolting. Also, it doesn't seem like many people eat here."

"I hired the place out for the night." He shuffled on his feet and bowed his head, wondering why he admitted that. "It's your night. I don't want to steal the spotlight."

A soft laugh escaped her lips. "You already have. I don't have to check behind me, but I'm sure everyone is watching us."

He looked past her shoulder and nodded. "Pretty much." All her guests had their eyes fixed on them, anticipating what would happen next. "The press will eat this up. Ramona will kill me." He caught sight of Pastor Sam and Mama Aida and gulped. "I doubt your parents would want me there."

"They'd love to see you again. It's Jeremy and Max you have to worry about."

A pang of guilt hit Nolan. "Guess the boys aren't my biggest fans anymore, huh?"

Serene shook her head. "Unfortunately not, but I'm sure they can handle being civil towards you for one night. So? Are you coming?"

Nolan caved. He couldn't bring himself to embarrass her by declining to go yet again.

When the crowd saw them approaching, they applauded. Nolan and Serene posed for photos and signed autographs. It took a good hour before everything settled down and the attention went back to the art. Finally, Nolan got to see the paintings up close.

Each one triggered a memory. *One Red Hue* was their story. She didn't pay much attention to him for the rest of the night, and he didn't expect her to. He just hoped that his appearance at the event would somehow help her reach her dreams. Serene deserved it, and despite his shattered heart, Nolan wanted that for her.

After all, she had once put all her dreams on hold just to make his come true.

five

THE ONE
WHO SHOT
TO SUCCESS

Critics praised Serene's art. The auction went far better than they could have ever expected. Seven out of fourteen of her pieces had sold at five-figure values. Two sold for one hundred thousand dollars — *Magenta* and *Cowgirl*. It was a silent auction, but she had no doubt in her mind which two people had won the bidding for those two paintings.

Weeks later, Serene still couldn't believe that Nolan had shown up. In fact, no one could get over it. It wasn't just art industry articles that covered his surprise appearance. Even entertainment outlets couldn't get enough of it. In the wake of Diana Rake announcing she and Nolan were together, Nolan showing up at Serene's art gallery was too juicy for the media to ignore.

Was Nolan Stone still in love with the Original Red even while dating the New Red?

Serene brushed away the conflict between what the media was saying and what Nolan had said about the nature of his relationship with Diana. Whatever he had with Diana was no longer Serene's business. She didn't care. At least she was trying not to.

Still, would it be appropriate to send Nolan a thank you note?

While Serene wrestled back and forth on whether to thank Nolan and apologize for all the trouble, the rock star's surprise appearance and the ensuing media attention thrilled Drew. More publicity meant more opportunities for Serene. Her art career could only skyrocket from there.

Serene wasn't sure how she felt about the entire thing. She should have been on some high. She had worked for this for years. Her art debut had been a challenge. It was almost impossible for most artists to catch a break in the world of modern art, and yet she broke through. She succeeded. And at the end of it all, Serene still felt aimless.

As she knelt on the floor one morning, Serene expressed her desperation to God. "Father, it's like I'm missing something, and I don't know what it is. Why am I like this? Do I not serve You and seek You? Aren't You supposed to satisfy? I've tasted success in both music and art, and I thank You. For most, it's so difficult to succeed in both industries, but You've given me Your favor. I'm grateful, but God, it doesn't seem to matter. It's all meaningless. What is it You want of me? Is this all there is to life?"

Deafening silence filled the room. Serene noticed the smallest of sounds. Every tick of the wall clock. The wind blowing against her apartment's window. Loneliness, as ancient as the fall of man, penetrated her soul.

Her phone buzzed on her bed. She grabbed it. The screen registered an unknown number. She answered the call.

"Hello?"

"Hi. Is this Serene Sinclair?" The voice was familiar.

"This is she," she said as she stood from her kneeling position to her feet.

"Ethan Caine here. We met at your art gallery. I asked Drew for your number. I hope I'm not intruding."

"Mr. Cai— Ethan. You're no intrusion at all." Serene sat on the edge of her bed, somewhat surprised that he had called. "To what do I owe the pleasure of hearing from you?"

"This may seem rather forward, but would you consider going out with me for dinner? On a date?"

Serene drew a breath. Would she? Was she ready for it?

"I know we barely know each other," Ethan added after a less than comfortable pause, "but I'm sure Caleb and Nova can vouch for me."

"It's not that. I just—" Serene didn't know what to say, because she wanted to say yes, but she wasn't sure if she should. Not when the image in her head at that very moment was Nolan watching her across the street from her art gallery. "Can I get back to you on that? I'd like to give Nova a call first."

"Certainly." His deep voice had the slightest quiver to it. "I'll wait to hear from you. Whatever you decide, know that I have the deepest respect and admiration for you, Serene, and I would understand your decision either way."

"Thanks, Ethan. I'm so flattered someone like you would view me so highly. It means a lot."

"You deserve it."

The moment they hung up, Serene made another call. The first thing she heard when Nova picked up was the loud wails of a baby. "Hello? Serene? Give me a minute."

Serene fell back on her bed and stared at the ceiling as she listened to Nova continue to speak.

"Yes. I'll be back in three hours. Nate is an angel during mornings. You shouldn't worry about him. He kept Caleb and me up all night, so I can't imagine him doing much of anything for a while. He should be zonked. Claudia though… yeah. She'll be fussy, but you're a baby whisperer. You know what to do."

Someone shut a door.

"Should I call back?" Serene asked.

"Sorry about that," Nova said. It sounded like she was walking. "Left the twins to a babysitter, so I can get some writing done."

"How are they?"

"Adorable!" The affection in Nova's voice was genuine. "Needless to say though, it has been exhausting for both Caleb and me, but never mind that. How are you? It's been so long since we talked. Christmas, right? That's I-don't-even-know how many months ago." A car door slammed shut.

"Life's been good," Serene said. "I might visit home one of these days. Get out of the city for a while. Figure life out."

"Girl, if you're back in town, promise to come visit us." Nova's voice sounded a lot more subdued. "I miss you. We need to catch up."

"I will come over for sure."

"Great, because you have to tell me all about your art. Nolan sent me one of your paintings, and it's gorgeous."

Serene's heart dropped. Nolan gave Magenta away? Why did this bother her so much?

"Okay, so I keep talking," Nova said. "I'm just so excited you called. Any way I can help you?"

Serene meant to say, "I wanted to ask about Ethan." Instead, she said, "I don't think I'm over Nolan. I want to be, but I'm just... not."

"Oh honey..." Nova sighed. "I wish I could hug you. I always wished you two would end up together. That's a lot of history right there, and..."

Nova continued to ramble. Meanwhile, Serene crumbled inside. *God, I followed You. I turned my back on someone I loved deeply. Why can't You just take these emotions away? Maybe I need to go out with Ethan. He'll help me get over Nolan.*

"Nova," Serene said once she finally got a word in, "what can you say about Ethan Caine?"

"Ethan? Caleb's boss? How do you even know him?"

"We met at my art gallery. He asked me out on a date."

"Wait. What? Serene, my mind just melted. How can you tell me that right after saying you're not over my brother?"

"I—" Serene swallowed hard. "I'm sorry?"

"Sorry? Why are you sorry? I have to admit it's weird to imagine you with anyone other than Nolan, but Ethan is a great guy. He's older than you — older than Caleb even, but who cares? He's handsome and a complete gentleman, and Serene, that man is a freaking genius. Not to mention he's rich and kind and did I mention rich? Like richer-than-Nolan rich. Old money, castle-in-Europe, rich."

"None of that matters to me. I guess it matters that he's kind and all that. I'm at ease around him, but if I'm not over Nolan, it would be unfair to Ethan if I go out with him."

"True, but if you're calling so I can vouch for the man, he's an amazing human being, and Caleb has been introducing him to Christ, so... Yeah. He's a catch. But, know that whatever you decide, I'll always see you as my family."

"It means a lot to hear you say that, especially after everything that happened between Nolan and me."

"I understand why you broke up with him. I don't like the way you did it, but I get it. Just know that you always have a seat at our table. Caleb and I love you."

"Thanks, Nova. One more thing though before you get back to your writing."

"My writing! I'm not even out of our driveway yet." The car started. "Make it quick. I only have so much time."

Serene laughed. She couldn't believe how much Nova had changed from the sullen teenager she used to be. Contagiously vibrant, permanently distracted, and absolutely beautiful. Nova Stone Grant. "Just one question. Would you trust Ethan enough to go into business with him?"

"One hundred percent yes."

With that, they ended the call, and for the first time since her art gallery, Serene got the slightest inkling what she wanted to do next. *God, direct me. Show me Your way.*

She had to be honest with herself. She had to be honest with Ethan. Had she been honest, had she just been upfront about what was in her heart, she never would have hurt Nolan the way she had. She probably never would have lost him, but she had, and this time, she would not leave her mind unspoken.

She made another phone call.

"Serene?" Ethan's deep, soothing voice calmed her.

"I considered your offer."

"And?"

"It would be unfair for me to date you. Not when I still have unresolved feelings for my ex."

"I see." He didn't sound disappointed. "I completely understand. Thank you for being straightforward and honest with me. A man like me can appreciate that."

"Thank you, Ethan," Serene said.

"Okay then. I don't want to take any more of your time, so—"

"Wait."

"Yes?"

Serene took a deep breath. "I would still like to have dinner with you. A business dinner."

"Oh?"

"There's something I want to get into, and I would like your help."

"Consider me intrigued."

Serene smiled. They set a date, and the faintest of ideas took form in her mind. She still didn't know what she wanted to do for the rest of her life, but she knew what she wanted to do next.

Nolan winced at Diana's outfit. "Do you mind if I ask you to cover up?"

"Why? Nothing you haven't seen before."

Nolan chose not to argue. He removed his jacket and covered her with it. "We need to talk." He gestured toward one of the sectional couches in his dressing room.

"What about?"

"We should stop doing this."

"Doing what?" Diana pouted.

"Don't play coy. You know what I'm talking about."

"I'm not sure I do." She plopped herself on a single couch and crossed her legs.

Nolan sank onto another seat and tried to angle himself where he wouldn't see too much of her skin. "We need to stop sleeping together."

She groaned. "We've been over this a thousand times." She cussed. "It's like they brainwashed you or something. We're not doing anything wrong. We're both consenting adults. Why are you complicating this?"

"How do I explain it to you, Diana?" He rubbed the back of his neck. *I'm sick of all this. I'm sick of you.* He hadn't been able to sleep for what seemed like months. Every bone in his body ached, and the last thing he wanted was to get up on stage to perform. "I want to stop. That should be enough explanation."

"You can't break up with me." Diana's face grew as bright red as her wild mane of curls.

"Technically, I'm not breaking up with you," he said. "We're not even dating. You said it yourself. It's just sex, and it's meaningless."

"But you said you grew up believing it can't be meaningless, so which story are you sticking with, huh?"

"Whichever one gets us to stop doing this, Diana. I need my soul back."

"What do you mean you need your— Ugh! Never mind!" Diana threw her hands in the air. "This isn't over."

"What do you mean this isn't over?"

She stormed out of his dressing room.

"Diana!"

With the show about to start, Nolan shrugged it off. They could talk about it later. She had to realize how serious he was about this.

By the time he was on stage, he was able to push Diana to the back of his mind. The crowd's energy gathered up in waves and crashed over Nolan and the rest of the band as they performed his classic song on stage — the one that shot *Red & Ice* to fame. Nolan played his part well and stared at Diana like he wouldn't be able to live without her. However, in his mind, he had never been able to sing that song for anybody else other than Serene.

Diana sang her part perfectly. Between her and Serene, Diana had the better vocals, and she knew how to play a crowd in a way Serene had never been able to.

Together, they were dynamite, and the crowd was blowing up. Unfortunately for Nolan, he couldn't stand Diana. Both her shirts and skirts were getting skimpier. Her actions on stage becoming more and more provocative. She swerved her hips and gyrated in front of Nolan as she sang her part.

It was just a performance, Nolan tried to convince himself, but he was of the mind that *Red & Ice* didn't need all these to make good music or pull off a great performance.

By the time they ended the song, Diana had herself pressed against him. As the music faded, she kissed him. When they broke apart, Nolan forced a smile.

Diana grinned and spoke into the microphone. "Why would you need to waste time rocking serene when you have me?"

His smile faded. Anger swirled within him. He backed away from her. Since she was leaning against him to support her weight, the moment he stepped back, she lost her balance and stumbled onto the stage's floor.

The tension that swept across the now-hushed crowd slammed against him as he realized what had just happened. Nolan helped Diana up. "You okay?" he mouthed at her.

She nodded. "Kiss me to make it all better. The audience will love it. Come on, Nolan. You and I belong together."

Nolan shook his head. "I can't. I'm serious, Diana. We have to stop this." Before he could think it through, he spoke into the microphone in his hand. "To clear things up, I just want to say something to all of you who have shown up here tonight. Diana and I make great music together."

"What are you doing?" Diana tried to grab the microphone, but he held her back.

"Relax, Diana," he said to her before once again addressing the crowd. "She's an amazing person, and I'm glad we found her. Don't you agree?"

The crowd cheered.

"She and I have to make a huge announcement."

Expectation and fear shimmered in her eyes. She brushed her fingers over his arm. "Nolan?"

"Unfortunately, this tour will be the last one *Red & Ice* will ever do. After this, Diana and I have decided to go our separate ways as artists and as a pair."

From his peripheral vision, Nolan could make out Ramona sending gestures for him to stop. Diana's shocked eyes etched itself in his mind. The way he felt at that moment must've been like what Serene had felt when she had broken his heart. It didn't feel good to hurt someone he genuinely cared about, but Nolan went on. "The news is bittersweet, but it's for the best. I hope we will remain as great friends, supporting each other. Diana is one of the most talented people I know, and I wish her all the best." He continued saying good things about Diana, but they had already cut the microphone off, and the band started to play the intro of a song by the opening band.

Diana stormed off stage. Nolan dropped the mic and followed, but he didn't bother to talk to her or comfort her. He brushed past her to get away from Ramona who was sending him a death glare.

"What was that, Nolan?" Ramona demanded in a deadpan voice that gave him chills. "Who agreed to that?"

"I don't want to talk about it."

"Stone, you just talked about it in front of twenty thousand people. Millions of people, actually, because you can bet all that was on video, and will be available for all the world to see before the night ends. This is something we will discuss, Nolan. Now."

Nolan stopped walking. He spun around to face her. "No, Ramona. Let me tell you how this will play out. If you want me to get back on that stage to finish this show, if you want me to get back on tour, you will end this discussion and leave me be. Now. Go to Diana, Ramona. See how she's doing. Do what you're best at. Do what I pay you for. Damage control. That's your job. Stop pestering me and get to it. I don't care what you have to do, as long as you leave me alone." Nolan stormed off to his dressing room, and the first thing he did was pour himself a glass of whiskey. And then another. And another. By the time the bottle was empty, all Nolan could think about was how much like his father he had turned out to be.

Nolan Stone. Brother of Nathan Stone. Son of Damien Stone.

Self-centered, alcoholic, godless musician.

Like father, like sons.

Only unlike his father and his older brother, Nolan was an actual star. He wasn't a failure. And he wasn't dead. Not yet.

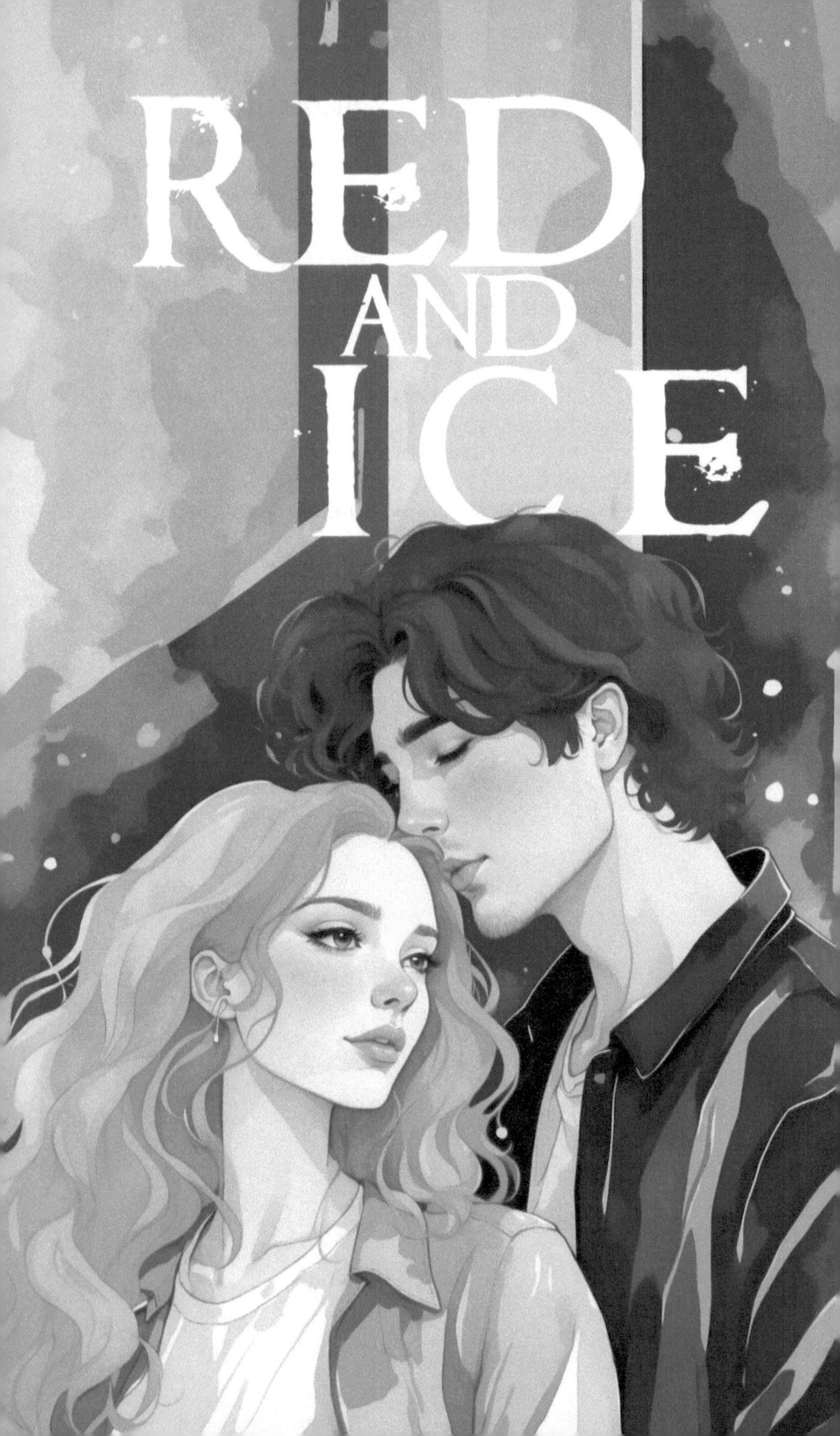

RED
AND
ICE

part two

PAST

EIGHTEEN YEARS AGO

six

THE ONE
WHO MOVED
NEXT DOOR

- NOLAN, 5 -

Nolan pasted his face and palms on the window of Neutron, their old, dirty-white family van. As they rolled into their new neighborhood, he gaped at the homes they passed — homes of all shapes and sizes, which all seemed to tower above the houses in the neighborhood they had left behind. No wonder his mother had been so happy about moving! He gawked at the ornate fences and landscaped lawns, transfixed by everything they passed, when— BANG!

He jolted in his car seat.

His ten-year-old sister, Nova, pressed her palms against the glove compartment to steady herself. "Was that Neutron?!"

Nolan giggled at the stunned expression on her face.

"Calm down, Nova," their mother said. "Yes, it's Neutron. Backfired."

Cheeks red, Nova sank in the front seat, so no one could see her from the window. "This is embarrassing. Why can't we change this stupid car?"

"Neutron's still running," Nolan and his mother said in unison.

Nova groaned. "I wish Dad would get us a new one."

"Your grandmother taught me never to let anything go to waste. Whether it be food or experiences," Ma said. "Neutron is just announcing our arrival. He's letting the neighborhood know: the Stones are here! And because they now know we're here, all our neighbors must give us some yummy food to welcome us. A casserole maybe. Or lasagna."

Nolan wrinkled his nose at the thought of anyone giving them food. No one ever did that in their old neighborhood. In fact, Ma always told him and Nova to stay away from their neighbors. Would it be different here? It sure looked different. Nolan pressed his nose against the glass and admired the nice grassy lawns and the clean exteriors. It wasn't like this at all where they had come from.

"Will Daddy or Nate ever come to visit us here?" he asked.

"Of course they will," Ma said.

Nova shook her head. "Dad will for sure, but Nate won't."

"Nova." Their mother's tone had an edge to it. "Your *kuya*[1] will return to us. Have faith."

Kuya. The Filipino word for "older brother" sounded odd to Nolan. He hadn't been able to use it since Nate ran away to become better at music than their dad.

"Ma, Nate's never coming back." Nova snorted. "You know I'm right."

"We'll talk about this later, Nova." Ma rounded a corner. "Right now, we have to find our house."

An image of Nate crossed Nolan's mind, and a heavy weight fell on his chest. Nolan wriggled his shoulders and forced another giggle. To banish the discomfort the mere thought of Nate brought about, he focused once again on the novelty of the scenes outside the car window.

A redheaded little girl stood on the porch of a large house. Her jaw dropped when she saw their car. She had one missing tooth. Nolan snickered

____

1 ku·ya /koo-yah/ noun; Filipino word for older brother.]

and waved at her as they passed by. She grinned and waved back.

To Nolan's surprise, his mother pulled over at the gablefront house right next door from the pretty house where the redhead lived.

Nova blew out a deep breath when they parked in the driveway of their new home. "It'll be so hard to make friends here. Especially if they find out where we come from."

"Nova Ramirez Stone." Ma tucked a stray strand of Nova's dark hair behind her ear. "Why so much negativity?" She twisted to her side and leaned her temple against the car seat so she could give Nova a better look. "Our lives are changing in so many ways. Can we not enjoy this, *mahal*[2]? Please?"

Nolan made a face when his mom said "love" in Filipino. *Mahal.* Ma usually spoke her native language when angry about something. Never for endearment. Ma was right. So much was changing. He stared at Nova long and hard before his gaze drifted out the window. The redhead jumped up and down her house's porch. A man strode ahead of her and opened a shiny black van parked on the driveway. Their vehicle put Neutron to shame.

Nolan sighed. He hoped what Ma said was true about their lives changing. He hoped there would be no yelling, fewer arguments, less pain. Nolan hoped, and as he did, he caught a glimpse of her again. The redhead with a missing tooth. She ran from the porch to the yard. As if sensing his stare, she stopped right in the middle. She glanced his way, and her face broke into a bright grin.

Nolan decided then and there that Nova was wrong. Making friends wouldn't be hard at all. In fact, he felt like he already had one. She had red hair, green eyes, a missing tooth, and a frilly green dress. Before the day could end, Nolan convinced Ma to let him pay their next-door neighbor a visit. By the time he got back home, he already had a friend named Serene.

---

2 ma·hal /mah–hal/ noun; love

- SERENE, 5 -

Serene didn't want to paint on paper anymore. She wanted the grown-up stuff, the ones her mother used for her masterpieces. The easel, the canvas, and the paintbrushes — Serene wanted them all. So, when her dad agreed to buy her a grown-up painting set of her own, joy bubbled from her chest and revealed itself in the bright smile on her freckled face. She rushed down the stairs and past the foyer. She threw open the front door, raised both arms in the air in a gesture of freedom, and twirled around on the porch.

"I'll be just like Mama Aida!" she exclaimed. "I'll paint the most beautiful pictures!"

She twirled around again and almost tripped on her feet, so she tried to balance herself by holding on to the nearest thing she could grab. That's when she saw the dirty minivan clunk its way past their house. She gawked at it as she held onto the wooden post supporting the roof of their porch. She had never ridden a car that could fall apart at any time, so she wondered why its passengers were so calm. A boy looked at her from inside the van. She blinked hard to make sure he was okay. She then smiled and waved at him. He waved back.

Serene's shoulders rose and fell as she breathed in a satisfied sigh. What a good day it was turning out to be!

"Serene?!" Her dad called out from inside the house. "Where are you? Are you ready to go?"

"As ready as I can ever be!" She jumped up and down.

At the sight of her, the muscles on his face eased into a bright smile. "There's my little artist!"

He picked her up and kissed her on the cheek. "Just give your mother time to get ready. She knows the materials you'll need a lot better than I do."

Serene threw her arms around his neck. "Thank you, Daddy! Thank you!"

He nuzzled his cheek against her hair and rocked her from side-to-side. "I love you, Serene."

"I love you too, Daddy."

Two craft stores and one hour later, Serene walked from the car to their house with her arms full of art supplies.

"Need help with that, kiddo?" her dad asked.

"I can manage," she said. "I'm all grown up." As she passed by their front lawn, she glanced at the house next-door to find out if the boy was there. What was his name? She would find out soon enough. Right now, she had a lot of painting to do.

Eager to get to her art, she set up her easel and canvas on the side of the front porch with the help of her mother. It took Serene only a few seconds before she decided what to paint: a clunky white car driven by a dark-haired boy off on an adventure to the moon.

She sang a song from Sunday School as she painted, a song about God's wonderful creation — butterflies, mountains, and seas. She decided she would one day paint them all, but more than anything, she wanted to paint something greater than the world she knew. Something unseen. Something beyond.

"Watchadoing?"

Serene yelped at the sound of the voice behind her. She spun around to find out who it had come from. Since she still held a wet paintbrush in her fingers, her slight leap in the air and sudden turnaround smeared blue paint on the face of the boy next door.

"Oops," Serene said.

The two stared at each other for a moment.

Serene blinked. "You have paint on your face."

"I know," he replied. "You have a missing tooth."

She giggled. "I know. What's your name?"

"Nolan. What's yours?"
"Serene. How old are you?"
"Five."
Her mouth dropped open. "I'm five too!"
"Do you want to be friends?"
Her wavy red ponytail bounced as she bobbed her head up and down. "I love new friends. Sorry for painting on your face."
Nolan grinned. "Don't worry about it." Before she realized what he was doing, he dipped his finger on her palette and smeared paint on her face. "Now, we're even."
In normal circumstances, Serene would've been furious. Why was he wasting her paint? But, she wasn't. Maybe because he smiled and said, "You look pretty, Serene."
And somehow, she felt like she made a friend whom she wanted to keep forever. For many years after, she always found reason to thank God for the day she accidentally painted Nolan Stone's face blue.

THE ONE WHO DECIDED TO MARRY HER

- ONE YEAR LATER; SERENE, 6 -

The bus that would lead them to the campsite where Connect Church held its annual summer family camp rolled along on the highway. It heaved up and down even as it moved forward, bringing them closer to their destination. Serene snuggled closer to her mother, who sat on the aisle seat beside her. Her head spun as she wrapped her arms around her stomach, clinging tightly. Every move the bus made blurred her vision. She kept swallowing, hoping it would help settle her stomach.

Squished between her and the window, Nolan sat in the same seat she was in. They had insisted even before they got on the bus that they would sit together no matter what; thus, the reason they shared one seat.

Nolan rubbed her back. "Get better, Serene."

Afraid of throwing up yet again, Serene just whimpered in response as she buried her cheek against her mother's thigh.

Mama Aida's fingers brushed her hair. "It'll be all right, darling. We'll get there soon."

As tears brimmed her eyes, Serene promised herself she would never ride a bus again.

"Yes, Jesus loves me." Nolan started singing softly. "Yes, Jesus loves me."

Serene angled her head down to peer at him. Rays of sunlight cast a glow on him as he observed the scenery they passed by and rocked his legs, his toes tapping against the seat in front of him, setting a beat for the song.

"Yes, Jesus loves me," he continued, unaware of anyone else. "The Bible tells me so."

A smile crept on her face as he continued to sing the verse. Drowsiness captured her, induced by his singing. It didn't take long before she couldn't sense the dizziness or the stomach ache anymore. She had drifted off to a land of dreams, to a mountainous grove where she saw a stunning woman with dark skin, a fair face, and an ivory white veil on her head. Riding on a horse, the intricate grandeur of her wedding dress didn't seem to faze the bride one bit as she held a sword in her hand and yelled into the horizon. A thundering quake shook Serene awake, causing the vision of the warrior bride to vanish in a blink.

Serene jolted up, her heart beating hard against her chest. Sweat dripped from her brow.

"It's okay, honey." Mama Aida comforted her. "We're here."

Suddenly, Serene's stomach turned, jolting her back into her nauseating predicament. "I don't feel okay," she moaned.

Nolan grabbed her hand. "Let's go out. Whenever I get carsick, Ma says all I need is fresh air."

Serene didn't have time to object, because he was already pulling her out of the bus. They squeezed past other passengers preparing to disembark. A few steps away from the bus, Nolan stopped pulling her. At the sight of her, his face fell. "Serene?"

To her horror, Serene threw up. Several chunks landed on his shoes. A tear fell from her cheek. "I'm so sorry, Nolan," she said when it was over.

Nolan handed her several tissues and wiped her face with one. "No use being sorry. It's all over now. We don't have to sit inside the mean old bus anymore. Now, we can have fun. What do you want to do?"

Get clean. Instead, she said, "Paint. I have to paint."

- NOLAN, 6 -

Nolan wrinkled his nose at the sour odor coming from Serene. No one could convince her to take a shower first. It didn't help that he had stood by her side and had defended her against all the adults when she wanted to paint first. He couldn't have known she would end up so stinky.

By the time Serene finished her painting, Nolan had already watched two afternoon cartoon shows on the clunky TV inside the family cabin where they were staying. Not how he wanted to spend their first day at church camp. They could hear Ma and Mama Aida's chatter all the way from the small kitchen shared by the families assigned to their cabin. Nolan's stomach grumbled. Hopefully, the mamas were making good food.

"All done," Serene announced. "I'll take a shower now!" She leaped in triumph, having done what she had set out to do.

Nolan sighed with relief.

Serene noticed.

He jolted up on the bean bag he had plopped himself on, his back straight.

The smile he was so familiar with brightened her already cheery countenance.

He relaxed.

"I stink." Serene wrinkled her nose.

He nodded slowly.

She shrugged and hopped to the shower. A few seconds in, she poked her head out of the door. "Sorry for the stink, Nolan."

"I don't mind," he said.

"It's not good to lie." She giggled.

Nolan grinned. She was his favorite for a reason.

With the sound of the shower and her hums as background, the painting captivated Nolan's attention. The dark woman with a white dress rode a black stallion, with a sword in her hand and a fierce look in her eyes. What was she fighting for? Who was she angry at?

"She's getting married."

Nolan leaped on his spot. Serene stood next to him. He hadn't even noticed her get out of the shower, much less get dressed.

"Do you like it?" Serene asked.

He nodded. "She's beautiful, but she looks like she wants to fight. My dad and mom are married. They always fight. Ma cries herself to sleep almost every night when he's around. Nova says she never wants to get married, because Dad and Ma are awful together, so there's no point."

The expression on Serene's face betrayed her confusion, like she didn't believe a word he had just said. "Daddy and Mama are married, and they're happy together." She shrugged. A smile spread across her face as if a series of fond memories had just played in her mind. "They always speak good things about each other and do nice things for each other. And they always say I love you. All the time. Daddy likes to kiss and hug Mama, and I suppose she likes it too. Sometimes, they surprise each other with little gifts for no reason at all. It's not even their birthday!"

"That doesn't sound like marrying at all." Nolan shook his head.

Serene stomped one foot on the floor. "I don't lie."

"What does it mean to get married, anyway?" Nolan asked.

"I heard all about it at church when Mama was teaching the youth group about love and marrying. The girl wears a pretty white dress, and the boy dresses up nice, and they promise to care for each other forever. And their mom and dad give them their blessing. And they must also both love each other." She spread her arms as far as she could reach. "A lot."

"I like your family's version of marrying. I'm sure Dad and Ma never promised all that to each other." His chest puffing out, determination coursed through Nolan. "When I get married, I'll love my girl, and her parents will give their blessing, and I'll promise to care for her forever. And I'll even give her gifts even if it's not her birthday. I like that kind of marrying."

"Me too." Serene agreed.

As they both nodded in unison, their hands found the other's, and Nolan decided right then he wanted to marry Serene.

He intended to state his intentions to her father, Pastor Sam, while they sat around a campfire later that night.

When Nolan arrived, Jake Harris, their worship pastor, was tuning his guitar and singing in a hoarse, off-key tone. One of their church elders, Marcus Grant, was making himself some smores. One of his sons, Caleb, sat next to him. Caleb lifted his glasses over the bridge of his nose as he used the firelight to illuminate the book he was reading. Meanwhile, Pastor Sam was opening another bag of marshmallows.

Nearby, the women had laid a picnic blanket on the grass near the lake. Two lanterns provided light to them. Mama Aida nodded at Ma as they discussed something about his dad. The two women rarely talked about anything unrelated to his dad. Nova sat akimbo not far from them. She hummed and rocked her head from side-to-side as she braided Serene's hair.

Seeing Serene reminded Nolan of what he had decided on. Nolan cleared his throat. "Pastor Sam?"

"Yes, Nolan?" He positioned a marshmallow over the fire.

Nolan took a deep breath, puffing his chest out to gather courage. He gave their pastor a curt nod.

"I want to let you know that I want to marry your daughter. I'd like to receive your blessing."

Elder Marcus coughed. Jake stopped playing. His head whipped to the side to regard Nolan. He then laughed and ruffled up Nolan's hair. The older men exchanged smiles and a few chuckles.

Pastor Sam narrowed his eyes at Nolan. "You want to marry Serene, huh?"

"How old are you again?"

"Six years old."

"Right. Same age as Serene. Why do you want to marry her? Can't you two just be friends?"

"We're already friends." Nolan frowned. "We will always be friends." He bit his lip and furrowed his brows. "Right, Pastor Sam? If I marry her, does that mean she has to stop being my friend?"

"Not at all." Pastor Sam shook his head. "Mama Aida is my wife, but she's also my best friend in the entire world."

"That's what Serene is to me! And I'm her best friend, too."

"You certainly are, Nolan."

"So can I marry her?"

"You can come talk to me again when you're a lot older."

"Like when I'm twelve?"

"No. More like when you're older than twenty-one. Nolan, you must understand how precious Serene is to Mama Aida and me. She's our little girl, and that means we want what's best for her. Maybe someday you will marry her, but—"

"I will." Nolan lifted his forefinger in the air. "I want to."

Pastor Sam smiled. "I can see that but not any time soon, kid. Not when you can't even get a job or earn money yet."

"My dad plays the guitar to get money."

"Your Ma told us. Do you know how to play the guitar?"

Nolan ran his gaze over the curvy edges of Jake's guitar. "I asked Dad to teach me a long time ago, but he never has the time. We don't see him around a lot, and when he visits, Ma asks us to stay away because he's often in a sour mood. My older brother and sister don't like him much. I don't know why Ma does." He gave a light kick to a small rock on the ground. "Can you teach me how to play the guitar, Pastor Sam?"

"I sure can, Nolan, but—" Pastor Sam reached forward to tap Jake on the back. "You've seen Jake in church every Sunday. He'll be better at teaching you to play."

Nolan turned his head toward Jake. "You play almost as good as Dad."

Jake grinned. "I'm glad you think so, Nolan. I'd be happy to teach you. Do you have your own guitar?"

Nolan grimaced as he slowly shook his head. "I don't. Ma doesn't like instruments inside the house. Nova has to leave the house if she wants to play loud music."

The men exchanged glances before Pastor Sam nodded and said, "We'll get you a guitar, and if your mom doesn't want you to play in your house, you can always practice in ours."

The next day, Pastor Sam gave Nolan his first guitar. It was just the right size for his age. By the end of the day, he already mastered the basic chords. By the last day of camp, Nolan could play most songs by ear, and no one present could deny what a gifted musician he was.

Connect Church had just discovered a virtuoso.

THE ONE WHO LEARNED TO WORSHIP

Mesmerized, Serene's eyes followed the quick movement of Nolan's small fingers on the guitar's strings. He had tried to teach her several times. Though she had quickly learned the chords and how to strum, she kept returning the instrument to Nolan. He was leagues better than her, and she enjoyed hearing him play.

Serene sat next to him on the wooden steps that led to the conference hall, the venue of their final camp meeting before they all had to leave for home the next morning. She couldn't be prouder of him. Nolan's eyes twinkled as he strummed the last note of the worship song Jake had taught him earlier. Delight spread across his face as he hugged his guitar tight. Inside the camp meeting hall, Jake started to lead worship. Serene covered her ears at the sound of his voice. Nolan giggled. She followed suit, and both broke into unstoppable snickers until a pang of reverence hit Serene's heart. She dropped her hands away from her ears and onto her lap.

"We shouldn't laugh," she said. "Jake is worshiping God."

Nolan stopped. Right at that moment, Jake sang a note off-key, and a smirk threatened to form on his lips.

Serene stood her ground and kept a reverent expression on her face. "Daddy said that Jake may not sing the best, but he is a gifted music man, and he has a worshiper's harp."

"Jake doesn't have a harp." Nolan started tuning his guitar.

"Maybe it was heart. I don't remember."

"Is Pastor Sam right about Jake?"

"I think so." Serene nodded. "Daddy is right about a lot of things."

"Yeah? Well, Pastor Sam said I can marry you when I'm twenty-one years old. That's a long time from now, but I think we can be that old someday. We just have to make sure neither of us goes to heaven before then."

"If Daddy says you can marry me, it's for sure we'll reach twenty-one years old. I know it." Serene inched closer to Nolan and leaned her head on his shoulder. "How long before we're twenty-one?"

Nolan stopped playing. His shoulders drooped. "I'm not good at math, especially takeaways."

"Me too." Serene scrunched up her nose in disappointment. "We'll be twenty-one someday. We just have to wait."

Cradling his guitar, Nolan rocked himself on the steps. "We should enter and worship."

Something deep within Serene soared at the suggestion. "Have you ever tried it before?"

Nolan shook his head. "We never worship in Sunday School. We just sing all the kid songs, but it's not like how Jake or Pastor Sam or Mama Aida do it."

"Let's go." Excitement filled Serene. She had worshiped with Daddy and Mama Aida before, but something about worshiping God with Nolan felt special to her.

They entered the hall, and Nolan handed his guitar to his mom for safekeeping. They headed straight to the front and mimicked everyone else around them. Dancing and raising their hands and singing, Serene had the time of her life, and it seemed as if Nolan did too. The music slowed down. A strange calm swept over Serene, and it stopped being just a fun thing to do. The playing morphed into a yearning deep within a child's heart. Tears ran down Serene's cheeks as she realized how much she loved Jesus. She experienced His embrace in an inexplicable but personal and authentic way.

She barely sensed time passing by. God was captivating her, and she lost awareness of everyone around her, His presence being the only thing that mattered. Her young mind couldn't comprehend it, but God had become as real to her as Nolan was.

Only when one of the elders, Marcus Grant, went up on stage and shared how God had brought him up to heaven, did Serene snap back to an awareness of where she was and who she was with.

As the respected elder shared his experience, right next to Serene, Rhoda Ross, their Sunday School teacher, nudged Nolan's Ma. "Impossible. If he did go to heaven, he should be dead. Do you believe him?"

Clara Stone nodded. "I don't see why he would lie, Rhoda."

Miss Rhoda tsk-tsked.

Whatever reason she had for not believing in what Marcus Grant said, Serene didn't care to know, but it intrigued her. What if Miss Rhoda's surly attitude toward people was the reason she couldn't find a man to marry her? It didn't seem so hard. Serene bumped Nolan's arm with her own. She was six years old, and she already knew whom she wanted to marry.

After the session on the last night of summer camp, Nolan rested on a picnic blanket his mother had spread over the grass. His brand new guitar lay next to him. As everyone in camp rushed to finish packing for their return home the next day, he decided he wanted to spend more time staring at the stars. Not long after he had made himself comfortable in a quiet spot, Serene found him. She followed suit and positioned herself on the blanket so that the top of their heads touched each other.

Nolan hummed a song Jake sang during the evening session. "He loves us more than the number of stars in the sky." He sang in a hushed tone. "He's the Father whose love we can't deny."

"Do you think Marcus Grant really saw heaven earlier tonight, Nolan?"

"I don't know." He shrugged. "Do you?"

"I don't know either. Miss Rhoda says she doesn't believe him."

"Miss Rhoda doesn't believe in a bunch of things." He giggled.

"You're right. But Nolan?"

"Yep?"

"I sure want to have a vision like Marcus Grant did. Maybe I can see heaven, too."

"Why do you want to see heaven, Serene?"

"So I can paint it. I want to be a painter someday. What do you want to be?"

"Easy. I want to be a pastor just like your dad."

"Don't you want to be like your dad instead? A famous rock star?"

"My dad isn't famous, and he's not a star. He's just—" Nolan shook his head. "He's a rock."

Serene giggled. "No, he's not. Nobody is a rock, Nol—" Her hand reached for him, her fingers soft on his cheek. "What's wrong? Did something happen?"

"I don't want to talk about it. I don't want to talk about him."

"Okay."

Silence swept over them as they kept their eyes on the stars. Nolan's eyelids grew heavier. When Serene yawned, he yawned as well. Not long after, he drifted off to sleep. When he woke up, the stars still glittered in the heavens. Nolan lifted himself up to a sitting position and scratched his cheek. His mother sat on a bench nearby, talking to Nova. Serene lay still on the blanket, a smile on her face.

"Sweet dreams, Serene," he whispered.

That's when the music drifted into his consciousness. Like a sound emerging from deep within. He picked up his guitar and played the song in his mind. The moment he did, goosebumps spread over his entire body. He rocked his head from side-to-side.

Suddenly, Serene jolted awake. Her labored breathing shot a sliver of worry within him. Did her dream turn into a nightmare? He was about to put his guitar aside, reach out to her to comfort her, but Serene's face lit up in a bright smile. She lifted her palm to keep him from approaching. "Don't stop playing, Nolan. What song is that?"

Nolan shrugged. "I made it up."

"Have you been playing it a long time?"

"No. I started playing just before you woke up. Why?"

"I dreamed of heaven, Nolan—" her eyes sparkled with wonder "—and I heard your song being played there. Did you go to heaven, too?"

Nolan winced. Had his best friend gone crazy? Was she telling tall tales?

Several days after camp, Serene asked him to play the song again while she painted. When she showed him her painting, a deep, ageless yearning awakened within Nolan: a yearning for the heavens. A yearning for home.

nine

THE ONE WHO DIDN'T DO HIS HOMEWORK

- ONE YEAR LATER; NOLAN, 7 -

Like every other Sunday, Nolan got up and jumped into his morning routine. He made his bed, entered the bathroom to brush his teeth and shower, and returned to his room to put on his Sunday best — black pants, a red shirt, white suspenders, and leather shoes. He took extra time combing his hair to the side. Satisfied with his appearance, Nolan grinned at his reflection in the mirror and stepped out of his bedroom and into the hallway that led to the stairs. Once he exited his room, however, he froze at the sight that greeted him.

His dad had Ma pressed against the wall. Their mouths melded together like they were trying to swallow each other up.

Nolan grimaced. "Ma?" His voice came out as a squeak.

Ma tapped his dad several times on the shoulder.

Damien turned his head to Nolan and grinned. "Hey, buddy. You look spiffy. Why are you so dressed up?"

"It's Sunday, silly," Ma said.

His face scrunched up in confusion. "So?"

"We go to church every Sunday. I told you about that, remember? Nova, Nolan, and I have been going to Connect Church. You remember I told you about our neighbor, Mama Aida? She's the pastor's wife."

"I remember you mentioning her, but you said nothing about bringing the kids to some church."

"Well, I'm telling you now. Nolan's playing the guitar for the first time on stage today. It's this incredible story with our pastor's little girl, Serene. She's Nolan's best friend, and at church camp, sh—"

"Yeah. I met her last time I was home. Just didn't realize she was a pastor's kid. And church camp? What the—" He uttered a word that made Nolan wince. "Why didn't you tell me about this earlier, Clara?"

"I don't know." Ma frowned. "I didn't think it was such a big deal. Can we discuss this some other time? Not in front of the kid?"

Damien's face softened. "I'm sorry. Just a little surprised, that's all." He winked at Nolan. "Aren't you going to give your old man a hug?" Damien crouched down and spread his arms to welcome his kid.

Nolan ran into Damien's embrace and wrapped his arms around his father's neck.

"That's my boy!" Damien exclaimed as he carried Nolan. "So handsome. And you're so big! How old are you now?"

"Seven."

"So your Ma says you play the guitar, huh? Just like your dad?"

Nolan nodded.

"That's great!" He walked down the stairs to the living room while Ma trailed behind them. "Can you play for me while Ma makes breakfast?"

Nolan hesitated. "You can watch me in church later. You'll go with us, won't you, Dad?"

"I wanted to talk to you about that, buddy. I'm home for just a few days, so I'm hoping we can skip church today and go on a little road trip as a family. How about a trip to Disney World, huh?" Damien tickled Nolan on the stomach. "What do you think?"

When Nolan's giggles subsided and Damien set him on the floor, Nolan shook his head. "I can't skip church this Sunday, Dad. Serene will paint the heavens again while I play the guitar. We started it at camp last year, and Pastor Sam saw us at their garage, and Mama Aida suggested we show it this Sunday. It's the first time we'll do it in front of the whole church!"

"So you're telling me you'd rather go to church than to Disney World?"

Nolan didn't even bat an eyelash. "I can't go to Disney World without Serene. We promised we'd go together. She hasn't been there either. And Sunday is for church. All the other days can be for Disney World."

Damien deadpanned. "Are you serious? What kind of kid would prefer church over an amusement park?"

Nolan didn't know how to respond, so he just stood on his spot and stared up at his father.

Damien scowled. "And what do you mean Serene will paint the heavens?"

Nolan grinned. "Come to church and find out."

Damien glanced at his wife, shook his head, and tsk-tsked at her. Ma winced as he walked past her. "I need a beer."

She cast Nolan an apologetic smile before following Damien to the kitchen. Nolan plopped himself on the couch. Within minutes, the arguing started.

"I thought we were done with all this Christian stuff a long time ago, Clara. You said so yourself: the way your church treated you when they found out I got you pregnant was nasty. Why would you even subject my kids to—"

"Wait. What? Your kids?! Are you kidding me, Damien? You barely know these kids! Nolan loves church, and Nova has made some great friends there. The past years have been tough for her, especially with Nate going off on his own. Let's not forget how that is your fault, Damien! You—"

A sharp slapping sound, a shriek, and a long pause followed.

"Don't you dare talk about Nate." Damien lowered his voice. "Not to me."

"We will go to church. You can stay here if you want."

"Clara—"

Ma returned to the living room. Nolan stared at the drop of red liquid on one corner of her mouth as she passed by him. "Ma, there's blood."

She quickly wiped it away and turned to face him. She smiled — or at least tried to. "It's nothing, honey. Don't worry about it."

Nolan's expression turned grim. "Did Dad do that?"

Ma shook her head. "No, of course not." She walked to him and kissed him on the forehead. "Wait here while I get ready for church, okay? Nova will be ready soon."

"I'm going with you." Damien leaned on the arches that led to their living room. He winked at Nolan.

Ma ignored him and climbed up the stairs. A blend of anger and sadness whirled within Nolan when his father didn't even bother to go after his mom. "Will you really go to church with us?"

Damien nodded.

Nolan didn't know whether to be thrilled or disheartened. He couldn't imagine his father in church at all, but they went, so Nolan got to play the guitar in front of Damien Stone for the first time.

The moment Nolan got on stage, the jitters flew away. All awareness of his earthly father's presence vanished. With eyes shut tight, Nolan's mind traveled heavenward, toward things greater than himself. He lost his worries in the music, his heart swept away by the wonder of reaching a God invisible yet present. When he opened his eyes, the first thing he saw was Serene's smile. His gaze drifted from her lovely, freckled face to her artwork: a portrait of a fantastical garden vibrant with colors that ignited his imagination. Her work was a promise of what awaited them someday in their true home.

Nolan then glanced at the applauding audience and immediately zoned in on his father. Slumped on his seat with arms crossed over his chest, he leaned to the side and said something to Ma. Her face contorted as she shot a glare at him.

"Damien," she mouthed.

Nolan never found out what his father said to his mom, but at the end of the service, his father made it clear: "None of you will go to church again."

From that day on, Ma stopped attending church. Not long after, Nova stopped too. Not Nolan. Every Sunday continued to start like any other Sunday. He got up and jumped into his morning routine. He made his bed, entered the bathroom to brush his teeth and shower, and returned to his room to put on his Sunday best.

No one could stop Nolan from attending church because for most of his years growing up, it was the only place he felt like he belonged.

Not even Damien Stone could stop him.

- ONE YEAR LATER; NOLAN, 8 -

Ma pulled over in their driveway in Blaze, the brand-new car Dad had bought for them before he returned to his tour.

"Tell Nova to come here and help me."

"Yes, Ma! I'll come back to help too." Nolan rushed out of the car and waved at Neutron, which they kept parked at their garage before hurrying to the front door. He wanted to help his mom with the groceries and then finish his homework so he could go to Serene's house after. He turned the knob and pushed the front door open. "Nova! Nov—" He stopped short when he found her at the entryway.

She was sitting on the last two steps of the staircase, sobbing.

"Nova?"

She raised her head from her crouched position, her mass of curls cascading down her shoulders as she did. Her tear-stricken cheeks paled as she hiccuped.

"Why are you crying?" Nolan asked as he approached with caution.

"Where's Ma?" Nova asked.

"Unloading Blaze's trunk. She needs help with the groceries."

Nova stood up and walked past him. "Ma!"

Confused, Nolan followed his sister outside and found her running into their mother's arms. Nova sobbed into Ma's shoulders while Nolan approached, unsure of what's happening.

"Honey, what happened?" Ma stroked Nova's long curls.

"Nate's friend called. Something terrible has happened."

Concern creased their mother's features. "Nolan, go to Serene's house right now."

"Even if I haven't done my chores and finished my homework yet?" Nolan couldn't keep the smile from his face.

"Yes, buddy. Go. Your sister and I need time to talk."

Nolan didn't miss a beat. He slung his backpack over his shoulder and ran to the house next door. When Serene opened the door for him, her bright eyes reflected the excitement written all over her. "Nolan! You came just in time!"

"For what?" Nolan asked.

"You know how I've been telling you that Mama has my baby brother inside her? He's coming out now!"

"Now?"

"Now! You're coming, right?"

Someone screamed from upstairs.

Nolan winced. "Who's that?"

"That's Mama, silly. She's in a lot of pain because my brother is trying to come out of her. Will you go to the hospital with us?"

Pastor Sam and Mama Aida emerged from the top of the stairs. Mama Aida's face twisted in pain as she clutched her stomach.

Nolan hesitated to go with them. "I don't know. I have to do my homework."

Serene grabbed his hand. "Nolan, please. I want you there with us so we can meet my baby brother together."

"I'll go ask Ma if she'll let me." Nolan rushed back to their house.

"Hurry!" Serene yelled out as he sped forward. "We don't have much time!"

Nolan ran as fast as his legs could take him. He arrived at their living room to find his mother and sister embracing each other. Their shoulders shook as they wailed.

"Ma? Nova? Why are you both crying?"

Ma reached out for him and included him in the tearful hug. Nova's arms wrapped around him too, and they caught him in their suffocating embrace of sadness.

"I want to go to the hospital." Nolan tried to squirm away. "Mama Aida is having her baby, and she's yelling out in pain. Can I go, Ma?"

"Nolan—" Ma closed her mouth and then nodded. "Okay. Go."

"What?" Nova asked between sniffles. "You won't tell him?"

"I'm not ready to explain. Are you?"

Nova shook her head.

"Go ahead, Nolan. Go to the hospital with them."

Nolan stood a step away from them and wondered what was going on. Something was wrong, but wasn't there always something wrong at home? He decided whatever they were crying about, there wasn't much he could do about it. So, he ran back in time to get in the Sinclairs' car and rush to the hospital with a family he considered his own.

That night, Nolan got to eat ice cream while they waited for Serene's baby brother to come out. Finally, when the long wait was over, he got to see Baby Jeremy for the first time. He wrinkled his nose and wondered why the baby's face was so crinkly. He didn't look at all like Serene. No way had she been as crinkly when she had been a baby.

All in all, despite all the crying back at home, Nolan considered it a good day. After all, he got to spend extra time with his best friend even if he hadn't yet done his homework.

The moment Serene met her baby brother, she adored him. He had Daddy's brown hair and had gray eyes, but Daddy said it would most likely be eventually green like hers and Mama's. He had the smallest round face and the world's cutest smile, at least in Serene's opinion. Dad told her Jeremy couldn't even smile yet — he was too young — but Serene refused to believe a word of it. Jeremy could smile! She had already seen it, and if it were up to her, she would never leave her brother's side. To her disappointment, however, soon after they brought Jeremy home, Nolan made it clear he wanted nothing to do with her new sibling.

"I'm going home!" Nolan stomped out of the nursery.

"Nolan, why?" Serene tiptoed to look over the side of the crib. She made a face at baby Jeremy before rushing out of the adventure-themed room to catch up with her best friend. "You said you wanted to spend the afternoon together."

He clenched his fists. His face turned red, and his cheeks puffed up. When Serene grabbed his elbow, he pushed her away.

Serene gasped when her shoulder hit the wall. "Why are you mad, Nolan? I don't understand. What did I do?"

Nolan stopped walking before he reached the stairs. He clung to the stair's rails. He took a stiff turn and faced her. His gaze softened when he looked at her.

Serene tried to keep the tears away. "You're never mad at me." Her lower lip quivered as she pouted.

Nolan flinched, but he didn't approach her like she expected him to. Instead, he stood his ground. Tears fell down his cheek. "Everything has changed. Since he came, I—" he shifted his weight from one foot to another and looked away "—don't belong here anymore."

"How can you say that? You're my best friend!"

"You have a brother now, so you don't need a best friend." Nolan shook his head. "I can't ever be a part of this family. Not anymore. Now that he's here, none of you need me, so I'm not coming back! I don't want to be your best friend anymore!"

Before Serene could say anything, Nolan turned and ran down the stairs. He almost collided with her father, who was climbing the stairs with a basket full of laundry in his hands. "Nolan!" he yelled.

Serene stood in her spot, frozen. She tried to wrap her mind around Nolan's outburst, but couldn't. When she heard the front door slam shut downstairs, she broke into a sob.

Daddy's brows creased when he saw his daughter's tears. He dropped the basket on the ground and rushed to scoop up his daughter in his arms. "Honey, what happened?"

Serene shook her head. "I don't know." Sobs wracked her small frame as she allowed her father to pick her up and rock her from side-to-side. When her tears subsided, Daddy put her on the floor and brushed the strands of her hair away from her face. "Would you like to tell me what happened?"

"He said he doesn't want to be my best friend because Jeremy's here now. Nolan says that means we don't need him anymore," Serene said between sniffles.

His eyes cleared. "I see. Do you want to go next door and visit Nolan and his mom? I've been meaning to check on Clara and Nova for weeks now."

Serene nodded. "But what about Jeremy?"

"Mama can take care of him for now. Come on." Daddy extended his hand for Serene to hold.

She took her father's hand, and they walked to the house next door.

Serene's chest tightened when she found Nolan sitting on the porch steps. He had his face buried in his palms. His shoulders shook. Serene acted on pure instinct when she ran to him and threw her arms around him. "Nolan, please stop crying. Please don't be mad. I never want us to stop being best friends."

Nolan lifted his face from his palms. His eyes widened with horror at the sight of her — even more so when he saw her father approaching. "Serene, you can't be here. Go. You and Pastor Sam. Both of you have to go now."

A loud crash echoed from inside the house, followed by loud yelling. Nolan's sister threw the door open and froze when she found Serene and her dad there.

A male voice swore up a storm inside before a woman yelled and something crashed.

Nova gulped. "It's not what it looks like."

Serene's dad rushed in. "Clara?!"

Serene wanted to follow her father, but Nova held her back. "It's best you stay here."

Serene stared at the open door, not knowing what to do. Nolan buried his face in his palms again. She sat beside him and hugged him. "Everything will be okay," she said, even if she wasn't sure it would be.

A few days later, Mama Aida sat down with her to explain to her what happened. Nolan's dad hit his mom, but that wasn't the worst the Stone family was dealing with. Nolan hadn't told a soul, but the day Jeremy was born, they received news that their older brother, Nate, had died.

Serene had gained a brother while Nolan had lost his. Mama Aida explained to Serene later that Nolan was dealing with a lot. They all had to be there for him and assure him that with them, he would always have a family. Jeremy's existence hadn't changed that.

But Nolan was never the same since that day, and though she didn't fully understand at eight years old, Serene felt her best friend's loss. Like that day took a certain level of innocence from both of them, and nothing could ever bring it back. From that day forward, Serene never saw the heavens again.

ten

THE ONE WHO KISSED & MESSED UP

- SIX YEARS LATER; NOLAN, 14 -

Early morning on their first day of high school, Mama Aida dropped Nolan and Serene off. The last time he was in that high school parking lot, Nolan was in his booster seat, and Ma had brought Nova to school. Nova had taken forever to get out of the car. Her eyes were wide with concern as she stepped into this world she hadn't felt like she belonged to. She had seemed so lost. Would Nolan feel the same way? Nolan got out of the car with a huge grin on his face. No way. Nolan had something Nova hadn't: Serene.

"You two behave, okay? And have fun!" Mama Aida said as they scooted out.

Nolan took a step toward the school building, expecting Serene to follow him, but she didn't budge. He took a step back and nudged her on the arm. "School is inside. That's where we need to go."

Serene breathed deep and hugged her colorful purse against her chest. "Is it weird that I'm a little scared?" The quietness of her statement made it seem like she had meant it as a whisper she hadn't intended for him to hear.

"Yes, it is." People were milling in and out of the school entrance, and Nolan couldn't wait for this brand new adventure with her. "It's just school."

"It's high school."

"So? I got you, Red. We're in this together."

Her brow rose. "Red?"

"We've been best friends for years. Don't you think it's odd we don't have nicknames for each other?"

"Not really." Serene shook her head. "Both our names are two syllables, Nolan. We don't need nicknames."

"I think we do, and that's what I'm calling you. Red."

"Okay then. I'll call you Ice."

"What? Why?"

Serene wrinkled her nose. "I don't know. It's the first three-letter word that came to mind. Also, your last name is Stone."

"What does that have to do with Ice?"

Serene's shoulders lifted as she made a face. "Hard as ice? Stone cold?"

Nolan chuckled. "I'm sure that makes sense to you, but whatever. You're Red. We can be like fire and ice." Nolan's gaze drifted toward the entrance to the school. "Can we go in now?"

Serene took a deep breath before she nodded. Nolan chuckled and playfully chucked her chin up with his forefinger. The moment they entered through the front doors, several heads turned. Most were guys, and they certainly weren't looking at him.

As they walked along the hallway, Nolan caught more glimpses of boys doing a double-take at Serene as they passed. It shouldn't have surprised him. She had already been drawing attention back in middle school, but something about that summer had transformed Serene. She had blossomed, and Nolan was well aware of how her presence could quicken a typical teenage boy's senses. After all, no matter how familiar he was with her, Nolan was no exception.

A sense of protectiveness came over him when he noticed how another guy's gaze swept over her entire form as they passed. Nolan bumped shoulders with her.

"What are you doing?" she asked, her voice laced with amusement.

"Please tell me you notice that," he said.

"Notice what?" Serene stopped to check the piece of paper that contained her locker number.

"I've seen at least three guys do a double-take when you passed by."

"It happens." She shrugged. "No big deal." She looked at the locker to her right and tapped it with her forefinger three times. "This is mine. Where's yours?"

Nolan shrugged. "Somewhere here." He let his stare linger on her.

"What?"

"Do you want to do something epic? Something they'll remember us by for the rest of our time here?"

Serene made a face. "What did you have in mind?"

"Just follow my lead at the cafeteria during lunch, okay?"

"Nolan, wh—"

"Do you trust me?" Nolan's senses quickened when she stared into his eyes and regarded him like she wanted to explore the depths of his mind and soul.

"You've never asked me that before."

"Well, do you?"

She smiled. "You know I do."

Nolan didn't overthink it. He just did it. He leaned forward and kissed her on the forehead.

Serene stepped back, but when he expected to find shock on her face, he found amusement. Her eyes narrowed as she giggled. She then nodded slowly as if trying to process what he had just done. Without a word, she turned to her locker and dialed in the combination. "Go look for your locker, Ice. I'll see you later."

Nolan smirked. "See you, Red."

He walked away knowing something had shifted between them. That one kiss, to him, was a promise of possibility. They could be more than friends. At least, that's what Nolan hoped it meant. All he could think about until lunch break was how much he wanted to kiss her, but he didn't push it. He drew confidence in the fact that none of these guys ogling her had the edge he had: time with her. History.

At the cafeteria later that day, Nolan flicked his eyebrows at Serene as they both set their trays on a table. "Ready?"

Her eyes popped open. "Ready for what?"

"Come on, Red." His shoulders sagged. "You said you'd follow my lead."

Serene chuckled. Her ponytail swayed as she bobbed her head up and down. "Fine, fine."

"Wait here a second."

"What? How—"

Nolan didn't wait to hear what she had to say. He ran to the music room, grabbed one guitar, and returned to the cafeteria. When she saw him approaching with the instrument in hand, she shook her head. "No way. What are you thinking?"

"You have a great voice, Red. Sing with me."

"We'll make fools out of ourselves."

"Maybe so, but no matter how this goes, we'll become legends. Unforgettable."

"Nolan—"

It was a risk, but he took it anyway. If he miscalculated, their new school would probably always view them as those two freshmen desperate for attention, but Nolan didn't believe for one moment that would happen.

He strummed the first chord and from that point on, there was no turning back. By the end of the day, the verdict was clear. Whispers of how two gifted freshmen would someday take the music world by storm scattered all across the school. But to Nolan Stone, it wasn't the music or the newfound popularity that was legendary about that day. No. The most legendary part of their first day in high school was after they waved goodbye to a bunch of their new friends and walked out of school together.

It seemed like the most natural thing to do when Nolan took Serene's hand. He expected her to pull her hand away. Instead, she looked at him with a flicker of wonder in her eyes and a huge smile on her face.

"What?" he asked.

"You're amazing, you know that?"

"Nowhere near as amazing as you are, Red."

Serene stood on her tiptoes and before he could figure out what was happening, she leaned forward, about to kiss him on the cheek. He hadn't intended to do it, but Nolan turned his head at just the right time and angle so that her lips landed on his lips instead.

He could never forget the way her freckles faded into the blush of her cheeks. Her mouth parted when she realized what just happened. "I—"

Nolan shook his head. "Don't you dare say sorry." He then held her waist, tugged her closer, and pressed his lips on hers. Her lips trembled and so did his. He didn't know what he was doing, and neither did she. He didn't know if the kiss was good to her, but to him, it was everything he dreamed of and more.

To him, their first kiss was precious.

Perfect.

Perhaps even legendary.

Serene fidgeted with the hem of her skirt as Mick Raymond drove the Jeep from their school to Brad Maxwell's house. Mick's girlfriend, Claudine Schafer, sat in the passenger seat in front. Serene sat in the backseat between Nolan and Trent. She squirmed closer to Nolan because Trent's elbow kept rubbing against her waist.

Nolan grabbed her hand and squeezed it tight. He leaned over and whispered in her ear, "I'm so glad your dad allowed you to come." He kissed the back of her hand.

Serene cringed. She had called home to ask permission to go to the party that night. Her dad said no, yet there she was — off to her first high school party.

"You're shaking so hard." Nolan's dark brow quirked up. "Nervous about tonight's performance?"

She nodded.

"Don't be. I'm right here with you."

His eyes had a sheen on them that betrayed his excitement over the whole event. She knew him well enough to recognize how important this was to him. It showed in the animated expression of his face when he had told her earlier that Brad Maxwell — senior, student body president, and arguably the most popular guy in school — had invited them to play at his party. Two freshmen at a senior's party. How could her father not understand how important this was to her? To Nolan?

Serene closed her eyes and prayed that her parents would understand.

"I can't believe Pastor Sam allowed you to go," Nolan said.

"He knows I'm with you." There it was. Yet another lie. Serene bit her lip as conviction swept over her. *I'm going to hell for this.*

"Here we are!" Mick announced as they took a turn and entered wide steel gates, kept open for the party.

Nolan peered outside the window and uttered, "Whoa."

Serene tried not to gawk. Brad's place was huge. The bass of loud pop music playing from inside the mansion thumped against their chests as they got out of the car.

They entered through the front door in time for Brad to step into the foyer. When he saw them, his face lit up.

"Nolan, my man!" he exclaimed. He bumped fists with Nolan and winked at Serene. "Hey, beautiful."

Serene smiled.

"Come in, come in." Brad ushered everyone in. "The guests will arrive in about an hour. You can rehearse until then. The stage is all set up in the living room." He pointed them there. "The instruments are ready. You can do whatever it is you do. Sound check. Whatever. Thanks for doing this on such short notice."

"Thanks for having me, man," Nolan said.

"I'm sure you'll rock it." Brad slapped him on the back.

Nolan and Serene headed to where Brad pointed. Mick, Claudine, and Trent trailed behind them. They had never played together before, but since the band Brad recruited hadn't yet arrived, he suggested Nolan and Serene play with Mick, a senior who played bass, and Trent, a sophomore who played drums. Nolan would play the lead guitar and sing while Serene would stay behind the keyboard and provide backup vocals.

They spent the next half-hour setting up and trying to sound like a band, but Nolan kept stopping everyone.

"Dude, we'll have to play soon," Mick said. "Make up your mind."

"It doesn't sound right." Nolan cringed.

Exhausted, Serene approached. "Nolan, what's happening? We can't be perfect right now. We have to make do with what we have. It's like church. You can bear listening to Jake sing, right?"

"Yeah, but that's church, Red."

"What does that mean?"

"You know." Nolan shrugged. "We compromise, and we give grace there, because it's the heart and the commitment that matters. It's different here. No one will care about what's in our hearts. They'll care if we're good."

"Are we rehearsing or not?" Mick asked.

"That's it." Trent threw the drumsticks on the floor. "I'm done." He walked off the make-shift stage. "I came here to party anyway, not to perform."

Mick watched Trent go and then shrugged. "Look. Nolan. You and Serene killed it when you pulled off that performance on the first day of school. I don't think you need us."

"Brad wants a full band though."

"Who cares what Brad wants? Do your thing, Nolan. You heard the man. He thinks you'll rock it. We all do."

Before they could object, Mick put down the bass guitar, hooked his arm over Claudine's neck, and walked away.

Nolan and Serene stared at each other. For a moment, Nolan seemed to hesitate when he took a step back and motioned to put his guitar down. However, something sparked in his eyes. He cradled the guitar in his arms and started playing an insane riff. He then smirked and peered at her through his long dark lashes. "Up for this?"

Serene rolled her eyes. "Guess I am."

She took her place behind the keyboard and performed with him, but by the end of the night, there was no doubt about it. Between the two of them, Nolan was the true star. And she loved him for it. She loved how he was so sure of himself, how he oozed confidence, and how at the end of it all, he wrapped his arms around her waist and kissed her.

With their set over, Brad's playlist blared on the house speakers. Their host approached to congratulate them. "Awesome job! Mad talent!"

With one glance at Nolan, Serene could tell he was drinking it all in. He loved this. On the other hand, with the adrenaline waning and Nolan's music replaced by music she didn't care about, her conscience found space to nag at her again.

She brushed her fingers on Nolan's elbow. "I think I have to go home."

"You mean now?"

"You're leaving? No, no..." Brad shook his head. He squeezed himself between them and placed his arms on their shoulders. "Not until you both have a beer. I insist."

Serene panicked. "I can't."

"Why not?" Brad brushed his thumb against her cheekbone. "Is it your first time? It's really not that bad."

"Come on, Red," Nolan said. "What harm would one sip do? Aren't you even a little curious?"

"I am, but..." *It's illegal. It's wrong.* Her cheeks flushed red. She couldn't believe Nolan was goading her into this. Her gut was screaming for her to say no, but Nolan made her want to say yes. "I'll take a sip if you take a sip."

"I love it!" Brad exclaimed. "Someone get these rock stars a drink."

Nolan brought her the plastic cup of beer himself. The excitement in his eyes, the grin on his lips, and an inexplicable fear in her heart made her take her first sip.

One of many that night.

Enough so that Nolan had to carry her to the Sinclairs' doorstep.

Enough so that the next morning, it felt like her body was trying to kill her.

Enough to break whatever trust her family had toward Nolan and herself.

Enough for her to regret for a very long time.

eleven

THE ONE SHE HAD TO BREAK UP WITH

A tense silence permeated the entire Sinclair household after Serene returned home from school. Not wanting to talk to anyone, she ran through the foyer and sped past her father on the stairs without acknowledging him. She proceeded to her bedroom and slammed the door behind her. She locked the door before plopping herself onto her bed face down. Tears soaked the fabric as she muffled her scream with her pillow. Minutes later, her father knocked on her bedroom door.

"Open the door, young woman. I won't tolerate this behavior any longer."

"I don't want to talk."

"Serene Sinclair." Her dad's deep, authoritative voice made her shudder. "Open the door. Now."

Serene dragged herself to the door. She braced herself for his fury before opening it. Instead of anger, she found pain and sorrow on his face.

She steeled herself from feeling bad for him. "What?"

"Come to the living room right now. Your mother and I want to have a word with you."

"I don't want to."

"Serene." He closed his eyes and took a deep breath. "Please don't make this harder than it already is for all of us. To the living room."

Serene gritted her teeth. "Fine."

She followed her father downstairs to the living room where Mama Aida was helping Jeremy with his homework.

"Go to your room, Jeremy," Mama Aida instructed. "We need to talk to your sister."

Jeremy made a face at her. "You're in so much trouble."

Despite the dread she felt, her little brother still made her smile. "I know, buddy." She ruffled his brown hair, locked him in a hug, and puckered up to kiss him on the cheek.

"Ew, ew, ew!" He tried to squirm away from her.

She planted a sloppy wet kiss on his cheek.

"Ew!" Jeremy broke away from her. He ran to the stairs, screaming, "You're a girl! Only Nolan likes to kiss you!"

Serene winced at that last statement before she turned to face her parents. Her dad wasn't even looking at her. He was on the edge of the sofa, staring straight ahead, breathing in and out deeply. Her mother sat next to him, brushing her hand up and down his back to soothe him.

Serene sat down on the single couch across from them. She had no clue what to say, so she remained silent until they spoke.

"Perhaps we should pray first," Mama Aida said.

The moment she spoke those words, Dad's face softened. He nodded. "Yes. Let's do that." He took her mother's hand in his and extended his hand for Serene to hold.

Serene hesitated but reached forward to hold both her father's and her mother's hands.

"Father, our family is Yours," her dad said. "In all its brokenness, it is Yours."

The moment he said those words, the Holy Spirit's conviction rushed over her, and tears flooded down Serene's cheeks. The rest of her father's prayer blurred in her mind, because a truth consumed her: to honor God, she needed to honor her parents. Even if what they were about to say to her was hard. This proved to be true because the conversation that followed was the toughest one Serene had to endure as a teenager.

Her parents addressed her lying, her disobedience, her drinking.

She acknowledged all of it as her fault, apologized, and agreed to abide by the consequences they felt her offense warranted. Only when they addressed her relationship with Nolan did she break.

"Your mother and I have agreed that it's best for you to keep your distance from him," her father said. "At least until both of you can earn our trust again."

"Dad, that's not fair." Her chest tightened. "Nolan did nothing wrong."

"By your admission, he encouraged you to drink. He's the reason you went to that party. Isn't that what you said?"

"Yes, Dad, but I told him you allowed me to go. If I told him the truth, he wouldn't have brought me to that party."

"Wouldn't he?" Her father's brow rose.

"We have no way of knowing now—" Mama Aida sighed "—but you said so yourself, Serene. Nolan goaded you to drink."

"He didn't goad me, Mama. All he said was—"

"Serene, those were your exact words." Her dad couldn't keep the edge from his tone. "He goaded you to drink."

"Well, then I used the wrong word. Dad, this is so unfair! This isn't Nolan's fault. We were just curious. He didn't force me to drink beer. I decided for myself. And now you want to separate me from my boyfriend — my best friend in the entire world — just because I made a mistake. One I regret and have apologized for! You can't keep me away from Nolan." Tears ran down her face. "Mama, please. What are you even trying to say? Can Nolan not come over anymore? Do you want us to break up?"

"Yes," her dad said. "I want you to break up with him. You're too young to be in a relationship, Serene, and if that boy is serious about you, he can wait for you. You're fourteen years old, and I don't want you walking into all kinds of temptation, which will surely come if you stay with him."

"Serene," her mother spoke in a much kinder, calmer tone, "we've talked many times about purity and how we honor God by keeping ourselves pure before marriage."

"We're not sleeping together!"

"We believe you, honey, but the temptation will come, and the Word of God tells us to stay away from temptation."

Serene shook her head. "I can't believe you're punishing me — punishing him — for something we haven't done yet."

Her father spoke through gritted teeth. "This isn't about punishment. This is—"

"Serene," her mother interrupted, "we love you, and we love Nolan too. He's been a part of our family for a long time. You know we care about him, but can you do your dad and me a favor and pray about this? I think you know in your heart of hearts what the right thing to do is."

Serene cringed. She didn't need to pray to God about it. In her heart, she knew. All those years she spent at Sunday School and at youth group had ingrained the principle in her head: to love God and honor Him above all. Was it time to let the principle go from her head to her heart?

Neither she nor Nolan had been honoring God, but how could they? How could they stay away from each other when she believed with every fiber of her being they were perfect for each other? And from what she could see, Nolan believed that too.

Her parents prayed for her. The final lines of her mother's prayer were, "God, give her a man who is handsome and kind, but most of all, a man after Your heart. She can't go wrong with a man like that."

Serene wasn't able to sleep a wink that night. She spent the rest of the evening and the wee hours of the morning on her knees, pleading to God to not make her do this. God's silence drew out her desperation until in her mind, she saw an image from a Bible story she had been taught in Sunday School countless times.

The image of Abraham laying his beloved son down on the altar in abject surrender to a God Who knew better than he.

Serene cried and groaned and wailed, but by dawn, she had come to a point of surrender.

When she saw Nolan at school, the first thing she said to him was, "I think we need to break up."

For the next two years, Serene and Nolan tried to be just friends. Being friends was better than being forced apart like they were the first few months after the night a tipsy Nolan took a drunk Serene home.

However, Serene didn't know how to be friends with Nolan anymore. Her heart raced whenever she saw him. With them not being a couple anymore, girls at school were a lot more vocal and forward about their attraction to him. Meanwhile, several guys had asked her out as well. Neither Nolan nor Serene ever took the bait.

Neither wanted to be with anyone else, and the more they rejected other people, the more it solidified the unspoken promise between them. They belonged together, and yet every moment she shared with Nolan felt like borrowed time, like a minute spent under a microscope. Throughout their freshman and sophomore years, rumors had circulated around church about their relationship — some true, some far too exaggerated.

Concerned people from church started giving them advice. They were too young. They needed to wait. Serene could handle that, but she hated how some painted Nolan like a villain, like he was a bad influence on her. He was proving to be his father's son — not good enough for their pastor's daughter. She could tell it bothered him even if he refused to admit it. One Saturday, while they were rehearsing the worship set for Sunday service the next morning, things boiled down to a point where he couldn't deny it anymore.

They had arrived earlier than everyone else. Her parents had some counseling to do. So, she and

Nolan had to watch Jeremy and his best friend, Max, while they waited for the rest of the worship team to arrive.

Serene dropped her weight on one of the cushioned seats in front. She kicked off her sandals and pressed her feet against the carpeted floor. Nolan climbed on the stage, with the boys trailing after him. He started plugging stuff in like he did every Saturday, setting up the stage and the sounds so that once everyone arrived, everything would already be ready.

Pride puffed up Serene's chest as she mused over the fact that her best friend did this week in and week out faithfully — despite all the criticism people threw his way. Sometimes, she wondered how he could still stand being in their church.

"What are you doing?" Max asked as he followed Nolan around the stage.

"I'm plugging everything in," Nolan replied.

"Nolan, could you teach us how to play guitar?" Jeremy brushed his fingers against the neck of one of the electric guitars.

"Jeremy!" Serene yelled. "Don't touch anything!"

The eight-year-old grinned at her and ran towards Nolan and Max.

"Can you teach us, Nolan? Please?"

"Uh, sure, buddy." Nolan scratched his head, his focus on the equipment he was setting up. "Not today though."

"Why not?"

"Jeremy." Serene rolled her eyes. Her brother had a peskiness about him that Serene somehow found endearing. "Stop bugging Nolan. You boys come sit with me here."

She didn't need to tell Jeremy and Max twice. They rushed toward Serene and sat on either side of her.

"Is it true you once painted the heavens, Serene?" Max asked.

Serene nodded. Longing coiled around her chest at the mention of something she never again could do. "Yeah, Max." Her voice broke. "I did."

"Why did you stop?"

Serene turned her head toward her brother. "You know the answer to that."

"I don't!" Max said.

"How about you two find something to do, huh? One that doesn't involve following Nolan around."

The boys exchanged glances.

"Tag?" Jeremy asked.

Max nodded.

"You're it!" Jeremy yelled before running off.

"No fair!"

Serene watched them go before she glanced back to the stage and caught Nolan staring at her. He smirked and winked. Her heart skipped a beat. He gestured for her to come up on stage as he picked up a guitar.

Serene stood up and didn't even bother to put her shoes back on as she jogged up the steps that led to the carpeted stage. Nolan sat cross-legged on the floor and invited her to sit next to him. She obliged and leaned her head on his shoulder. She glanced at the time on her phone. They had at least half an hour before anyone would arrive.

Nolan plucked a tune. "I wish you had an easel and a canvas here," he said. "Maybe we can try to reach the heavens again."

"I'm not sure if that's possible. Not anymore."

"Why do you think it stopped?"

"I don't know. Is it possible neither of us have enough faith?"

"Could be for me, but you?"

"God is distant to me too, Nolan. I sometimes wonder if He's even there. I don't see Jesus or any of the fruits of the Spirit in the lives of so many of the people who profess to follow Christ."

"Well, as Pastor Sam said, we're all works in progress. We all fall short."

"Yeah, yeah." Serene snorted. "Don't start with the Christianese, Nolan. Just play me a song, will you?"

"As you wish." He started fooling around with the electric guitar, playing one riff after another.

Serene laughed and slapped him on the shoulder. "I want you to sing!" She yelled out the words over the loud music.

"You sing!" He yelled back, his brown eyes twinkling.

She then saw it. Something changed in his countenance. This strange, disturbed calm came over his face as he shut his eyes and continued to play. The music took over, and it felt to her like she had lost him. Serene drew a gasp of breath at the pain that swept over her. The mere thought of losing him knocked the breath out of her.

Nolan's fingers moved with precision along the guitar's neck. He played every chord to perfection. The overwhelming sense of love and loss she had for him brought Serene to tears.

When he opened his eyes, he furrowed his brows at her. "Serene, why are y—"

"What is going on here?!"

Both turned their heads to find Mrs. Rhoda Petersen and her daughter, Rachel, standing in the middle of the center aisle.

Serene flinched at the lividness on Mrs. Petersen's face.

"Why are you playing worldly music here?" she demanded. "It's one thing to listen to it on your own time, but this is holy ground, Mr. Stone. Don't bring your father's music here."

Nolan's back straightened. Serene could sense the tension oozing out of him as his knuckles whitened from how he gripped the guitar. She stroked his back to calm him down.

"Mrs. P., Nolan was just playing me something," Serene spoke up. "I asked him to. He wasn't playing any specific song. We were just—"

"Why are you two even alone in here?" Mrs. Petersen said. "Weren't you forbidden from being in a relationship?"

"Mrs. P., we're best friends," Serene said. "We have been since childhood. You know this. Why are you so upset?"

Nolan scoffed. His nostrils flared as his breathing grew heavy. He shook his head and got on his feet.

"I'm out of here," he said before turning toward Serene. "Are you coming with me or not?"

"Nolan, what do you mean you're out? We have to practice for tomorrow. Who will play the guitar when—"

"I don't care." Nolan didn't bother to wait for her. He walked out of the hall.

Serene didn't know what to do. Shocked, her gaze drifted from Nolan's absence to Mrs. Petersen's presence. "How is any of this Christ-like?" she asked.

Mrs. Petersen shrugged. "Don't give me that tone, young lady. Someone has to speak up. You shouldn't be using church to flirt with that boy."

Serene chose not to respond to the unreasonable accusation. With tears rushing down her face, Serene chased after her best friend. She caught up with him at the parking lot.

His labored breaths and tense shoulders incited her cautious approach. "Nolan?"

"I've had enough, Serene. What have I ever done to these people? Who are they to look down on me this way? How can one worship God when His people are nothing like Him?"

"Nolan, the team needs you to play tomorrow. You know that. You can't just skip practice, because Mrs. P. said something rude. She's rude to everyone." Serene brushed her palm over his arm. "Remember that God doesn't act the way she does."

He scoffed.

Serene squeezed his arm. "Please come back inside. We need you."

His eyes searched hers. "I'm going back for you, Serene."

The vacant emotion in Nolan's eyes bothered her.

Worship practice that night proceeded without a hitch. The worship the next morning gave Serene goosebumps, but the expression on Nolan's face reflected how God's presence didn't affect him whatsoever. He could hide it from them, but not from her. She prayed a prayer for him during the service, but after everything, Nolan made it clear to her why he was still there. During a stolen moment backstage after he made sure no one was looking, Nolan grabbed her waist with one hand and caressed her neck with the other.

He then claimed her lips with his. Tears streamed down Serene's face as she responded to the kiss. Yearning and passion built up over the two years they needed to always be on guard because being around each other felt like committing a sin. In that reckless moment, it seemed Nolan stopped caring, and she tried to catch up with him, afraid that one day, she would no longer care as well.

When he pulled his lips away from hers, his fingers tangled with her hair, he drew her closer and pressed his lips against her forehead.

"I'll marry you someday, Serene, and I promise you. No matter what anyone here says, you won't regret it. I love you, Red."

Lips trembling, senses tingling, Serene wrapped her arms around his waist and pressed her face against his chest before kissing the line of his jaw and then his lips. Gentle, this time. Breathless, she pressed her cheek on his shoulder, her forehead touching the side of his neck. "I can never regret being with you. I love you too, Nolan."

Though Serene didn't realize it as it happened, in the months that followed, their relationship with God spiraled until one day, she went to church, and Nolan was no longer there.

- SERENE, 16 -

After a summer spent tagging along on the tour of his father's band, Nolan returned home with a red pickup truck named Sasha, a smug smirk on his face, and a gift for his girlfriend.

Serene had pined for him all summer only for conviction to overcome her after attending their four-day annual camp. It had happened on the last day. During worship time, a simple question from Above had grazed her ears and had gripped her heart: *"Are you satisfied with My love?"*

Serene should be satisfied, because God was more than enough, but another love — one she couldn't let go of — had been distracting her heart.

The question still burned in her mind on their first day as seniors in high school when Nolan pulled over in the parking lot, with her in the passenger seat of his new car. He glanced her way, grabbed a large bag from the backseat, and handed it to her.

"I wanted to give this to you yesterday when I arrived," he explained, "but Ma told me you had relatives over, so I figured I'd give it to you now."

Serene took the bag from him and set it on her lap. "You know you could still come visit even if we have guests over, right? You are still welcome at my house."

"We've been over this, Red." A stony look came over his face. "I don't want to deal with all those suspicious looks your parents throw my way."

"Come on, Nolan. They don't do that. In fact, Mama has been asking about you."

"Oh yeah? I assumed she had given up on me already. Especially after I snubbed all your dad's attempts to reach out to me."

"She cares, Nolan. I understand it's hard to believe after everything that's happened, but many people at church care about you. Jake, Vic, the worship team... We miss you. I miss you."

"Yeah?" He smirked. "You see me every day, Red."

"Not this summer." She shrugged.

"Come here. I missed you too." He held the back of her head and bent forward to kiss her.

Serene gasped when their lips touched. She pulled away. "Stop."

Cheeks flushed, he tried to catch his breath. "What's going on?"

"I—" She swallowed hard. "I think we should tone it down. Not get so physical for a while."

He looked at her funny but didn't respond. Instead, he gestured at the gift. "Well? Open it?"

Still uncomfortable, Serene opened the bag. She laughed when she saw what was inside.

Nolan grinned. "You like?"

"I guess?" She retrieved a red leather cowgirl hat from the bag. "I don't understand though. Why?"

"I remember one of your paintings was of a cowgirl riding a spaceship to the stars. She had a hat similar to that."

"The painting I made the day we met."

"Yeah. The one you painted after you made one with me riding Neutron to the moon."

"Who said the boy in that painting was you?" She smirked as she put the hat on. "You like?"

"I love." He tipped the hat a little to the right. "Admit it, Red. That was me on that painting. You were obsessed with me even then."

"Arrogant much?" Serene caught a glimpse of something on his wrist. "Wait. Nolan, is that a tattoo?"

She grabbed his arm and looked. The words "Red & Ice" were tattooed on the side of his wrist.

"I have another one here." He lifted the left sleeve of his shirt to show her his bicep. He had the head of a lion and the word, "Courage", tattooed there. "What do you think?"

"I like it," she traced her fingers over the one on his wrist and the one on his arm. "Has your mom seen these?"

"Oh yeah. You should have seen her face when I showed her! Like she was about to just keel over in front of me, but at this point, there's not much she can do. Not like she can erase the tattoos. She gave my dad an earful though."

"How is he?" Serene ran her thumb on his jawline. "Your dad."

Nolan shrugged. "Let's just say I understand why he would rather be on tour than be with his own family. I'm not saying it's right or that I approve of his lifestyle. I just understand him more now."

A flicker of longing in his eyes shook her. Would Nolan follow his father's footsteps? Could she follow him there?

"So?" Nolan asked. "Ready for senior year?"

She nodded. "So ready."

"Keep the hat on, Red," he said. "For me. I love the way it looks on you."

Serene obliged. They held hands as they entered the halls of the school they loved and that loved them in return. She didn't know how to live in this inner paradox of longing to break up with him but having the willingness to follow him anywhere he would lead her.

Serene couldn't break up with him, and in the days that followed, he made it even more difficult for her to do so.

twelve

THE ONE WHO MADE HER PROMISE

- ONE YEAR LATER; NOLAN, 17 -

Nolan took a deep breath and leaned his forehead against the fine mahogany of the Sinclair family's front door. He pressed his palm on the carvings that adorned the entry to the house that had been his second home since they had moved next door. He balled his hand into a fist and listened to the sound of his knuckles moving against the door.

Get a grip, Stone, he told himself. *Swallow your pride and admit you need help.*

With a deep breath meant to summon courage he wasn't sure he had, Nolan knocked.

The door swung open to reveal Mama Aida's sweet face. "Nolan." Her face softened in an affectionate smile when she saw him. "You get more handsome every time I see you. How are you?"

Despite the urgency behind his visit, Mama Aida's kindness was still far too disarming for Nolan to ignore, so he held off on the reason for his presence there and obliged her with an answer. "I'm doing well, Mama Aida," he replied. "As well as I can be, at least."

"You haven't come over in quite a while. I wish you would. I miss all those times you played music for us."

Nolan forced a smile. "I miss those times too, Mama." For reasons he didn't understand, her words choked him up. He missed Mama Aida, but could she still say all that if she found out about all the sneaking around he had been doing with her daughter? "I've been busy with school. It's senior year, so I'm focused on preparing for college. That's all."

"Well, you're always welcome here." Mama Aida's brows rose as she gasped. "How rude of me! Would you like to come in? If you came to see Serene, she isn't here. She's babysitting. Jeremy is with her. It's just me and Sam."

"Great." Nolan bit his lower lip. "I came to talk to you and Pastor Sam, actually. It's urgent. About my dad." He swallowed the tears back and thanked God that his voice didn't break. He straightened his spine and squared his shoulders.

Mama Aida's face crumpled up with a look of concern. Within a few seconds, her countenance cleared as if understanding came over her. She nodded. "Of course. Come in." She stepped back and opened the door wide for him. "Is everything okay?"

Nolan shook his head as he walked in.

"Okay then." Mama Aida shut the door. "Make yourself comfortable in the living room while I go fetch my husband. I'll bring you refreshments in a bit."

He opened his mouth to protest, but Mama Aida already rushed up the stairs before he could. He made his way to the living room and sank on the couch. *What am I doing? How can I run to them with this when I've been stabbing them in the back with Serene?*

Taking several deep breaths, Nolan leaned back on the couch and stared up at the ceiling. He shut his eyes. *God, please. I haven't been a good Christian or even a good person lately, but please… For Ma.*

"Nolan, what's wrong?"

The moment Nolan heard his pastor say his name, he fell apart. "Pastor Sam, I need you to come with me. We need help. My dad. He's—" Nolan stopped speaking to collect himself.

"Calm down, Nolan. Where's your father?"

"In the hospital. It doesn't look good, Pastor Sam. I came to ask you to come visit and pray for him. Ma's not taking it too well. We're—" Nolan gulped. "Can you come? Please?"

In the quarter-hour drive between their neighborhood and the hospital, Nolan kept praying for God to spare his father. He believed God would answer. He had to. Did He not listen to prayers?

Nolan's world fell apart when they arrived at the hospital, and he saw his mother's tear-stricken face. Nova shook her head to indicate what had happened. Their father had passed away for the same reason their brother had.

Nolan wrapped his arms around his mother and wondered where God was. Why didn't He do something? God didn't even bother to let Pastor Sam say a prayer for his father. Where was Damien Stone now? He hadn't been a good husband nor father. Why did God allow this to happen? Why didn't God give him another chance?

The rest of the day passed by in a blur for Nolan. Everything happened too fast. Ma was in a daze the entire time, so it was Nova and the Sinclairs who arranged to transfer the body to a funeral parlor.

Nolan didn't want to have anything to do with the arrangements. He wanted time on his own, but he didn't even get that because Serene found him in a secluded spot at the neighborhood playground.

She didn't say anything when she found him. She sat on the swing next to the one he was on and bent and stretched her legs to propel the swing in the air. After several minutes passed, she stopped swinging. The soles of her shoes dug against the sand beneath her.

Serene then reached out to him and squeezed his arm. "I'm so sorry, Nolan."

"Why?" He scoffed. "It's not your fault. I blame God for all this."

"Don't say that. This isn't God's fault."

"Yeah? Why not? He could've saved my dad, but he didn't. Serene, where is He? I haven't been able to connect to God in years."

"You used to, though. Every time you led worship in church, you took people into God's presence. If you were able to connect with Him then, why wouldn't you be able to do it now?"

He shook his head. "I don't think it can happen again. Not after we started dating in secret. Besides, my heart isn't in it, Red."

Her silence spoke volumes.

Nolan chuckled wryly as a tear rushed down his cheek. "Serene, what if He was never there all along? What if we made it all up? What if you imagined the heavens and everything else was just sensation and emotion? How do we know for sure that there's a God out there?"

"I don't know what to tell you that you don't already know, Nolan."

"My dad's gone, Serene. And so is my brother. They both died of a drug overdose. Serene, if I embrace what we believe in, then doesn't that mean they're in—" His lip twitched. He couldn't bring himself to say the words out loud, but he questioned why he had ever even gone to church. Had it been for God? Or had it always been for Serene?

Cool air caressed Serene's soft skin. She searched her heart for words to say, but couldn't find it. What did she know about God, church, and the Bible that Nolan didn't? How was she supposed to comfort him when she herself harbored doubts about God and His existence? How could a worship leader and the pastor's daughter even speak out their questions and misgivings about the faith they had grown up in?

Nolan steadied himself on the swing and set his feet firm on the ground. He placed his elbows on his knees and leaned forward, with his hands clasped together. He bowed his head and closed his eyes. Inaudible whispers came out of his lips, and tears rushed down his face.

Serene stood up from the swing and knelt in front of him. She held his clasped hands between hers and pressed her lips against his intertwined fingers. She couldn't tell for sure if he was praying, but she started to. *God, we're sorry. Please help us through this.* As she joined him in his tears, she became aware yet again of what had been pulling them away from God since they had started a romantic relationship. They had been living in disobedience and deception. They needed to break up, but how was she to say that to him? She trembled as she prayed. When she said, "Amen," she looked up at Nolan's tear-stricken face.

"I need to talk to your parents," he said. "We need to come clean."

Relief washed over Serene as she nodded. "Yes, I agree. We can't keep doing this, Nolan. We should—"

"Tell them we're in a relationship and hope they'll give us their blessing."

"What?" Serene frowned. "Nolan—"

"Don't worry." His expression darkened as he swallowed hard, his eyes fixed on the space past her right shoulder. "I know what to do. They'll accept us, Red. You'll see."

Serene didn't have a doubt in her mind she loved Nolan Stone with all her heart. However, in that moment, for the first time since she had met him, she felt like she didn't know him.

"Red, I need you to promise me something."

"What is it?

"No matter what, promise me we'll stick together. I can't lose you, Serene. Not after this. Always together?"

Something inside her raised objections, but the desperation on his face tore her up inside. She couldn't bring herself to tell him what she thought they needed to do, so she nodded in agreement. "I promise."

The moment she said the words, Nolan's face softened. He tucked a strand of her hair behind her ear and leaned forward to kiss her.

His lips had become familiar to her. She used to enjoy his kisses, but not this time. Something was different about that kiss, like the kiss was his, not theirs.

When Nolan pulled away from her, his countenance changed. Hardened. Determined.

Serene shuddered. She wasn't sure what Nolan had planned, but she didn't quite expect what he did later at his father's wake.

That evening, Serene sat next to her mom and Jeremy in a pew at the funeral parlor where they held a service for the wake of Damien Stone. Nolan sat at the front row with his sister and mother — both in tears. Not Nolan. When called upon by their pastor, Serene's father, he stood to his full height, with his father's acoustic guitar hanging from a strap on his shoulder. He had this unnerving calm on his face as he propped himself up on a barstool.

Before he said a word, Nolan cast a glance at her and gave her a curt nod, like he assumed an understanding just happened between them. Only Serene didn't understand. He cleared his throat and Serene blinked her eyes because she wasn't sure if she imagined it, but for a moment, it seemed as if he sneered. After a blink or two, however, his face showed a deep, heartbreaking sorrow.

"I grew up feeling like I was fatherless," he said.

Murmurs spread across the room.

"And now, I am. All my life, Damien Stone chased his music. One gig after another, musical tours that never quite reached the heights he hoped it would. He lived a life of disappointments, away from those who only longed to love him and be loved by him. I don't understand why he allowed his life to end the way it did. I've asked God countless times why He didn't give my father a second chance, but though I don't understand, I need to trust that God knows what He is doing. Job 13:15 says—" Nolan pulled out a piece of paper from his pocket and read what was on it *"—Though He slay me, yet will I trust in Him: but I will maintain mine own ways before Him."*

Serene shifted on her seat. Did he even know what that verse meant? Did she?

Nolan scanned the crowd. "In the pain and the grief, I choose to trust God and believe He is my Father. I have never been and will never be fatherless." He then sang an old hymn: It is Well with My Soul. By the end of the song, everyone was in tears. Including Serene.

Later, after the service, Serene embraced him. "That was beautiful, Nolan."

"I told you I had a plan," he said.

She pulled away from him. "Wait. So, Nolan, everything you said— You meant it, right? About trusting God and Him being your Father?"

A serious expression came over his face. "Sure." He nodded. "Every word."

Serene winced. Did he?

He kissed her on the lips and leaned his forehead against hers. "I talked to your dad. I'll come visit to discuss our relationship with them after everything settles down."

When that day came, he showed up at their house and talked to her parents. They confessed everything they had been doing, how they had been dating behind everyone's backs. Nolan even teared up when he explained how much he loved Serene, how much he wanted to be a part of their family, how he wanted to marry her someday. He asked for her parents' blessing.

To Serene's surprise, her parents agreed, with the caveat that he would agree to let her father mentor him and that he return to church.

In the next month, they saw a complete turnaround in the way the church treated him. Especially after rumors spread about how he had worshiped God even through his father's death.

Several girls from church even expressed envy to Serene about it.

"He's so strong in the faith, Serene," they said.

Suddenly, it seemed Nolan became worthy of her in their eyes. Their fascination with Nolan grew further when not only did he return to church and renew his commitment, he also convinced his mother and sister to go with him. Meanwhile, Serene found herself breath-taken by this new side of her best friend she didn't realize existed — a side of him capable of lying, wearing a mask, and making a performance out of worship and religion. Because in their private conversations, whenever she brought up God and the things he said in public, Nolan always diverted the topic to other things.

When she asked him point-blank if he believed in God, Nolan responded with, "I believe in us."

In the months that followed, Serene would listen to people tell her how blessed they were by Nolan and how much he changed after his father's death.

Serene agreed. Nolan changed, but not in the way they perceived.

Everyone looked back at that night at his father's wake as the night Nolan transformed into the man God wanted him to be. Serene looked at it as the night Nolan lost his innocence. The night he started to pretend to be everything the church asked him to be just so they couldn't prevent him from being with her.

thirteen

THE ONE WHO SURPRISED HER

The moment Serene woke up on the day of their graduation, a mixture of anticipation and dread swept over her. Like an omen warning her of things to come, a crack of thunder rumbled in the sky, making her jolt up in her bed as she checked the time. Thunder? Today of all days? She rose and made her bed before peeking through the curtains at the world outside. A slight drizzle introduced her morning.

Serene frowned. *Hope it stops.* She prepared for the rest of the day. By the time she rushed down the stairs, Nolan was already waiting for her.

He smiled at the sight of her. "Hi, gorgeous," he greeted.

He still made her blush. They shared a quick peck on the lips. He placed his arm over her shoulder. They made their way to the dining area where Mama Aida already had breakfast prepared. Her eyes softened when she saw Serene. "My lovely daughter. You're graduating! You too, Nolan! Oh, oh! Let me take a photo of you both! Jeremy, come help your mother snap a photo."

Jeremy slid off the barstool and helped his mother figure out how to use her new Nokia phone.

"I can't believe we can take pictures with phones now!" Mama Aida exclaimed.

Nolan and Serene exchanged glances and giggled. Breakfast passed by in a flash. After, they got in their own cars and drove to the graduation ceremony via convoy. Nolan drove his mother's car. Serene sat shotgun while Clara made herself comfortable in the backseat. They followed Pastor Sam's van. Silence filled the vehicle as Nolan drove.

Serene glanced his way and stared, her heart full, but her soul in turmoil. She stared at the man Nolan had become.

"God, give her a man who is handsome and kind," Mama Aida had once prayed, "but most of all, a man after Your heart. She can't go wrong with a man like that."

In Serene's eyes, Nolan was definitely handsome, and he had always been kind to her. As far as she knew, he had slighted no one. But was he a man after God's heart?

Short glimpses of him leading worship that Sunday rushed through her mind. "You're blessed to have him," Mrs. Petersen, of all people, had told her after the service. "I love it when he leads the worship. So powerful."

Serene had tried not to wince at their former Sunday School teacher's statement. "Praise God," had been her reply. She didn't tell anyone that whenever Nolan led worship, she couldn't concentrate enough to focus on God. Her mind would always drift to the man on stage. How was he capable of refusing to talk about God in private and worshiping the way he did in public?

"Red, what?"

Serene blinked her eyes. "Hmm?"

"You've been staring for the past— What? Ten minutes?"

"Sorry." She shifted her attention toward Clara in the backseat. "You sure you're okay there?"

"I am, honey." Clara nodded. "Don't worry about me. I prefer it here." She had positioned herself so she had her back against the car door and her legs stretched on the entire seat. "Comfy." A flicker of sadness crossed Clara's eyes with one glance at Nolan. She had often been on the melancholic side since her older son's death.

"Is Nova coming?" Serene asked.

"She'll be there," Clara replied.

"She said she might even bring a date," Nolan said. "Caleb Grant."

Serene's eyes widened as she turned from Clara and leaned back on the front seat, eyes straight ahead. "Caleb? From church? Olivia's Caleb?"

"He and Olivia broke up ages ago. He's Nova's agent or something, and they're coming to our graduation together. I don't even know why, so I figured they're dating."

Caleb and Olivia broke up. Serene had looked up to them as a couple. If they couldn't make it, was it possible she and Nolan wouldn't either? Rain poured, its pitter-patter on the hood entranced her into the future and what it had in store for Nolan and her.

They had planned their lives around each other, choosing to go to the same university. Serene would take up Architecture and Interior Design. Nolan would take up Marketing. They had chosen those courses because they figured they could use it in pursuing both art and music careers. All their plans included each other. That they would end up together seemed inevitable, so Serene didn't know why she found it so shocking that after their graduation ceremony, surrounded by chatter, congratulations, and picture-taking, Nolan pulled her away from the crowd to somewhere more private. And for reasons beyond her understanding, their families allowed them to go.

Beneath a sky that paused from raining down on them, he stole a kiss from her. He then took a step back and grinned.

Serene's brows met. "What?"

Nolan narrowed his eyes. "You know I love you, right?"

"Yeah." Serene chuckled. "So?"

"Shouldn't you say something back?"

"I think it should go without saying, Nolan."

"Yeah, but I still want to hear you say it."

"Okay then. I love—" Serene's eyes popped open when she remembered the present she had for him. It would be the perfect time to give it to him. She had saved up for it for quite some time. Jeremy had even pitched in some of his piggy bank savings to help buy it. "I have something for you!"

A soft groan escaped Nolan's throat. "Come on, Red. Forget that. Say it."

Serene froze. "Nolan, what's going on?"

He tucked his hands behind his back, sealed his lips shut, and rocked forward and back, forward and back.

She relented. "I love you."

The grin that spread across his face was unlike anything she had ever seen before. Delight and excitement danced behind his brown eyes. "I was thinking of some grand gesture to do this, Red, but I always end up going back to today. Graduation is an end of a season in our lives. I went through that season with you beside me every step of the way. And Red, I want you to be in every season in my life, so before we begin this new leg in our journey, I wanted to ask you—" He brought out a purple velvet box from behind him, knelt on one knee, and opened the box to reveal a ring. "Serene Sinclair, my Red, will you marry me?"

Serene's heart sank as her mind whirled with one question after another. "Nolan." She gazed into his brown eyes and brushed her finger against his hair.

Nolan was the love of her life. How could she say no?

Nolan had a darkness in him that only she could recognize. No matter how she prayed for it to disappear, it remained. How could she say yes?

Not a single person had expected Serene to say no. Especially not Nolan.

As he knelt on the ground, he stared up at the love of his life and admired how beautiful she was. Aware of how blessed he was that she was with him, he expected her to say what he wanted to hear.

Instead, she fixed her eyes on the wet ground, clenched and unclenched her hands, and said, "I can't."

Her words caused thunder within him. As if hit by lightning on the spine, he straightened his back and tried to burn his stare into her. "Red, what do you mean you can't?" Nolan reached a sudden awareness of all the people who had taken notice of them, throwing stares at them, whispering about them.

"I don't think there's anyone else for me but you, Nolan, but—" Serene bit her lip. "I don't know what to say."

"Say yes, Serene. If you think we're meant for each other, why can't you say yes?"

"Because—" Her lips quivered. "Nolan, I love you with everything I am, but—" She stomped her foot on the ground.

Nolan's cheeks burned red as he stood up, the ring still in its velvet box, the velvet box still in his hand. He let his gaze hover over the gentle contours of her heart-shaped face. He tried to hide the hurt in his voice when he asked, "Don't you want to be with me?"

"Nolan, don't say that." Her voice broke, and tears formed in her eyes. "I want to be with you. I do, but I can't marry you. Not yet. It's too fast. We're too young. I've only ever been here. There's an entire world out there, and I want to explore it with you, but I'm not ready for marriage, and I don't think you are either."

He winced as he gripped the velvet box tight. "I could see the entire world and meet all its people, Serene. It wouldn't change a thing. You will still be the woman I want to marry."

"I'm so sorry, Nolan." She broke into a sob. A flicker of fear set her eyes on fire. "Please don't break up with me."

Nolan swallowed back the hurt her rejection caused. "What are you talking about? I just proposed to you." He pulled her into a hug, engulfed her smaller frame, and brushed his palm against her hair. "Always together, remember?" In one swift motion, he yanked himself away from her, while his hands gripped her arms. "Red. Come on. This is us. If you're not ready, you're not ready. It doesn't mean we can't be together." He wiped her tears away with his thumb. He didn't know how she did it — how she made his heart hurt and swell with so much love for her at the same time.

Serene's sobs subsided. Red hair wild, freckles highlighted by the glow of the sun on her face, she raised her gaze to him and took his breath away.

Nolan kissed her on the lips and shoved the velvet box in her hand.

She stepped away and raised her hand to reveal the box on her palm. Her lips pursed, her eyes narrowed, her expression spoke out her questions.

"Keep it. Let my question hang in the air for as long as you need it to. Once you're ready to say yes, wear the ring, and I'll know."

At first, he thought she would say no again. Instead, she nodded and slapped him on the shoulder hard.

He creased his brows at her and smirked. "What was that for?"

"Why did you propose? Now my makeup is ruined." She wiped the rest of her tears away as she chuckled. "How could you surprise me like that?"

"Trust me, Red. As long as we're together, you can expect more surprises."

Her face broke into a smile that made his heart race and his pulse quicken. "In that case, it's my turn to surprise you." Serene grabbed his hand and pulled him toward their families, who were waiting at the parking area. They were still quite a distance away when Nolan saw Jeremy standing by Serene's car, holding something Nolan had wanted for years.

Nolan stopped walking, causing Serene to boomerang to him, unable to pull him forward. He fixed his eyes on the *Les Paul* guitar Jeremy had in his hands. "Red?"

Serene smiled. "Lots of babysitting money. Dad and Mama pitched in a little too. Jeremy even broke open his piggy bank to get it for you. It's our family's graduation gift to you."

If it weren't for her parents standing just a few feet away, he would've pulled her into his arms and kissed her hard, but he tried to get a hold of himself. He squeezed her hand and walked toward their loved ones. He headed straight for Pastor Sam. "Thank you so much, Sir."

"Congratulations on your graduation, Nolan," their pastor said. "We're proud of you and Serene."

Nolan hugged Mama Aida next. "You've been such a blessing to me."

"As you have been to us, young man."

Nolan took the guitar from Jeremy and chucked him lightly on the jaw with his fist. "Thanks, kid."

"When you get tired of it, will you let me keep it?"

Nolan chuckled. "I doubt I'll ever get tired of it."

Nova cleared her throat. She and Ma cast a questioning look at him. He shook his head. They checked Serene's ringless finger and exchanged confused glances.

"I see you didn't say yes." Pastor Sam sounded relieved.

"We're still together," Serene clarified. "Just waiting for the right time."

Pastor Sam took her in his embrace and rocked her from side-to-side. "I love you, Serene."

"I love you too, Daddy."

As Nolan watched the tender scene between father and daughter, two opposing thoughts roiled within him: One, how much he admired their relationship. Two, how much he couldn't wait to get away with Serene.

That night, Nolan crashed into his bed and stared up at the ceiling with a huge smile on his face. For someone whose marriage proposal got rejected, Nolan hadn't expected to still be so elated, but how could he not? He had a brand-new *Les Paul* and an amazing future to look forward to with the love of his life.

Confident that nothing could tear him and Serene apart, he drifted off to dreams of a life full of surprises and possibilities: a life rocking the world with Serene. The next morning, he woke up with a song in his head. He jotted it down and by the end of the day, he finished writing a song he entitled, *Rocking Serene*.

fourteen

THE ONE
WHO ROCKED
SERENE

- TWO YEARS LATER; NOLAN, 20 -

Nolan drew a deep breath before stepping inside the amphitheater-styled classroom.

"Art needs a level of restraint," Serene's professor said. "Go ahead. Paint outside the lines, innovate, but writing, or any art form, needs its boundaries, its rules, its ways of harnessing the wildness of imagination and— Excuse me? Who are you? What are you doing?"

"Hello, Professor." Nolan nodded at the teacher, walked to the front of the class, and took out his guitar from its case. "This is a song dedicated to my beautiful girlfriend. Consider it a demo of unrestrained art. Isn't that the topic you were discussing, Professor?"

"Mr.—" A blank expression formed on the professor's face as Nolan plucked an upbeat tune on his guitar. "You can't just do this."

Nolan started singing.

"Hey now, let's make some noise."

Nolan winked at Serene, who was giggling at the back of the class.

"You get me going, baby, I don't have much choice."

"Miss Sinclair, do you know this guy?"

"Yes, ma'am. I do," Serene said. She then jogged down the steps.

Nolan expected her to stop him, but instead, she retrieved a sketch pad from her backpack, sat cross-legged on the floor and sketched. Though he hadn't yet played the song for her before, it wasn't long before she harmonized with him as she drew a picture inspired by his music.

"You come with calm, I come with chaos.
Red and ice, nothing can stop us.
Let's open up the heavens and discover wonder.
You summon peace while I cause thunder.
Our love will paint the world a scene.
Let's spend our lives rocking serene."

The professor had no clue what to do when the music drowned out her objections. Some students watched, amused. Others pumped their fists in the air in time with the beat. A rush swept over Nolan as he played the song. He had written the song as an anthem dedicated to his love for her, but upon seeing the reactions of those who listened, Nolan could tell in his gut it would be so much more.

He didn't expect that someone would take a video of his spontaneous classroom performance. Whoever had taken the video uploaded it online that night. By morning, the video had gone viral. And that was where *Red & Ice* began. That was where life as Nolan thought it would be ended.

As great as it had been and as instrumental as it haad been to his career, several years later, Nolan would look back at that day and wonder if it was the day he started losing Serene.

- ONE YEAR LATER; SERENE, 21 -

Serene had wanted nothing more than to marry Nolan Stone, but she had said no to him because she feared the day would come when he would live up to his full potential. And once he did, she wouldn't be able to keep up with him. He had embarked on the road to the day she feared when he sang *Rocking Serene* in public for the first time. Nolan had sung his composition with the sole intent of interrupting her class to surprise her, but the song became an anthem of freedom to those who listened. *Rocking Serene* spoke of pushing one's limits and going beyond what the world allowed or expected. Rebellious and full of angst, what Nolan meant as a love song turned into a rebel anthem for those who wanted to disrupt the peace and shake current establishments.

They became a duo — *Red & Ice* — but Serene held no delusions that any of it was because of her. The star of their duo was Nolan, no doubt about it, but he acknowledged her as his muse — the girl behind the music.

Nolan became the center of their newfound fans' universe, but he never failed to make her feel like the center of his. His adoration intoxicated her enough to stay. So, *Red & Ice* became online sensations, and all signs indicated they were only at the beginning of their road to fame.

"Cut! That's a wrap! Perfection!"

The sultry look in Nolan's eyes switched to concern as he helped her get out of the back of the red vintage pickup truck. "You okay?"

Serene nodded. "I'm fine."

He placed his hand on the small of her back and kissed her forehead. "You did an amazing job. You looked so hot up there."

Serene wrinkled her nose at him. "You never used that word to describe me before."

"Well, that's what you've always been, babe."

Babe? Since when did he talk like this?

Their friend, Mick, approached. He had been talking them into making an official, professional music video. They had crowd-funded it, and after weeks of planning and preparation, they finally pulled it off.

"This will go viral, man," Mick said as he hugged Nolan. "Thanks for letting me do this."

"What?!" Nolan flashed that easy, charming grin of his. "Dude, thanks for talking Serene and me into this. What an experience! You're so creative!"

"Hey, it was a great collaboration. I'm still floored by your girl's amazing input." Mick winked at Serene.

Serene tried not to wince. More and more, people had begun referring to her as Nolan's girl. Like she didn't have an identity apart from him. The bothered feeling disappeared when she glanced at Nolan and saw how he looked at her with fire in his eyes. He placed his arm over her shoulder and pulled her closer. "You have no idea how blessed I am to have her by my side."

Just like that, Nolan had her willing to do anything to be with him. As sure as Mick predicted, the music video hit a million views within a few hours of being posted. Nolan showed up at Serene's dorm the moment it did.

"We have to celebrate!" he exclaimed as he twirled her around, catching the attention of several people milling along the hallway outside her door.

Serene loved seeing him so happy, but she shook her head. "Nolan, I can't."

"What? Why not?" He set her back on the ground.

"I have to study. I have a bunch of exams coming up, and my grades are already going down the drain as it is. Don't you have exams coming up too?"

Nolan rubbed the back of his neck and squinted his eyes at her. "I dropped my classes."

"What? Nolan! When?"

"Just before I came here, but before you freak out on me, hear me out because I have the best news. A label called. They want to offer us a deal, Red. They think Red & Ice will be a huge deal in the music world. Can you believe it?!"

Serene took several harried breaths as she tried to process the information he had given her. "Nolan, I— Congratulations?"

He paused. The smile faded from his face. "You don't seem thrilled."

"I am! This is amazing." She sighed. "Unbelievable. I mean, this doesn't happen to just anyone."

"We're not just anyone though, are we? We're *Red & Ice!* Why aren't you crazy excited about this?"

Serene winced when she noticed several of the people in her dorm glancing their way. She tugged on his sleeve. "We should talk about this somewhere private." She nodded her head toward her room. They entered, and she shut the door behind her.

"I didn't expect you to react like this," Nolan said.

"I'm sorry. It's going too fast, Nolan. You've always dreamed of this, but—"

"You didn't." Realization cleared his eyes. "Serene, I—" He shifted his weight from one foot to the other. "I should have—"

"Hey, come on." Serene forced a smile and lifted her hands in the air, palms facing him. "This has been an amazing ride with you. I'm swept away, that's all. I'm finding it hard to catch up. If I'm not mistaken, you're talking about dropping out of college at this point. Am I ready for that? Would my parents even approve?"

"Come on, Red. We're adults. We should be able to make these decisions for ourselves. I mean, you said it yourself. No one just gets opportunities like this. Serene, I can become what my father never was, what he only dreamed he could be. I can succeed where he failed." He lowered his gaze. A muscle in his jaw twitched. "This can be my chance to regain my family's dignity."

"Nolan, when did your family ever lose dignity?"

"My father and my brother both died of drug overdoses, remember? Ma still hasn't recovered. All the tears she has shed—" He shook his head. "Nova's going through her own personal crisis with her career right now, and I think our family needs this."

Serene tried to understand, to comprehend. Her mind whirled at the notion of what he was asking of her. "Nolan, I need time to pray about this."

He snickered.

"What?"

"I didn't think you still prayed."

"Why would you think that?"

Nolan shrugged. "I don't know, Red. The fact that we've barely talked about God? We don't even go to church anymore."

"Nolan, we don't talk about God, because you act all dodgy when I bring Him up. And we stopped going to church because we had trouble finding one that's like the one we had back home. Doesn't mean I've given up on my faith. Wait. Nolan—" she cringed "—have you?"

"All I know, Serene, is that all my dreams are about to come true. I don't think God had anything to do with that. We — you and me, Red — we did that. You can pray about it if you want to, Serene. I'll give you time, but please remember we may not get this chance again. I've made my choice. You make yours, but I challenge you, love. Ask God tonight to show you the heavens again. If He's around, does He even still care? What if He's abandoned us? Or what if we were just young and naïve? Maybe the paintings and music from the heavens were just you expressing your art and me expressing my music in an environment that — let's face it — restrained our creativity."

"Nolan, it kills me to hear you say these things. We've been Christians since childhood."

"I don't know if I'm still a Christian, Serene. We've met unbelievers who are so much more loving and less hypocritical than those we left in church. Take Mick for example. Great personality, creative, kind, and cool. Atheist. Compare him to Mrs. Petersen who would probably send me to hell if she could."

"Nolan, where's this coming from? You and Rhoda have had a great relationship, especially after your dad's death."

"Yeah, Serene, because since my dad died, I fought hard to fit into the mold of what our church saw as acceptable. I did it so they would let me be with you."

Chills ran up and down Serene's entire form. There it was, spoken out loud: the truth.

Desperation crossed Nolan's face when he realized what he had just admitted. He took a step forward, held both her arms, and pulled her to him. "Please, Serene. I know it's a lot to ask, but when you make your decision tonight, remember how much I love you. We belong together, Red."

Yet again, he swayed her. He rocked her beliefs and her convictions. He inclined her towards him because of how much her heart leaped and her senses awakened when she was anywhere around him.

"Give me tonight," she said. She stepped away from him before he could make her lose her senses yet again. "If tomorrow you see a painting of the heavens in this room, then you'll have your answer."

His face tensed as he nodded. She thought she saw a flicker of worry cross his face, but it disappeared and turned into stone cold determination. "I'll see you tomorrow."

He left her feeling hollow.

She pushed back all thoughts of her exams and his dreams away. She knelt on the ground and tried to pray.

The heavens remained silent. Resentment grew in her heart and because she didn't hear an audible voice from above, she reasoned God had given her freedom to make her own choice. In doing so, she ignored the still, small voice of reason that was telling her the way to go.

The next day, Nolan arrived in her room and smiled when instead of a painting of the heavens, he found her bags packed. She was ready to follow him anywhere he intended to go.

Serene Sinclair couldn't imagine a world without Nolan Stone in it, so to keep herself in his world, she dropped everything and followed his dream.

fifteen

THE ONE WHO SHATTERED DREAMS

- SEVEN MONTHS LATER; SERENE, 21 -

The energy inside the stadium transformed Nolan every time they got on stage. As Serene took her place behind the keyboard set on the back of a red pickup truck in the middle of the stage, she glanced at Nolan. He smiled at her. The steady beat of the drum made her heart pound. The rhythm of the bass followed. Soon after, the violin dipped and climbed. Serene played her first key, and Nolan positioned his fingers on his new state-of-the-art electric guitar.

In an instant, Nolan, the sweet boyfriend she had grown up with and adored, disappeared. In his place was Ice, the rock star. Serene barely recognized him. She barely recognized herself. Wave upon wave of euphoria climbed from the wild audience to the stage, and he was riding every minute of it.

Nolan gave everything to every single performance the powers-that-be of the music industry had given them the opportunity to make. He lived for each night they stepped up on a stage to perform for thousands of people. Of course, Red & Ice was still just the opening act for world-famous female rock star, Desirée. But Nolan often said it would only be a matter of time before he and Serene would headline their own show, their own tour.

Serene rejoiced for him. This was his element, and she loved seeing how swept up he was in the thrill of it all. She, however, languished with every moment she spent playing a part she never dreamed of playing.

"That was incredible!" he exclaimed as they returned backstage.

Serene trailed behind him, her hand limp in his grip.

"Wasn't this the best night so far?"

Her eyes tired, her response listless, she forced a smile and gave him a half-hearted, "It was amazing."

The angles of his face tensed with concern as he studied her. He gave her a quick peck on the lips and squeezed her hand. He cocked his head to the side — a gesture for her to follow him.

"Dude, what a show!" one of the roadies patted him on the back. He then grinned at Serene. "Delicious eye candy as always, Red."

He meant it as a compliment on her looks, but Serene winced. She felt like Nolan's accessory.

Nolan tugged at her hand. They headed to the dressing room after going through a few more cheers of encouragement and pats on the back. The moment Nolan opened the door, Serene rushed inside. Nolan shut the door and turned to her as she plonked herself on the white leather sofa. A deep sigh escaped her lips.

"You okay?" He sat beside her and angled himself to face her.

"Yeah. Just tired."

"I am too!" His eyes widened. "That was such a trip! Talk about energy, but yeah." He brushed a thumb over her freckled cheekbone. "At least we have some time to rest now." He drew a short intake of breath. He caught several strands of her hair and twirled it around his forefinger.

Serene still blushed at the awareness of his gaze hovering over her appearance.

"You look gorgeous," he said.

She ran her fingers over the stubble on his jaw. "So do you. A lot of girls out there seem to agree."

"And yet I only have eyes for you."

Serene's shoulders sagged. She leaned her head on the arm he had draped over the backrest of the sofa. "Don't do that, Nolan."

"Do what?"

"Be so perfect."

He smirked. "Kinda can't help it."

Serene rolled her eyes. "Arrogance." She blushed at the way he stared at her lips. Within seconds, he had her in his embrace, his lips claiming hers with an intensity that left her gasping for breath when she pulled away from him.

"Serene." He tried to pull her back against him, but she resisted.

"Nolan, we can't."

"Come on, Red. Let's do this."

The moment he said the words, her entire world spun out of control in one dizzying second before everything came to a full halt — her breath, her pulse, her heartbeat. The words got stuck in her throat as she stared at him, unable to recognize him as he freely used his eyes to explore her. She gasped for breath to push back the shock. She forced herself to speak because she needed an answer. "Nolan, what do you mean let's do this?"

"We're virgin rock stars, Red. The idea's ridiculous."

Serene pressed her palms against his chest and pushed to get herself out of his lap and stand up. She drew several breaths as she paced the floor. "I can't believe you said that. Are you asking what I think you're asking?"

Nolan leaned back on the sofa and chuckled. "Serene, relax. I know you. We can get married first. This shouldn't come as a shock. You know how much I want you. I don't understand what we're waiting for. It's torture to see you as stunning as you are and not be able to even—" He creased his brows. "Are you crying?"

Serene wiped away the tear that came unbidden. Love and anger warred within her. Her soul felt so sensitive, she feared a single misplaced word or action from him would be a pinprick that would make her explode. Everything caught up with her. She had brought this upon herself. She allowed this to happen. A touch here, a kiss there. With one little compromise after another, she had reached a point where she couldn't remember how to live, trust, and believe like a child anymore. Never before had she longed to paint the heavens more than she did at that moment.

As if suddenly realizing how shaken she was, the fire in Nolan's brown eyes vanished. "Serene? Hey, if you don't want to, I understand. Red, you know me. I wouldn't ever pressure you into something you don't want to do."

His words broke her heart because it was true. Nolan had never intentionally pressured her to do anything, but on multiple occasions, she had bent her will, her ways, and her beliefs to adjust to his lifestyle. She couldn't go on like this anymore. She had reached the point where she couldn't bend without breaking. Because if she were to be honest with herself, she couldn't tell what shocked her more: that Nolan asked her to sleep with him or that she had to fight back every instinct she had to keep herself from giving in.

"It won't happen," she said. "I can't sleep with you, and I can't marry you." She shook her head. "This is all too much." She tried to walk past him and head for the door, but his strong arms caught her and pulled her to him.

"Hey, Red, come on." Nolan drew her close and shook his head. "I told you. I'm not pressuring you or anything. Sorry if I'm being a little too impatient. You understand, right?"

She tried to wiggle away from his embrace, but he wrapped her in his arms until she stopped resisting. She buried her face on his chest and encircled his waist with her arms.

"Serene? You understand me, right? You get why I asked?"

His tone seeped beneath her skin and penetrated her bones, making her aware of how easily he could get to her. "I do," she said. "I understand."

Nolan kissed the top of her head. "You and me, Red." He embraced her, rocked her, and swayed her.

How was she to respond without lying?

He said the right words to soothe her, to calm her, but this time, unlike every other time Nolan Stone took her in his arms and told her what she needed to hear to make her stay, Serene didn't fall for it.

Something had snapped within her, and she realized the truth: she didn't want to marry Nolan. She had been stringing him along. She had been stringing herself along. No matter what she felt for him, she couldn't live this life with him.

She stepped back and straightened her clothes. "We're okay, right?"

Serene forced herself to look him in the eye. She nodded. How could she tell him she didn't want this life? How could she make him choose between his dream and her?

Serene opened her mouth to speak, to tell him why she didn't think all of this would work. Instead, she succumbed to her cowardice and appeased him for another night. "I'm sorry I can't give you what you want, Nolan."

"As long as I have you," he said. "I have you, right?"

"I can't remember a time when you didn't. We'll forget this ever happened. Tomorrow is a brand-new start."

For the rest of the concert, she convinced herself that she didn't lie. She did intend to forget, or at least try to. Tomorrow was a brand-new start — one that wouldn't include him. Tears threatened to fall from her eyes as they returned to the tour bus, but she held them back. Her mind ran ahead of her and devised her escape.

Past midnight, she rose from the single bed stuck to the wall of the bus rocking them to sleep as it rolled along a stretch of highway. She peeked outside. They would pass by a town soon. She would figure out from there how to get home.

Loud snores greeted her as she snuck into the small room Nolan shared with several other musicians. She placed the letter over his chest and kissed him on the cheek. In fear of second-guessing her decision, she hardened her heart and fought back the tears.

"I love you, Nolan," she said, "but I have to go."

Serene asked the driver, Ray, to pull over at the next town. It took an hour's drive before he did.

"Does he know?" he asked.

"Please tell him in the morning."

"I have half the mind to tell him now."

"Please don't."

"Why are you doing this?"

"Because I don't want to lose myself."

Something lit up in Ray's eyes. He shrugged and pulled the lever that shut the doors of the bus.

The first signs of dawn lit her way as she searched for a hotel where she asked directions from. By nightfall, she arrived at their front yard. Just one glance at the house next-door made her heart ache on Nolan's behalf. She dragged herself toward her parents' front yard, stepped up on the porch, and knocked on their mahogany door.

When Mama Aida opened the door and saw her standing there, her mother's eyes lit up with pure delight, but the delight vanished when finally, Serene cried.

"It's over," she said. "We're over."

She spent the rest of the night and the wee hours of the morning updating her parents about everything that had happened. She told them the little details she kept from them whenever they had gotten in touch.

They listened and cried with her when she admitted that she didn't think she believed in God anymore. Neither did Nolan. Sam and Aida Sinclair remained silent. Not a word of judgment or condemnation came from their lips as Serene poured her heart out. By the time she finished speaking, her parents were on either side of her, embracing her, praying for her.

Wrapped up in their love and their embrace, Serene broke down in tears in a way she never had before, and for an instant, Serene felt it again: God's presence. The atmosphere shifted, and all it took was a glimpse for her to believe again.

She neither saw nor painted the heavens that night, but she caught a revelation of the love God had for her — a father's love, so great, it could lead her home no matter how far she strayed.

So, as much as it broke her heart, Serene returned to bed aware she needed to let go of Nolan. She prayed to God to give her the strength to stand by her choice. She had left him behind, but she knew he would come for her. This battle was far from over.

Nolan kept a tight grip on his steering wheel as if it could somehow save him from losing his sanity. What happened? Why did Serene do this? She said they were fine. She said she understood. Why then did she go?

He couldn't reach her phone, couldn't talk to her, couldn't understand. The shredded piece of paper that was once her letter provided no answers, just more questions. He had read it over and over again before tearing it to pieces.

My dearest Nolan, it said. *No words I say can explain what I'm doing. I am truly sorry for the hurt I am causing you. I'm losing myself, Nolan. You mean the world to me, and I think that's the problem. You can't be my world. I barely know who I am anymore, and I don't even know how to explain that to you. I love you so much, it hurts, but I can no longer be with you, Nolan. Please continue to pursue your dream and try to forget me. Red & Ice doesn't need me. Nolan Stone has always been the star of the duo and rightly so. I will always believe in you and love you, but I have to find my way home. Love, Serene*

The words circled his mind. Each one felt like a taunt. Fear gripped him. She couldn't do this to him, could she? She promised him they would stick together. Why would she abandon him like this after everything he did to win her over?

A familiar monster haunted him yet again — that sense of unworthiness. How could someone like him ever deserve someone like her? He reminded himself things were different now, he wasn't just the boy next-door anymore, not just her childhood best friend. He was a rock star — or at least he was well on his way to getting there. Did she not see how many people adored him and his music? Was that not enough? Wasn't he enough?

The road stretched for hours, and every minute without her was torturous. He threw all caution to the wind and ignored all calls from their manager the same way she ignored his.

He considered calling her father and mother to ask if she was home but didn't have the guts to speak to them. Instead, he called her brother.

"She's with us," Jeremy said. "What did you do? She said she didn't believe in God anymore, and that you two are over. Did you break up with her?"

"What? Kid, no. Me? Break up with Serene?"

"Well, she broke up with you then, because she doesn't want to be a rock star or something. You screwed up, Nolan."

Every word Jeremy spoke was a stab in Nolan's chest. Tears threatened to fall. What had he done to deserve this? He slammed his palm against the steering wheel. Why hadn't Serene said anything? Question after question flooded his mind and stirred up his soul.

By the time he passed the welcome sign that led to their hometown, he had fire in his eyes and thunder in his chest. He took several turns from the highway before he arrived at an establishment all-too-familiar: Connect Church. He had no doubt her family had dragged her there for Sunday Service.

Nolan entered the lobby. Worship music played inside the main hall. An usher saw him coming, and her mouth dropped wide open. He had never seen the usher before and didn't know if she reacted the way she did because she recognized him as a celebrity or as the boyfriend of their pastor's daughter. Or was it ex-boyfriend now? The notion made Nolan clench his fists and grit his teeth.

Not caring anymore how the church viewed him, he geared himself up to demand answers and force her to tell him why she had broken his heart this way. He stormed past the ushers and walked through the aisles as worship went on.

Vic, the worship leader's eyes widened at the sight of him. Nolan and Serene had taught him everything they knew about leading worship. Nolan cast a sharp glare at Vic before heading right to the front row where he assumed Serene would be. He was wrong. He reached the front row to find Pastor Sam and Mama Aida there. The sight of Mama Aida's sweet smile made him wince.

"Nolan!" she exclaimed in a hushed whisper while brushing her fingers against his arm. "You look more handsome than ever. Your mom and sister are somewhere here."

"I'm here for Serene." Nolan tried to keep a brave, gruff tone, but it was hard to remain so intense when around Mama Aida.

"Of course. She didn't want to sit with us today, though. Said she wanted to sit way at the back. Don't ask me why."

"Thanks, Mama Aida," Nolan said, his heart softening at the affectionate gaze she was giving him. He turned to leave before she could get under his skin, but just as he twisted on his heel, he saw Serene standing midway down the aisle. Her eyes moistened as she stared at him.

Nolan's entire body tensed at the sight of her. He shook his head, unable to hide his anger. People started to notice. Whispers spread among those who could see them. Serene didn't even flinch as he marched toward her. Once he reached her, the fury he felt drained away at the sight of something he hadn't seen on her face for a long time: peace.

The moment he reached her, all he could say was a broken, "Why?"

Her lips trembled as she nodded at him. "We should talk outside."

Part of him wanted to say no, to make a scene, to show everyone what was going on, so they wouldn't have to speculate and gossip about it later. Instead, he watched her turn and followed her to the parking lot. Before they reached the lobby, they saw Jeremy following Mrs. Price out of the hall.

Anger flashed in Jeremy's face when he caught sight of his sister. He shot a glare at Nolan.

Nolan wondered why. All he saw was the back of her head. Was Serene in tears? Did this whole situation distress her as much as it distressed him?

She dragged him all the way to the parking lot, and there, his rage surfaced.

"I don't understand, Serene. Why would you do something like this? If something was wrong, why didn't you just tell me?" He cussed loudly.

The foul expression made her flinch.

"I don't think I deserve this, Serene."

A tear ran down her cheek, but she quickly wiped it away. "You're right. You don't. And I'm sorry, Nolan. I should have clued you in on what was going on within me, but—" Serene bit on her lip to keep it from trembling, to keep herself from tearing up. "I love you, Nolan, but *Red & Ice* isn't the life for me. It's like every moment I spend going on with this whole rock star thing is a moment I lose who I am."

"Then why didn't you say that, Serene? Why not discuss it with me?!"

"Because I wanted to want it, Nolan. For you. And I didn't want to make you choose."

"What do you mean by that? What do you mean choose?"

"Between me and your dream."

Nolan froze. He tried to understand, but the heady mixture of hurt and anger made it difficult for him to comprehend.

"I didn't want to make myself choose either."

"Between what?!" He spat out. "Between me and your church?"

"Nolan, it's not like that."

"It is." He cussed again as he threw a glare at the building. "I've always feared I would someday lose you to this self-righteous bunch. Just didn't think you would do it this way, Red. Or can I still call you that? I love you, Serene. I'm not sure I'll ever be able to stop loving you, but you broke me. Remember that when you think back to this moment. You tore me up, and you didn't even flinch doing it. I did everything to keep you, but I've stopped refusing to let go. Goodbye, Serene."

"Nolan—" Her voice broke, and her resolve to hold back the tears vanished. She grabbed his elbow, but he shrugged her touch away. Without another word, he returned to his car and drove back to his dream. It didn't take long before he had to pull over on the side of the road to break down in tears, because losing Serene felt like the shattering of all his dreams.

part three

PRESENT DAY

CIRCA
LATE 2000'S

sixteen

THE ONE WHO SHOWED UP

- SERENE, 23 -

Dressed in a pinstripe pencil skirt and a white blouse, Serene shifted on her seat as she drummed her fingers on top of the hotel restaurant's fine mahogany table. She checked the time on her phone and winced. Five minutes past the time she set with Ethan. Was he standing her up?

The time went up another minute. Serene blew out a breath and took a drink from her glass of water. She tapped her foot on the marble floor and winced again. The bracelet on her wrist caught her eye. Maybe it would have been better if she had worn a watch. More formal and business-like. What if this was a mistake? Ethan Caine wanted to date her, not work with her. Was it even wise for her to go into business with him? Besides, what would she know about running a business?

The doubts assailed her, but in her mind, she once again glimpsed into the future and all the possibilities it held, all the lives it could change, all the dreams it could help fulfill. Her heart skipped a beat when in her mind's eye, she relived the memory of Drew telling her she would have her first art show. She smiled and allowed her shoulders to relax as she leaned back in her seat and crossed her legs. The image of the beam on Nolan's face when their first video had gone viral flitted across her mind. That video had launched him into the future he had always yearned for. Thrive was the future she wanted, not only for herself, but for so many others, and Ethan was a valuable resource if she wanted a head start toward her vision.

Serene closed her eyes and shut down all the doubts with a prayer: Abba, this idea has made my heart come alive in ways I never expected. You've blessed me so much in so many ways, and I pray that this vision that You ignited within me — one I believe is from Your heart — will glorify You and bless many more of Your children.

"I have to know what is causing that beautiful smile."

Serene opened her eyes and found Ethan sitting across the table from her. Her cheeks flushed red. "Mr. Caine!"

"I'd tell you to call me Ethan, but since you've clarified that this is a business date, Mr. Caine it is. Forgive me for being late, Miss Sinclair. I got a little tied up at the office. I asked my assistant to let you know that I would be late, but it somehow slipped her mind. Work has been busier than usual, but this meeting has been at the forefront of my mind all day. I am beyond curious. How can I help you, Miss Sinclair?"

A surge of purpose unlike anything she had ever experienced came over her. She straightened herself in her seat and cleared her throat. "I want to invest my earnings from being a part of Red & Ice and from One Red Hue towards starting a—" she caught herself. "I'm so sorry."

"Sorry for what? Please... Continue."

"Shouldn't we order first? You must be starving after such a busy day."

The easy smile on his face warmed her heart and put her at ease. "I actually am."

They called in a waiter and made their orders. As soon as the waiter left, Ethan goaded Serene, "Please. Satisfy my curiosity and tell me what you have in mind."

Encouraged by his interest, the words flew out of Serene's lips. "I want to start a company called Thrive, where struggling artists who can't seem to get a break can be nurtured and supported in their craft. I will search for hidden gems — the ones who have skill, talent, or something to say, but somehow can't catch a break — and then invest in them, use my connections to help them."

Ethan nodded. "Like an agency?"

"Yes." Serene paused and gulped. "Kind of. But for all forms of art. Musicians, writers, painters... It's not just about supporting them financially. The goal is to provide a space for them where they can hone their skills and earn while they are at it."

"Like an incubator."

"Right. I guess. What's an incubator?" Serene's heart sank. In her mind, her idea had sounded so innovative, so fresh, so original. She was never more aware of her naiveté and inexperience, sitting there in front of Ethan Caine. He must have thought of her as such a child. Only then did she realize just how much she had wanted to impress Ethan.

He shifted in his seat and leaned forward on the table, laying his elbows on top of it, with his fingers clasped together. "An incubator is where an owner of an establishment provides a space — sometimes, even the equipment — for small businesses or startups to develop an idea. In exchange, the investor receives a percentage of the earnings of the business for a predefined amount of time. Is that what you have in mind?"

"Yes. Kind of." Serene took a deep breath. Before she could say anything else, the waiter came with her pesto and his steak.

"Thank you." Ethan smiled at the waiter. He then looked at his food and then at Serene and asked, "Shall we say grace?"

"Please. Do the honor."

As Ethan bowed his head and said a prayer, Serene tried to get back to a place of peace. Just because her idea wasn't as original as she had first assumed, it didn't mean it wasn't from the Lord. Having always been uncertain of or skeptical about what she was doing or why she was doing it, Serene wasn't very well-acquainted with the sense of confidence that came over her at that moment. By the time Ethan finished praying, she already had a smile on her face.

She picked up her fork from the table and placed a piece of penne in her mouth. "So? What do you think?"

Ethan chewed as he nodded slowly. She could almost see the wheels in his head turning. "It's ambitious, and it will require quite an eye for talent. There are a lot of artists out there who have the potential, but it's not wise to invest in potential. You need to be able to recognize the real thing and how to invest wisely in it."

"So... It's a bad idea?"

"Not at all. I admire you for wanting to do this, but it will take a lot to make it happen. You would have to be committed to your vision and passionate about the people you put your money into. Why exactly do you want to get into this, Serene?"

She dropped her fork and gave it a moment's thought. "I've been so blessed, Ethan. Getting a break in both music and arts in my early twenties, I'm amazed by it, but being in both industries, there's always been a restlessness in me. Like all of it is for a purpose greater than just my dreams or ambitions. I've had people who have invested in me, and I wouldn't be where I am if it weren't for them. I want to do the same for others."

A wide grin formed on his face. "How noble, but if I may, Miss Sinclair, how do you see me fitting into all this?"

"I don't want to go into this blind. I know nothing about starting or running a business, so I need to work alongside someone who does. Mr. Caine, I was hoping to propose a partnership with you."

"You're asking me to be your partner?"

"I guess so. Yes."

Ethan shook his head. "I can't. As much as I am flattered that you would ask that of me, this vision is yours. It's not mine. It's not something I can run with in the long-term."

Her mouth formed an O as she processed what he just said. How would she do this without him?

"I can't be your partner, Miss Sinclair. I'm sorry. However, what I can do for you is to mentor you, mainly because I have a high degree of respect and admiration for you. And if I'm to be frank, I wouldn't mind more of your lovely company."

The last sentence made Serene cringe inside. Despite Nova's assurances that Ethan Caine was a good and trustworthy man, his attraction to her — and how vocal he was about it — gave her pause.

"So what do you say, Miss Sinclair? Would you want me to be your mentor?"

Serene flashed a smile. "Given the caveat that we keep it one hundred percent professional, it would be my honor, Mr. Caine."

His jaw twitched. "Hundred percent professional. Of course."

One hundred percent professional. They could do that, right?

Later that night, after getting back to their apartment and filling Laila in on her meeting with Ethan, Serene threw a throw pillow at her roommate.

Laila caught the pillow, rolled her eyes, and snorted. "One hundred percent professional. You said so yourself. You think he's attracted to you."

"I could be wrong."

"He asked you on a date, which you turned into a business meeting. How could you be wrong? He's into you. What I don't understand is why you don't just date the man."

The words she had told Ethan came back to her as she leaned back on their couch. "I still have unresolved feelings for my ex." There was no way in the world she would admit that to Laila. Though from the way Laila was narrowing her eyes in scrutiny of Serene, it didn't seem like she would need to admit anything.

"Are you still into Nolan?"

Serene gulped.

Laila threw her hands in the air. "I knew it!"

"No. Laila, it's not what—"

"It's impossible that you weren't at all affected by him showing up at your art show."

"It means nothing. Nolan and I are over. There's no way of repairing that bridge. He did a kind thing for me to be there, and it brought up some things that I thought I'd already dealt with, but apparently haven't. Nolan hasn't even bothered to reach out to me since, so... It's nothing. Just unfair to Ethan or to anyone if I date them when I'm aware that Nolan can still affect me this way."

Laila crossed her legs in the loveseat across the couch, hugging the pillow and leaning forward to tease Serene. "Affect you what way, exactly?"

"You're impossible." Serene chuckled and shook his head.

"Know what? It doesn't even matter. If you have unresolved issues, you should resolve it."

"Finally. Something we can agree on."

"And how exhat? Drew and I have tickets to a Red & Ice concert this weekend. You should come with us."

At that, Serene laughed. "Right. That's going to happen. You're hilarious."

"I'm not kidding."

Serene deadpanned. "In that case, no."

"Come on! Why not?"

"For one thing," she said as she lifted a finger in the air, "I'm not a fan of Red & Ice. I left, remember?"

"Yeah, but think about it, Serene." Laila clutched the floral-printed throw pillow close to her chest. "You are the original Red. If we show up with you to a Red & Ice concert, that's automatic backstage VIP passes. For sure!"

"Or you get kicked out of the venue, because they won't allow Nolan Stone's ex-girlfriend there."

"That is so not going to happen." Laila shook her head. "That's bad publicity all around. They will never do that. Also, please. Serene, did you even watch The New Red?"

"Of course not." Serene grimaced at the mention of the reality show that revolved around Nolan choosing a replacement for her — the one Diana had won.

"The whole point of the show was how much he loved you and doubted anyone could replace you," Laila said. Her eyes sparked with wonder. "Imagine what it would be like." She waved a hand to create an arch in the air. "You show up to his concert, and there's this moment of reconciliation between you and him. And we all get backstage passes and perhaps even get invited to the after-party."

"You don't understand. I'm nobody. Ramona would never even let me anywhere near Nolan. You're painting this in your head like some dream reunion, but I may do more harm than good if you take me there."

"Fine. Whatever. Still, in my opinion, the only way you can deal with your unresolved issues is to face Nolan again. Besides, this concert is one of the last for Red & Ice."

Serene froze. "What do you mean by that?"

"Haven't you been keeping up? Nolan broke up with Diana onstage — well, kind of. It's not clear if they were ever even together in the first place. I'm sure he wasn't trying to, but he humiliated her and announced that this will be their last tour before Red & Ice will be officially disbanded."

Serene sat still. "That doesn't sound like him at all. Do you know how the label has reacted to the news?"

Laila shrugged. "Just a generic official statement about how the talent is under a lot of pressure and that nothing is final." Laila bit her lip and tilted her head to the side. "So? Are you coming to the concert with us then?"

Serene wrinkled her nose and shook her head. "No."

"I can't believe I'm here." Serene crossed her arms over her chest as she stood in line with Drew and Laila for the *Red & Ice* concert. She had convinced herself the reason she had agreed to go was to get Laila and Drew off her back, but staring at the images of Nolan and Diana around her as she lined up, she knew it was more than that.

Nolan had supported her. Perhaps in some small way, coming to the concert would be her way of showing support for him.

Serene genuinely believed that her presence wouldn't cause much of a scene, but they had been in line for barely five minutes when Drew and Laila's predictions had proved to be true.

One fan pointed at her. "You're Serene Sinclair! You're the original Red!"

Eyes went her way, and a crowd gathered. If she should fear for her life, Serene was yet to find out. Were the fans still angry at her for breaking up with Nolan? At first, a few fans snapped photos of her. After, some approached to ask to be in the picture with her. Soon after, chaos ensued. Her presence caused enough of a commotion to grab attention from the concert organizers and just as Drew and Laila had hoped, they received backstage passes just to save Serene from getting mobbed.

Security personnel asked them to stay and wait at one area backstage, so they could figure out what to do with them. Drew and Laila watched everything going on around them with unabashed fascination. Serene rubbed her palms over her arms. Cold and out-of-place, she considered ditching her friends to go home. After all, she had already gotten them backstage.

"Unbelievable," a familiar voice said.

Serene lifted her gaze.

Ramona was approaching. "I had to see for myself. You're actually here."

Serene gave her former manager a reserved smile. "Hey, Ramona."

"I have missed you, even if you were quite a headache back then, Sinclair."

"I missed you too, Ramona, and all's good, right? You turned your headache into a reality show and got a much more talented rock star out of it."

"Yeah. That sums it up pretty well. You're not mad about that, are you?"

Serene shook her head. "Nah. You saved Nolan's career. I didn't want him to lose his dream because of me."

Ramona's expression softened as her shoulders sagged. "For all it's worth, it's good to see you again, Sinclair. There's nothing like the original." She narrowed her eyes before opening her mouth to say something then shutting it again. She bit her lip and regarded Serene for a long moment. Finally, she nodded. "I need your help. Nolan doesn't want to perform tonight. Can you talk to him?"

Serene froze. "What? Why me?"

"There's a greater chance he'll listen to you."

"Why would you assume that, Ramona? Nolan and I are still not on good terms."

"Please. He made a hit out of your art show, didn't he? Do you have any idea what that side outing of his did to our tour schedule?" Ramona tsk-tsked. "Now, come on."

"No. I'm the last person Nolan would want to see right now."

Ramona laughed. "Oh, honey, you haven't changed at all. You're still so naïve. Please, Serene, come and do me this favor."

"I'm not sure you deserve a favor from me."

"Yeah, but you're a Christian. Don't you believe in loving people even when they don't deserve it?"

"I'm telling you. This is a bad idea."

"Still worth a try. Come on, darling." Ramona approached and pulled her out of her seat. She then linked arms with her and dragged her forward. When she came across one of her assistants, she instructed her, "Raina, Serene's friends are somewhere backstage. Their names are—" she snapped her fingers.

"Drew and Laila," Serene said.

"That." Ramona nodded. "Find them and take good care of them. VIP treatment. Give them front row seats, soda, a five-course dinner, whatever. Just make sure they're taken care of. Where is Nolan?"

"Still locked in his dressing room."

Ramona swore and glanced back at Serene. "He's turned into such a diva since you left. Come, come."

Serene held her breath. She almost wished they would never reach the dressing room. Her heart pounded against her ribcage when they did.

Ramona slammed her palm repeatedly against the door. "Nolan! Open up! Someone's here to talk to you."

"Go away, Ramona!" A voice spoke from inside. "I don't want to talk, and if it's Diana, tell her I'm sick of fighting with her."

At Ramona's nudging, Serene moved closer to the door and knocked gently. "Nolan, it's Serene."

A long pause came from inside the room.

"Hey, Stone! You still alive?" Ramona pounded on the door again. "Are you letting her in or not?"

"I don't believe you." Nolan's voice sounded like he was standing right next to the door. "She wouldn't come here."

"Well, she did." Ramona huffed. "Open the door and find out for yourself."

The knob turned, and the door creaked open. Nolan's eyes widened when he saw Serene. "What are you doing here?"

"I—" Serene couldn't speak. The sight of his sullen face and the bags under his eyes took her aback. What happened?

"How could you pull her into this, Ramona? Desperate move." Nolan shook his head, swung the door wide open, grabbed Serene's wrist, and pulled her inside. He then slammed the door shut and locked it before Ramona could follow in. "How did she talk you into coming to this concert?"

"She didn't. I came because—" What could she say? That she had unresolved feelings for him? "It doesn't matter why I'm here. What happened to you? Haven't you had any sleep at all?"

"Don't change the topic. It matters to me why you're here." Nolan winced and looked away. "And don't judge me. You don't get to do that."

"I'm not. I'm just asking you a question."

"You're telling me you came here just for kicks? You wanted to watch the concert?" He paced the floor.

Serene backed away from him so that her back was against the door. She told him a partial truth. "Drew and Laila convinced me to come. They figured they would have a good chance of getting backstage passes if they were with me. Clearly, they were right."

"So you came with him?"

"Yeah. Him. Drew. And his date, Laila, in case you missed that part. Why do you even care if I'm dating anyone? You told me you're sleeping with Diana, because you're over me."

Nolan stopped pacing. His jaw twitched. "Are you dating someone?"

"No. Are you still sleeping with Diana?"

He winced and paced again. "Not anymore. Not in a long time."

Serene winced. The ache in her chest was for him. "How are you functioning like this?"

He laughed. "Functioning?" He stopped pacing and faced her. "I hate that you're seeing me like this. You shouldn't have come."

"Well, I did, and I'm worried by what I see. All this time, I hoped you were living your dream. Whenever I imagine you, I wished you happiness with her."

"Don't do that. Don't pity me."

"I don't. More like disappointed."

"Geez. Thanks."

"What happened, Nolan? The Nolan I knew was stronger than this. The Nolan I knew manned up when his brother and father died. He didn't make excuses. He rose and fought to reach his dreams. I don't understand what I'm seeing right now."

"What if I was never what you thought I was?"

"You never were what anyone thought you were, Nolan. You kept surprising us and going beyond what anyone imagined you were capable of."

"Capable of what?" Nolan hiccuped. "Of being an alcoholic like my dad and my brother, dead of some addiction at some point?"

At his words, a coupling of fear and rage took over Serene. She had only seen Nolan this way once before, and the memory was at the core of all her unresolved issues about him. Before she could talk her way out of doing it, Serene strode toward him and slapped him on the cheek.

A moment of shock followed as their gazes met. The sting on her palm sent waves of panic into her brain. What had she done? Why had she done that? The one answer that came to her was heartbreak. She hated seeing Nolan this way, and the only person who could help Nolan was Nolan. Still, never before had she done anything like this to him. How would he respond?

Serene swallowed hard when Nolan's entire form tensed, his fists clenching. His tightened jaw twitched as he took a step forward to close the distance between them.

Though tempted to back away, she held her ground and stared him straight in the eye. She squared her shoulders as she gathered her thoughts to vocalize why she had reacted the way she did. "I refuse to let you talk about yourself that way, Nolan. You're better than this. Don't be an idiot. Get yourself out of this rut you fell into."

Nolan flinched, broke eye contact with her, and shook his head. "You don't know me anymore, Serene."

"You're brave and strong and good. No matter what happened between us, I will always believe that."

His lips quivered. His brown eyes moistened. He shook his head to fight back the tears. "You were always too good for me."

Serene looked down, ashamed of the history that convinced him of that lie. "That's not true. You fought for me every step of the way, and I failed to value it. I'm so sorry, Nolan. I hurt you deeply. After everything you did for me, I abandoned you, and—"

"Please stop." His shoulders sagged and before her was once again the boy she had once painted blue. So broken down beyond recognition, but in a snap second, the boy manned up. His eyes cleared, and he stood straight. Nolan then looked her in the eye and stepped forward.

For a moment, Serene feared he would kiss her, and her heart stopped. This time, she backed away.

Nolan's jaw clenched before a soft smile appeared on his face. "I can't believe you slapped me," he said. He then rubbed his face with his palm. "That hurt."

"Sorry," she said. "You have to admit. You kind of needed it. This isn't you. The Nolan I know would man up and get on that stage to give all those people the show they paid to see."

He drew a short breath. His gaze swept over her as if he was seeing a different person. "You will never cease to amaze me, Serene. I will always regret the day I lost you."

His words made her heart jump. *Calm down, Serene. This is Nolan. He says stuff like that. Don't let it get to you.*

"Could you do me a favor please?" he asked. "I deserve nothing from you, but—"

"What is it?"

Nolan smirked and looked away. "Pray for me?"

Without hesitation, she took his hands in hers, closed her eyes, bowed her head, and prayed a simple prayer: "Father, tonight, I pray that you would remind Nolan and me what it is like to experience music while in Your presence."

Little did she know how quickly and how powerfully God would answer her prayer.

seventeen

THE ONE WHO KISSED & MESSED UP AGAIN

"Father, tonight, I pray that you would remind Nolan and me what it is like to experience music while in Your presence."

To Serene's prayer, Nolan nodded and said, "Amen," even if he wasn't entirely sure if he agreed with her. Had he ever experienced God's presence? Or was all of it just goosebumps and chills, sensations brought about by the environment they had created around them? Still, he had asked her for a prayer. He should at least say amen. The tender smile on her face made the prayer worth it.

"Thank you," he said.

Someone knocked on the door.

Nolan's jaw clenched. *Please let it be Ramona.*

"Nolan? Are you ready yet?" Diana's tentative voice came through the door.

Nolan grimaced. "Yes! I'll be with you in a bit!"

"Can I come in?"

"I should join my friends," Serene whispered.

"No. Wait." Nolan brushed past her to crack the door open. The moment he did, Diana forced her way in.

At the sight of Serene, Diana froze. "So it's true. She's here."

"Hi, Diana," Serene said.

"Ramona asked her to come talk me into going on stage."

Diana spun around to face him. The tears rushing down her cheeks made him step back in surprise. "I gave you everything you could've ever wanted, and still, you choose her?!"

"Whoa." Serene raised her arms in the air. "It's not what you think."

"Hey, hey..." Nolan brushed his palms against Diana's arms. "Diana, calm down. What is going on with you?"

Between sobs, Diana said, "Why can't I be your Red?"

Nolan's heart dropped. Why couldn't she be indeed?

Serene tiptoed past him and cast him a sympathetic glance as she mouthed, "I should leave."

He nodded and mouthed back, "Thank you." He then pulled Diana into his embrace, as he watched Serene close the door of his dressing room. Serene's absence in the room changed the atmosphere. Somehow, the room became colder and emptier without her — a stark reminder of how Diana could take the place of Red, but she could never be Serene.

"I'm so sorry, Diana," was all he could say. She had offered herself to him, and he had taken what she offered, even knowing that he could never love her the way she wanted him to. And now, he had broken her. "I wish I could make it better."

Diana's form stiffened in his embrace. She pushed him back and wiped her tears away. This time, her cheeks flushed red with anger. "You wish you could make it better?! You've ruined everything!" She pressed her palm over his chest to push him back.

"I'm sorry."

She shook her head. "Not good enough."

His jaw twitched. "I know."

"It's her, isn't it? It's Serene. You don't want to be with me because of her."

"It's not like that." Was it? Nolan shifted his weight from one foot to the other. Did seeing Serene again prompt him to let go of Diana? Did she have that much power over him? Nolan clenched his fists and shook his head. "It's not her, Diana. I ended us because I've never been this unhappy my entire life."

Diana's face contorted from shock to pain to anger. Her palm landed sharply against his cheek.

Nolan's head spun as it registered the sharp sting on his cheek. He flexed his jaw. What was with these women slapping him that night?

"I'll make you pay for this," Diana said. She spun around and rushed to the door.

"Diana…" He followed her out the door and to the stage.

When Ramona saw them approaching, relief washed over her face, but the moment she saw Diana, concern replaced whatever calm the relief brought with it. "What is going on?" she asked Nolan as he tried to catch up with Diana.

"I doubt it's good," he said.

They finally caught up with his costar, who had stopped at the side of the stage as the opening band finished their set. Ramona brushed her shoulder. "You okay?"

"Totally fine." She flashed a smile, her eyes vacant.

A chill came over Nolan. Was she?

"You sure?" Ramona pushed.

Diana nodded. "Relax, Ramona. Tonight will be a show to remember. I'll make sure of it."

Before either of them could react, the opening band finished the set, and way before their cue, Diana just walked on to the stage.

Taken by surprise, Ramona just glared at Nolan and said, "Go! Now!"

Nolan rushed to follow his costar.

Diana already had the microphone.

The sight of them livened up the crowd.

"Are you ready to rock?!" Diana yelled.

The audience went wild.

"Ice and I are giving you a show you won't ever forget!" She tossed the microphone over to Nolan.

He scrambled forward to catch it and blew out a breath when he did. He narrowed his eyes at her as she marched toward him. What was she up to?

Diana grabbed his arm and pulled him close so that her lips were close to his ear, her breath hot against his earlobes. "Follow my lead, Nolan. Or else." Her cutting tone was nowhere near as sharp as the glare she shot him when she let go of his arm.

Nolan replaced the microphone on its stand and cleared his throat before speaking into it. "Guess tonight will be a night full of surprises." He grinned at the audience as an attempt to lighten the mood. Serene was sitting in the front row. Concern laced her eyes.

He picked up his electric guitar and swallowed hard. He turned to check on Diana. She had already taken her place on the drum set. She slammed the drumsticks together. One, two, three.

Nolan played his chord. Expecting a solid drum beat — Diana style — he couldn't have prepared himself for the noise that assaulted his ears where music should have been.

Fury blazed in Diana's eyes. One by one, she stabbed her drumsticks into each piece of the set before flinging the cymbals randomly into the air, not caring where they went. Their bass guitarist caught one. Meanwhile, the other crashed into some lights. Finally, Diana flipped the drum set over.

A piece of the set rolled to his feet. Nolan's jaw dropped at the gaping holes on it. It was possible to poke holes into drums like that?

Diana grabbed her microphone and screamed into it. "See that drum set?! That's what this man did to my heart! He used me and disposed of me once he didn't need me anymore! Nolan Stone is not a rock star! Sex, drugs, and rock-and-roll, remember? This Jesus Freak doesn't do any of those! I'm done with this! *Red & Ice* is over! Diana out!"

Nolan felt like the world had just crashed on him as he watched her walk off the stage. The silence of the entire stadium magnified the oddness and sadness of the situation. Never had he felt so sorry, so guilty over the pain of another person. Nolan started to chase after Diana, but from the side of the stage, Ramona motioned for him to stay where he was.

"Fix! This!" She mouthed the words and accompanied it with hand gestures like she was hammering something in the air. "I'll take care of her."

What did she expect him to do? Diana had lost it. How was he going to perform a *Red & Ice* concert without Red? Serene. He glanced at her. As if reading his mind, she shook her head.

There was no way she would ever get on that stage, and he was aware of it. For the first time in his career as a musician, he had to take the stage alone. He gripped the neck of his guitar, nodded his head once, squared his shoulders, and faced the microphone on the mic stand.

Only then did he realize that most of the crowd had everything Diana just did on video. "Forgive Diana, please. Forgive me also for what just happened."

"Now what?!" someone in the crowd yelled out.

"What did you do to her?!" another chimed in.

A commotion followed and the rumble of the crowd grew louder and wilder by the second.

Serene had her eyes closed, her lips moving.

Out of the pure desperation of that moment, Nolan shut his eyes and said one short prayer in a whisper only he could hear: "God, if You're listening, please. What do I do?"

At that very moment, a faint recollection of his childhood drifted on his mind. How music used to come to him. Music from somewhere other than his own self enveloped him, silencing — at least in his mind — the noise surrounding him. Losing himself in the music, Nolan's fingers moved effortlessly, plucking the guitar's strings and playing a song never heard before.

The audience grew silent.

The band picked up their instruments and accompanied him.

At first, only the melody. After a few seconds, the words eased into his soul like a sweet promise from heaven.

"One battered rose in a cluster of thorns," Nolan sang into the microphone. "Where does the blood go once a heart is too worn?" The song expressed the sorrow of his heart over both the women whom he had pulled into being the Red to his Ice. At the end, he drew a breath and let his ears absorb pure silence. He had no idea whether the song was any good. What did it matter? It was true.

Applause erupted across the stadium until the mention of his name, uttered by one voice, morphed into a chorus of voices.

"Nolan! Nolan! Nolan!"

"It's time to go solo!" a random voice rose above the chants.

From the front row, Serene had a big smile on her face and tears in her eyes, and to Nolan's surprise, so did he. Nolan placed his forefinger over his lips. "Shhhh..."

Like a wave, one by one, the audience hushed across the stadium.

Nolan, however, could clearly hear the thumping of his heart against his chest. He cleared his throat and wiped a tear away. "I'd like to say a few words before we all figure out what we will do tonight." He checked the side of the stage and found Ramona there, nodding for him to go ahead. Where was Diana? With a heavy heart, he continued to speak. "Diana Rake and I have been through a lot. Many of you joined us on our journey through The New Red. To be honest, she was right when she said that I did hurt her. That is something that I will always regret. On behalf of Red & Ice, to all of you who have supported us and loved us as a duo—" his gaze swept across the crowd "—I apologize. This tour has been difficult on both Diana and me. Even now, standing here—" He choked. He paused to get a hold of himself and reel the tears back in.

"We love you, Nolan!" a female voice boomed from somewhere in the audience.

The statement genuinely warmed his heart. A light chuckle escaped his lips. "I love you guys too. Thank you for all the support you've given us and our music." Again, he cleared his throat. "Ultimately, that's what we all came here for, right? The music. That's what this is all about. The original Red, Serene

Sinclair, whom you all may already know was my childhood sweetheart, is here right now. And no. She will not perform tonight. Her days as a rock star are over. She can, however, attest to the fact that I have always loved music and will always love music. I'd like to give my solo spin to the music of *Red & Ice*. Tonight will be the debut of Nolan Stone. Solo artist. You came for a concert tonight, and if you let me, I'll give you one."

A numbing silence filled the auditorium before a commotion in one area of the stage distracted the crowd. A clump of Diana's hard-core fans stood from their seats and began demanding a refund. Some of the audience began to respond to those walking out with derision and more than a few boo's.

"Please." Nolan lifted his arms in the air in a motion for them to stop. "Let them be. Anyone who wants a refund can have it." Once again glancing backstage, Nolan found Ramona's eyes growing wide as she mouthed, "What?!"

He shrugged at her before refocusing on the audience. To his relief, most of them were still there.

"Just play," Serene mouthed at him.

And so, he did. He turned toward his band and instructed them to follow his lead. Never had he been more thankful for how supportive and professional they were.

Nolan plucked a tune and belted out a note, and the moment he did, the crowd was his. He performed only his originals, the ones he had written without Diana's input. A lot of them were Red & Ice classics. The audience was right there with him as he improvised each performance, making up for Diana not being there.

However, when he started playing the intro of *Rocking Serene*, the song that shot *Red & Ice* to fame, one lone voice crying out, "Sing it with Serene!" became a chant that filled the stadium: "Sing it with Serene! Sing it with Serene! Sing it with Serene!"

Nolan cast an apologetic look at her. Her cheeks flushed red as she closed her eyes. She looked terrified. He stopped playing and lifted his arms toward the crowd. "Hey, guys. Come on. We can't force—"

The audience began to cheer.

To his surprise, Serene was approaching the stage. Elated, Nolan rushed to her and extended his hand to help her climb up the steps.

"This is crazy!" she exclaimed as she steadied herself on stage.

"I know!"

She threw her arms around him, sending the crowd into a frenzy. She whispered into his ear, "I'm so proud of you, Nolan."

"It means the world to me to hear you say that."

They pulled away from each other.

He winked at her. "Ready for this?"

Serene laughed. "I don't think I'll ever be ready for all of this, but I trust I'll be okay if I follow your lead."

The statement both comforted and burdened his heart. "Okay then." He smiled at her and played the intro, memories of the first time he had ever performed the song flooding over him.

Something about seeing Serene on stage with him just felt so right. Nolan lost himself in that performance and in the span of one song, convinced himself that he and Serene belonged together. How could they not? With the crowd cheering and her standing right there, they sang out the last line of the song, staring into each other's eyes. Swept away by emotion and the sensation of once again performing with her, Nolan kissed her.

The audience loved it, but the look of pain and betrayal in Serene's eyes was enough to tell Nolan he had just made a horrible mistake.

Serene brushed her trembling fingers over her lips. She gazed up at Nolan. The fire in his eyes and the disappointment and awkwardness that followed crushed her soul. One sensation after another hit her like waves. The crowd cheering. Her skin tingling. The energy ramping up from the impromptu performance she never imagined she would ever have to do again. The unexpected kiss that he had stolen from her.

"Sorry," he mouthed.

"It's fine," she said. It wasn't. "I'd like to rejoin the audience now."

"You sure?" His voice sounded choked. "It might be safer for you and your friends backstage."

"I'm sure." She nodded.

Nolan extended his hand toward her. "I really am sorry."

"I know." She took his hand, and he led her to the edge of the stage.

She was about to go down the steps when he squeezed her hand. "Let's talk after the show. Please."

Serene bit the corner of her lower lip. He understood, or at least she hoped he did. He let go of her. She was trembling so hard, she feared her knees would give way beneath her.

Upon her return to them, Drew and Laila made no effort to hide their elation.

"Does this mean what I think it means?!" Laila exclaimed loud enough for people around them to hear.

Trying not to embarrass Nolan, Serene fought hard not to shake her head. She pulled Laila into a tight embrace and whispered, "No. He made a mistake, and he knows it."

Laila froze against her embrace, but quickly hugged her back and nodded over her shoulder. Laila squeezed her arm and said, "We'll talk later."

The show wrapped up, and Nolan himself invited them to the after party. Drew and Laila wanted to go, but Serene decided not to. Not after that. Drew and Laila, being the good friends they were, skipped the after party as well and took her home.

Nolan called her several times that night. She rejected each call. She was about to turn the phone off when another name registered on her screen. Ethan Caine.

"Hello?"

"Serene! I have great news."

"What is it?" The words came out in a much higher pitch than her normal voice. An attempt to lighten her tone.

"We're expanding our publishing arm, and Caleb has been scouting new business locations we could use as headquarters. We checked three locations today and have already made our decision where to go. One location we didn't go for, however, made me think of your incubator. It's the perfect spot, Serene."

"That's great news!" The excitement eased the heaviness of what happened at the concert that night.

"I mentioned it to Caleb. I hope you don't mind."

"Not at all."

"He said he can set up an appointment for you and him to go check it out next week. Are you up for it?"

"Of course! Yes. Totally. Thank you so much, Ethan." This time, the light tone of her voice was genuine.

"Anything for you, Serene."

Her heart stopped. Was she beginning to owe Ethan too many favors? Serene plopped down on the bed and buried her face in her pillow before letting out a strangled yell. But even then, her lips remembered Nolan's, and a tear trickled down her cheek.

God, why is it so hard to stop feeling this way for him?

Immediately, she knew the answer. Because once in her life, she loved Nolan more than she loved God.

eighteen

THE ONE WHO CHOSE TO MOVE ON

Serene shifted in the driver's seat. She checked the time on her watch. Almost four o'clock. She wasn't late. Caleb would arrive soon. She stood waiting on the sidewalk of the location Caleb had sent her. From the outside, she wondered why Ethan thought it would be a good incubator. It looked like some warehouse that needed looking after. The location was also in the suburbs away from the city. She would have to relocate should she choose to take a lease on this place.

Caleb's van showed up. Serene had to smile when Nova waved at her from the passenger seat. She waved back.

As soon as the van's motor stopped running, Nova bounded out of the vehicle and rushed to Serene, pulling her into a hug. "Serene!"

"So glad you're here, Nova." She hoped she sounded convincing. The irony that she was hugging Nolan's sister wasn't lost on her. Caleb and Nova's presence reminded her of how intertwined her life was with Nolan's. She bit her lip.

"I told her it was a business meeting. That didn't stop her. She insisted on coming anyway," Caleb explained.

"I'm glad you did," Serene said. "I feel like it's been ages since I last saw you. How are you doing?"

"As good as I can be while juggling the twins and work. It's difficult, but I'm not complaining. I love my life. And you?" The spark of concern in Nova's eyes told her that Nova knew about what had happened at the concert. "I can imagine it might have been a rough week."

The words hung inside Serene, unable to come out.

"That's not what we are here to talk about." Caleb came to her rescue. "Hello, Serene." He hugged her. "We miss you."

"I miss you guys too."

"You should have seen Ethan's face when he saw this place. He immediately thought of you."

Ten minutes later, they were with the real estate agent, exploring what looked like a rundown warehouse from the outside, but inside, Serene saw what Ethan had: potential.

The place used to be the headquarters of a startup tech company that made it big. All around, the space breathed innovation and creativity. Brick walls on one side and concrete on the rest, the first thing that would greet someone coming in was one wide open space with offices on an open second floor, seen through full glass windows. In one area were a few rooms and alcoves for those who wanted more privacy. Artful graffiti filled the concrete walls. Serene could picture what it would look like if it became her incubator.

"There are also residential apartments right across the street," the real estate agent said. "Mr. Caine mentioned you may want to keep some staff in-house, or maybe consider moving here. The building doesn't look like much from the outside, I'm aware, but that's because the company that first used this as a business space wanted to focus more on the interior. They didn't need something big and flashy back then."

"It's why we didn't go for this place," Caleb added. "We needed something more presentable to clients from the outside. But for an incubator—"

"It's perfect." Serene nodded.

"And it's so close to home." Nova hooked her arm over Serene's. "We'll see you a lot more often."

"That's a definite perk." Serene leaned her head on Nova's shoulder. "I love the place."

She loved it so much, she walked out with a five-year lease on the commercial space and a contract for one penthouse apartment across the street.

Still, her concerns over both Nolan and Ethan dampened Serene's excitement over this new venture.

"Why the long face?" Nova nudged her shoulder as they walked past the door and to their vehicles. "We should be celebrating. Serene! A new business!"

"I'm thrilled!" Serene said too enthusiastically to be convincing. "I'm excited about all the possibilities. I am. It's just—" She shook her shoulders. "I need to shake some things off and be in this moment. That's all."

Concern brushed through Nova's eyes, but a smile pushed it aside. "We don't even know what your business is. Ethan refused to fill us in on any details regarding what you had in mind for this space, so I'm dying to know what you need an incubator for."

Caleb chuckled as he leaned back on their van. "It's one reason she insisted to come with me today."

"I'd love to tell you, but you guys probably need to go by now."

"Do you have plans tonight?" Caleb asked.

"I was thinking of dropping by my parents' place."

"Have you told them you were coming?" Nova asked.

"No, but—"

"Then please have dinner with us?" Nova gave her a pleading smile. "Ma is there taking care of the twins, and I know she would love to see you."

Serene wasn't sure if she could handle a night with Nolan's family, but just like her brother, Nova was notoriously difficult to resist when she wanted something. "I would love to."

Half an hour later, she was at Nova's kitchen, helping to prepare dinner with Nova and Clara.

"Still lovely as ever, Serene," Clara said.

Serene looked up from the stalk of celery she was cutting. "Thank you, Clara. You're so kind."

Clara waved her knife in the air and shook her head. "Never could understand why that son of mine allowed you to slip through his fingers."

"Ma." Nova's eyes widened. "We talked about this. Also, stop waving sharp objects around."

One of the twins began to wail.

"Nova!" Caleb's voice boomed from the second floor.

"What's happening up there?" Nova chuckled. "Serene, do you mind stirring the soup for a bit?"

"Sure." Serene put her knife down and took the long wooden spoon from Nova.

Silence filled the kitchen after Nova disappeared. Clara finished cutting the chicken and proceeded to marinate them in soy sauce and vinegar.

Clara was making *adobo*. Just the thought of the dish made Serene's mouth water and her eyes moisten even as one childhood memory after another, spending time at the Stones' house, came to her.

"Serene?" Clara eventually spoke up.

"Yes?"

"Your mom and I often pray for our children together. You and Jeremy. Caleb, Nova, their twins, and that boy of mine." She sighed. "Nolan. Did your mother mention we were doing that?"

"No, Mama Aida has never mentioned it. Thank you for praying for us. It's encouraging for me to hear."

"Sometimes, God has funny ways of leading us right where we should be. I feel like He wants me to tell you right now that He knows your heart, Serene. You shouldn't always feel so guilty."

Serene choked back a tear. She stopped stirring the soup and held on to the edge of the counter. Clara's words hit her hard. From Nolan's mother, it meant the world to Serene to hear that.

The doorbell rang.

Serene turned to Clara who lifted her hands, which was as marinated with soy sauce and vinegar as the chicken.

"I'll go check who it is," she said. Before heading out of the kitchen, she stopped beneath the door post, did a one-eighty, walked back to Clara, and kissed her on the cheek. "Thank you, Clara. I love you."

"I love you too, Serene. You'll always be family to us."

The words warmed her heart as much as it crushed it. Serene forced a smile. So overwhelmed by emotion, when she reached the door, she didn't even bother to check who it was through the peephole. She just swung it open and found herself standing in front of Nolan.

At the sight of Serene, Nolan's entire body turned numb. What was she doing here?

"Hey." He shifted his weight from one foot to the other as he rubbed the back of his neck with one palm. He squirmed and squinted an eye. "Am I in the right house? This is Caleb and Nova's house, right?"

Whatever guilt he carried from what he had done during last week's concert washed away when her squared shoulders relaxed and her shocked expression morphed into a chuckle.

"You're in the right place. They're upstairs taking care of the twins. Your mom is here, too."

"Great." Nolan tried not to focus on the fact that all of that other information was normal. It was Serene's presence there that was wrinkling his brain. "So, yeah. Can I come in?"

"Right!" Serene swung the door wide open. "It's your home more than it is mine."

"Pfft. You're family to us." Nolan brushed past her.

"Your mom's in the kitchen." Serene shut the door behind her.

He turned to face her. "About what happened—"

A pained smile appeared on her lovely face. "Let's not make tonight awkward."

"I understand. Just wanted to say thank you for performing." Nolan meant it — even if the mere sight of her still felt like reopening an old wound.

"Nolan!"

He turned to find his older sister coming down the stairs with his nephew, Nate, in tow.

"There she is!" Something about seeing Nova and her family always provided him a blanket of comfort knowing that at least someone in his family wasn't living a messed-up life. "Ramona agreed to give me a break while she negotiates a deal for my solo career, so I figured it's time I give my favorite *Ate* a surprise visit so we can celebrate."

"Ate." Nova raised a brow at the Filipino word for older sister. "You haven't called me that in years."

Nolan shrugged and grinned. Warm affection spread on his chest at the fond smile Nova directed at him.

"I'm glad you're here," she said, squeezing his bicep. "And a solo career! That's amazing!"

"Can't complain." He pulled her into a hug, while trying not to crush his nephew between them. Nate squirmed and tried to push Nolan away.

"He has no clue who I am."

"It's not you. He's grumpy right now. Claudia is the one who's in a good mood."

Nolan smiled at his nephew. "Why so grumpy, Nate? Aren't they feeding you?"

"Do I hear my son's voice?" Clara appeared from the kitchen almost at the same time Caleb descended the steps with Claudia in tow.

Seeing his family altogether — the people he cared about the most — enveloped him with so much warmth and made him feel like he hadn't in a long time: safe.

Even with Serene there.

She had always blended in so well with his family, and that night was no different. His family acted like she was their family, and he found that surreal, because she no longer felt that way to him.

After dinner, Nolan managed some time alone with his older sister when he volunteered to help her serve dessert. It was the perfect opportunity to bring up the presence of his ex-girlfriend.

"So—" he brought out the mango graham cake from the fridge "—Serene is here. Why?"

Nova filled him in on her new business venture and how they got mixed into all of it. "Caleb's boss is into her."

Nolan's jaw clenched.

Nova brandished a cake knife from the drawer. "Jealous?"

Nolan cocked his head to the side as he watched her cut the cake. The familiar tightening of the chest at Serene being with anyone other than him was absent. "Strangely, no."

"What was going through your mind at that concert, Nolan? After what happened to Diana, you kiss your ex on stage? Seriously?" Nova emphasized her words by waving the knife in the air. "You shouldn't have done that."

He laughed at the way she was swinging the knife at him.

"What's so funny?"

"You're so much like Ma." He mimicked her.

Nova stared at the knife, dumbfounded. She narrowed her eyes at him. "Don't change the subject. Are you still into Serene?"

"Honestly?" He shrugged. "I'm a mess whenever I'm around her. One moment, I'm just hurt that she's not with me. The next, I'm almost on the verge of getting on my knees to ask her if we can be together again. Nova, she was the one. You saw us back then, how we were. It's hard to see her moving on, but after that kiss, and after I saw the look on her face when I did it—" his jaw twitched "—I have to let go of her. She deserves happiness."

"You deserve happiness too, Nolan."

"Maybe, but for that to even be a possibility, I need to deal with my feelings for her. I need to deal with my own issues. Otherwise, I'll just keep hurting people I care about. I can't stand how much I hurt Diana, and now, I have to process and look back to what went on with Serene and me. Was I more at fault than I would care to admit? Nova—" His voice cracked. He let her name stay frozen in the air as he sought the courage to admit to one of the few people he fully trusted what he was there for. "I need help, Nova. That's why I came here. I need help. All the things I've done—" He shifted his eyes away from her and fought back the tears. His voice came out strangled. "I don't want to turn out like Dad and Nate."

The curves of Nova's face softened as she laid the knife down on the table and rushed to pull him in an embrace. "That won't happen, Nolan," she said as she brushed her fingers against his hair. "We won't let it. I'll talk to Caleb. You can stay here with us as long as you need to."

"Thanks for the offer, Nova." He nodded as he gently pulled himself out of her embrace. "But I'm staying with Ma. I'm sure she'll let me. She lives next door to Pastor Sam, and it's him I need to see."

"Nolan." Nova reached out for his hand and squeezed it in a firm grip. "I'm glad you want to seek help, but are you sure this isn't just about Serene?"

"No," he said with complete resolve. "I'm seeking out Pastor Sam, because he's the healthiest father figure I've ever known. He's the only one I would be able to trust with everything that I've done. Believe me. Once he finds out what I've been up to, there's no way he would ever let me be with Serene." He took a deep breath. "In a lot of ways, me going to him is my way of letting go of her."

The color drained out of Nova's face as she looked past him. Nolan turned around, dreading who he would see there.

Serene was standing beneath the door post. She opened her mouth, but brushed three fingers over her lips instead.

Nolan didn't know how much she had heard of what he had said, and he didn't need to know.

"Your mother and Caleb had their hands full with the twins, so they asked me to—" Serene winced. "Should I leave?"

"That would probably be best." Nolan nodded.

"Nolan." Nova's voice came with both a tone of reprimand and resignation. "Serene, you don't have to go."

"I think I do. Thank you for the lovely evening, Nova. I appreciate it." Serene then fixed those green eyes on him. She smiled. "Goodbye, Nolan."

He gave her a short, courteous nod. "Goodbye, Serene."

The words had a ring of finality to it that broke his heart all over again, but this time, it felt like the breaking was necessary for the process toward wholeness to begin.

And so, he watched her go and forgave her completely. Now, all he had left to do was forgive himself.

nineteen

THE ONE
WHO NEEDED
A FATHER

Reliving one of the darkest moments of his youth, Nolan stepped up the front porch of the Sinclair residence, shut his eyes, and took a deep breath. He summoned courage and knocked on the door. The last time he had seen Pastor Sam and Mama Aida had been awkward. What would he say to them to justify how he had dragged Serene's name through the reality show that had launched Diana to fame? He didn't have much time to think about it, because the door swung open, and there before him was Jeremy Sinclair.

The teenager's face grew grim at the sight of Nolan. "You have a lot of nerve showing up here."

Nolan flashed him a grin. "I'm aware." He buried his one hand in his pocket and brushed the side of his hair back. "Is your father here?"

"What do you want?" Jeremy crossed his arms over his chest.

"Hey, Jeremy, what's taking you so— Oh." Max stopped in his tracks. A smile lit up his face. "What's up, Nolan? What brings you here?"

Jeremy glared at him.

"What?" Max shrugged. "He's a rock star! People like Nolan don't just show up on people's doorsteps." He pointed at Jeremy with his thumb. "He still listens to your music."

"What are you doing, man? Have you forgotten what he did to Serene?"

"Showed up to her art show and made it a hit?"

"It's her art that made *One Red Hue* a hit, not me." Nolan had to interrupt.

"You still sure helped." Max shrugged.

Nolan forced a grin. "Great to see you again, Max." He shuffled on his feet. "Is Pastor Sam home?"

"Now, I am."

Nolan turned around to find Samuel Sinclair assisting his wife up the front steps. Aida Sinclair looked pale, but the usual soft smile on her face widened at the sight of him. "Hi, Pastor Sam." Nolan gave the pastor a curt nod. "Mama Aida." It hurt to see her looking so frail. "Is everything all right?"

"Of course, it is." Mama Aida pulled him in for a warm embrace. "It's so good to see our Nolan again. How I've missed this amazing, talented worshiper."

Wrapped in his arms, Mama Aida seemed smaller and frailer than he remembered. Serene's art show hadn't been that long ago. Pastor Sam's eyes moistened, his gaze fixed on his wife. Pride and deep affection shone on his face, reminding Nolan of why he had always wanted a marriage like theirs.

Mama Aida pulled away from their hug and grabbed hold of his shoulders and looked up at him with undeniable delight. "Clara told me everything. We're so glad you're here! How are you? It's a pleasure to see you."

"I'm great, Mama," Nolan said. "And you?"

"I'm very well. Thank you for asking." She tapped him on the shoulder before brushing her fingers over his cheek. "Still so handsome. No wonder my Serene could not resist you."

"Aida." Pastor Sam's expression was a mix of affection and sternness.

Nolan ignored the way Mama Aida's last sentence made his heart flutter and extended his hand for the pastor to shake. "Pastor."

"None of that." Pastor Sam rejected the handshake and pulled him in for a hug. "We have missed you in this household."

While he expected it from Mama Aida, the kindest and most affectionate woman he had ever met, a warm welcome wasn't something he expected from their pastor. Pastor Sam's firm embrace melted Nolan's defenses. Memories of Damien Stone revisited Nolan's mind. Not once had his own father ever hugged him the way Pastor Sam was doing now. All pretense fading away, in Samuel Sinclair's arms, Nolan broke into a sob.

Instead of pulling away, Pastor Sam held him tighter. "Shh... It's okay, son. God will work everything out for your good."

A series of sobs wracked Nolan's chest as years of pent-up tears rushed from his eyes to his pastor's shoulders.

"We're out of here," Jeremy announced. "Mama, Max and I are taking a walk while you guys figure this one out."

"Jeremy." Mama Aida's tone was sternness mixed with affection, echoing Pastor Sam's reprimand of her earlier.

"Too much drama for me, Mama."

Nolan's awareness of their short exchange helped him recover his composure, so he could avoid embarrassing himself further. He pulled away from Pastor Sam and tried to pull himself together. "I'm sorry," he croaked out. "I don't know what came over me."

"Son, we have a lot to talk about."

"You two go ahead to Sam's study." Mama Aida waved them away as she walked through the front door. "I will make dinner."

With an arm over his shoulder, Pastor Sam led Nolan to his study — the venue of many mentoring sessions Nolan had forced himself to sit through, so he could be with Serene. This time, however, he wasn't there for her. He was there for himself.

Once they settled on their seats, Pastor Sam placed his elbows over his knees and gave Nolan an intent stare. "So what can I help you with, Nolan?"

Nolan winced. Why did he think this would be a good idea? What did he expect a pastor to do for him other than tell him to believe in Jesus? He cleared his throat and searched within for an answer. "I don't know, Pastor Sam. I've just fallen so far away, and the things I've done—" Nolan tensed in his seat, his face numbing as he recalled the first time he slept with Diana or the first time he got so drunk, he passed out. One after another, flashes of the things he had been doing ever since Serene had left him filled his mind. Once again, a tear ran down his cheek. "Pastor Sam, this may sound ridiculous, because the only reason you ever paid attention to me before was Serene, and now that she's not in my life, you don't need to mind me whatsoever since I'm not even in your church anymore, but—"

"Now, stop right there, Son." Pastor Sam's expression softened. He seemed almost hurt. "Nolan, you have been a part of this family for almost two decades. I watched you grow up with my daughter. I watched you become the man that you are now. Whatever happened between you and Serene, it doesn't change the fact that Aida and I care deeply about you. Like you are our own son. Whatever you will ask of me, know that you will always have a place at our table, Nolan. We love you. I love you."

In that moment, it was as if the grief he had over the loss of Nate and his father came to him in full force and there was no way Nolan could hold back the tears. "Pastor Sam, you've been a father to me all these years, and I think I need one right now, because I don't know what to do. I'm falling apart."

The much wiser man rushed from his seat and sat next to Nolan on the couch and pulled him in a hug. "Everything will be okay. Our Father in heaven loves you, Nolan. You'll get through this."

Somehow, Nolan believed that he would. A familiar, but still strangely exhilarating sensation came over him. It was one that he could only remember feeling when he was a child. Like he had somehow touched on something greater than him, something eternal. He knew what he had to do next. "Pastor Sam, I think I have to rededicate my life to Jesus. Can you please pray with me?"

This time, a tear trickled down the pastor's cheek. "It would be an honor."

And so, with head bowed and heart humbled, Nolan Stone said a prayer he had uttered so many times at Sunday School as a child. This time, however, it was different. It was real.

Loved by the Father Above, Nolan Stone was about to become a changed man.

Swept away by the demands of her new venture, Nolan's stolen kiss morphed into a distant memory Serene didn't bother to deal with. Entertainment outlets made a lot of noise about it for a while. Speculations circulated about her and Nolan. Had they ever really broken up? Had the whole concert been just one big media stunt to promote Nolan's solo career? Had Diana sensed it; thus, her meltdown?

It didn't matter. What she heard him say to his mother in Nova's kitchen often haunted her: *"In a lot of ways, me going to him is my way of letting go of her."*

Hopefully, "him" was God, but she didn't intend to find out. Whoever it was, if Nolan was intent on letting go of her, she had to find a way to let go of him.

Serene blocked it all out and focused on *Thrive*. Soon, people closest to her realized she would avoid any talk of Nolan Stone, and she created for herself a Nolan-less bubble.

Until he started attending church regularly.

"I don't know why it bothers you," Drew said as he and Laila helped her transfer heavy suitcases inside the elevator that would lead up to her new apartment. "Don't you want him to know Christ?"

"I do." Serene huffed as she dragged the last box inside the elevator. "It's just hard to see him." She pressed the letter P on the panel of buttons. "He doesn't even look at me. It's like I'm not there."

Laila stepped into the elevator. "You're not making any sense. If you don't want him to communicate with you, then isn't that a good thing?"

"Yeah, but if he's there every Sunday, the whole out of sight, out of mind thing can't work for me. If I see him all the time, how can I stop thinking of him?" Serene crossed her arms across her chest. "Let's stop talking about it."

Drew laughed. "You're the one who brought it up, Serene."

She pouted.

The elevator bell chimed to indicate they had reached the penthouse. The spacious living area lightened her mood. It had taken several months of renovations before she could get it the way she wanted it to be. Her first home that was completely her own.

Drew and Laila stayed to help her unpack and put everything in its place. Recently engaged and planning their wedding, Drew would soon move to Laila's apartment to take Serene's place.

Everything had worked out well for everyone.

Laila embraced Serene when it was time for them to go. "I will miss you as a roommate, but I know we'll still see each other a lot. Because you have a lot of work to do for my wedding."

Serene laughed. "Don't worry. I won't abandon you. Thanks, guys! Are you sure you don't want to go out for lunch? It's my treat."

"We're sure." Drew gave her a side hug. "We have dinner tonight with the parents. Hers and mine. We need to drive back to the city and prepare for that."

Laila rolled her eyes. "He says he needs a lot of emotional preparation."

Serene chuckled. "I'm having coffee with Ethan this afternoon to discuss the incubator. I feel like I'm in over my head with all these applications. This is so unexpected."

"We're still not sure why you're so surprised." Drew made a face. "Your name recognition is huge in both the music and art industries. You released a video saying you want to pay it forward and help hone the talent of artists—"

"Not to mention house them and finance their work," Laila piped in.

"Yeah. That." Drew nodded. "Of course you will get a ton of applications."

Serene cringed as she scratched her head. "Still, I have my work cut out for me."

"You'll do amazing." Drew patted her on the shoulder. "We believe in you."

"Thanks, guys. It means a lot to hear you say that."

They said their goodbyes, and the couple went on their way, leaving Serene with a dream in her heart, a place to call home, and a mind she needed to fill with the next thing, so it wouldn't wander off to issues she didn't want to deal with.

By the time Serene met Ethan at a coffee shop, she had also already spent two hours whittling down applications to the ones that most spoke to her heart.

"This is great art." Ethan said as he scrolled through her laptop to view the portfolio of Jon Abraham, a barista struggling to make ends meet as he tried to finish his graphic novel.

"Right? The concept alone takes my breath away." Serene took a sip from her apple cider. "It's stunning. His writing leaves a lot to be desired though, so I figured I could put him through creative writing courses. And—" she angled the laptop to face her, so she could bring up another portfolio "—there's this girl, Piper Lacey, who sent in her writing. Her dream is to collaborate with other artists to create interactive stories. The only problem is she's a great writer, but can't draw to save her life. Her story ideas are amazing though. Imagine if we could bring all these artists together and give them space to see if they're creatively compatible." Serene's soul lifted just talking about it. "The possibilities are endless."

"It is." Ethan leaned back on his seat. "But you're seeing this whole thing from rose-colored glasses,

Serene. You're putting together all these people from different backgrounds. They have different personalities, creative mindsets, and frankly, real issues. Do you understand how that could be a recipe for disaster? You're assuming everyone will just get along."

"I'm hoping things will go well, of course, but as enthused as I sound, I understand it will be challenging. There's a reason we have the tortured artist stereotype. I don't doubt it will be difficult in ways I couldn't even fully imagine, but I also want to help them through that. To give them a safe space to create their art and feel supported, like they matter, like they're worth fighting for."

"That's admirable, Serene, and it's because of this that I want to bring up that you make *Thrive* a non-profit organization instead of a business."

"I've taken that into consideration, Ethan, but that's not what I want to do. *Thrive* has to become a profitable business, not one that's running from charity. The work of these people can turn a profit. I have to believe that."

"You asked me to mentor you, Serene, and I'm telling you that businesses are rarely successful when you run them from the heart. It's a worthy cause, but it's a lot of money spent without a promise of profit any time soon. Let's be real. How much of your savings did you lose getting the lease for the incubator and your apartment?"

"I'll be fine. I—" Something unexpected caught her eye. "No way. Is that—" She blinked her eyes to make sure she wasn't just seeing things. Sure enough, on the far end of the café, tucked in a secluded corner, was Nolan and her father.

Following her gaze, Ethan twisted his torso to look behind him. "That's Nolan. Isn't that your dad?"

"What are they doing?"

"Why don't you go say hi?"

"I don't want to."

"Why not?"

"I can't."

"I'm going then."

"No. Don't. Ethan, please." She frowned. Nolan laughed at something her father was saying. "I think they're studying the Bible. That's so odd. I mean, Nolan's been attending church, but I thought it was only because he's been living with his mother." She pried her eyes away from them and fixed her stare on Ethan. "Why didn't Dad tell me about this?"

Ethan shrugged. He then raised a brow at her and straightened his shoulders.

"What?" she asked. She stole another glance at Nolan.

"You're still so in love with him."

Serene's cheeks heated up. Immediately, she stared Ethan dead in the eye. "No. You're reading this wrong. I'm just intrigued to find him having one-on-one meetings with my dad."

Ethan chuckled. "If you say so, Serene, but the way your face lights up at the sight of him, it's a clear sign to me I have zero chance with you."

That gave her reason to pause. "Ethan, we agreed that—"

"One hundred percent professional. I remember. Still, can you blame me if I held onto some hope? Don't mistake my intentions. I'm helping you out because I admire your passion, and I believe in your vision, but I'm attracted to you, Serene. I don't mind admitting that; however, it's clear to me you still have eyes for someone else. It's hard to compete with that kind of history."

"It's not—" Serene lowered her gaze and stared at her fingers as she rubbed her right thumb over her left hand's palm. "Nolan and I have said our final goodbyes to each other. There's no hope of us ever getting back together."

She dared glance Nolan's way again. Something about him was different. His countenance was much lighter than what it had been at the concert. The way he smiled. She hadn't seen that smile in a long time. Perhaps even ever.

Despite her pronouncement, Serene couldn't deny how at the sight of Nolan, her pulse doubled, her heart rate accelerated, and her hope flourished.

God, remind me why Nolan and I can't be together, she prayed later that night.

And to that, she was sure that God's response was, "Child, I never said you can't." After all, didn't God give Isaac right back to Abraham?

twenty

THE ONE
WHO GOT
A MAYBE

Nolan leaned against the elevator wall, his palms sweating, his pulse quickening. He gripped the sides of the platter of lasagna Caleb had prepared for Serene's house blessing. He had never been more nervous to see his ex.

"Relax, Nolan. You look like you're about to hyperventilate." Nova made a face at him. "What is wrong with you?"

Nolan kept his mouth shut. He couldn't admit to Nova that the last time he had talked to Pastor Sam, he had broached the topic of dating Serene again. To his surprise, Pastor Sam's response was, "You can ask her. You have my blessing, but how she responds is up to her." Pastor Sam had reminded him that Serene still didn't know they had been meeting.

It had been months since his first meeting with Pastor Sam, and the last session they had was the first time Nolan ever talked about how he still had feelings for Serene. He had been trying to avoid it the entire time, hoping to focus on his issues with his father, Damien's and Nate's deaths, all the temptations packaged with the career he had chosen, and his regrets over Diana. But Serene? She was a terrifying subject to broach to her father until it was Pastor Sam who brought it up himself.

And so, that Friday evening, he squeezed himself inside an elevator with his sister's family and his mother, hoping by some miracle, he could get back in Serene's good graces.

The elevator door slid open. Nolan held his breath as they walked into the cozy, well-lit hallway that had a single door for them to knock on.

Caleb knocked.

Pastor Sam opened the door. His face lit up. "Ahh!" he exclaimed. "Our beautiful next-door neighbors. Come in. Come in. Serene and Aida are still in the kitchen."

Nolan let out a breath of relief as he gave a nod of respect to their pastor who clapped him several times on the back.

"Nervous?" Pastor Sam quirked a brow, a glint of amusement in his eyes.

Nolan grinned and said through gritted teeth, "Terrified."

Pastor Sam laughed. "It'll be fine. Everything will fall into place in its own time. Let me get that for you." He gestured to reach for the platter in Nolan's white-knuckled grip, but stopped short. "You should take it to the kitchen yourself."

Before Nolan could react, Pastor Sam diverted his attention to the twins, who had just learned how to walk. Little Nate and Claudia were hard to compete with for attention, so Nolan snuck into the kitchen with no one noticing. At the sight of Serene, he could barely breathe. How had he allowed himself to lose her?

Serene brushed a stray strand of her hair away from her face and tucked it behind her ear as she smiled at Mama Aida. Something was different about her. Her countenance had changed so much from how she had been when they were on tour as Red & Ice. Had she always looked this way since she had left him?

The familiar pangs of betrayal and bitterness hit him, but he warded it off with a deep breath. He then cleared his throat and flashed a smile.

Serene lifted her gaze from the vegetables she was slicing. Her expression remained stoic. Almost as if she didn't recognize him.

"Nolan!" It was Mama Aida who acknowledged his presence. "What do you have for us?"

"Caleb made lasagna. Where do I put it?"

"Why don't you put it inside the oven to keep it hot? There's a spot there among the other dishes. I love Caleb's lasagna. Still trying to get the recipe from him."

Nolan smirked. "Not even you can get that secret out of him, Mama Aida."

Mama Aida wiped her hands on her apron. "I'll go welcome Caleb, Nova, and the twins." She flashed a smile at Nolan. "Your mother's here, right?"

"Yes, ma'am."

"Wonderful. I hope you don't mind helping Serene while I greet our guests."

"I—"

"Mama—"

Nolan and Serene locked eyes, blushed, and looked away in the span of several seconds. Meanwhile, Mama Aida had already brushed past Nolan and glided into the living room. The sound of her cooing over the twins made Nolan even more aware of Serene's presence. His nervousness around her was a stark reminder of how they had grown apart. Part of him longed to go back to the way they were when they were children, but the greater part of him embraced the tension. This was where they needed to be to find out if what he believed for so long was true: if they really belonged together.

"Hey." He scanned the kitchen. "I'm not sure what I should do."

"I don't think you should do anything." Serene finished slicing the celery and moved on to cutting tomatoes. "Pretty sure Mama just wants us to talk."

"I wonder why."

"You tell me." Serene shrugged. Her grip on the knife tightened, made evident by the way her knuckles protruded and the veins on her wrist stuck out.

"Everything okay?"

She stopped cutting. Her fingers trembled. She closed her eyes, placed her hands over the edge of the counter, and took a deep breath. A smile appeared on her face and when she opened her eyes, she looked at him. "I'm fine. I just have a lot to process. That's all."

"Sure?" Nolan asked.

"I'm sure."

In hindsight, it was probably the worst timing he could have picked, but Nolan blurted it out anyway, "Serene, go out with me? On a date? Saturday?"

The color drained from her face as she stared at him with unmistakable surprise. "What?"

"I want to take you out on a date."

"Last time we were in a kitchen together, you were telling your sister you were intent on letting go of me."

Nolan squared his shoulders and nodded as he walked to the counter and stood across from her. He leaned over the edge and nodded. "I did say that, and I tried to, but so many things have changed over the past few months. I'd like to think I've changed, and I'm sure you have. Maybe I had to let go of the Nolan and Serene of our childhood to start afresh and find out if who we are now can be together."

"Nolan, we've been through so much, so you can't blame me for asking. All these Sundays you've been going to church, it's not just to have a chance with me again, is it?"

His heart sank. Defenses threatened to come up, but Nolan took a breath and tried not to entertain the notion she was trying to attack him or his motives. He grew quiet and gave it some thought before shaking his head. "No. I've been going to church, because God came through for me even when I don't deserve it. That night at the concert, that song I sang after Diana stormed off—" a soft smile appeared on his lips "—it didn't feel like it came from me. That moment when the crowd hushed up and listened, it felt like a divine moment, an embrace from Above. Like I wasn't alone, and I never have been. Looking back at that night, it could've gone in so many ways that would've ended everything and ruined my career, but now, Ramona is negotiating a record deal better than anything *Red & Ice* ever had. I believe God did that."

Serene's brows knitted, but her eyes cleared, as if she was seeing him for the very first time.

"That's why I've been going to church, Serene. Not because I have to or because I want to see you — though I admit seeing you every Sunday is a perk. Still, I'm there because I've realized that even if I grew up in church, I still don't know who God is. And I want to get to know Him. For real this time."

She sighed. "Don't you think us dating would distract you from doing that? From focusing on God, I mean?"

The question gave him pause. Nolan swallowed back his disappointment. "If you believe that to be true, then I understand if you say no." He tried to smile. His mind raced to find another topic, so he went for the most obvious. "Beautiful place you have here. Can't wait to see the incubator."

The stoic look on her face made him want to bolt.

Nolan couldn't remember a time when Serene had ever made him this anxious.

"I never said no," she said, her eyes downcast, a strand of her hair falling to frame her face.

Nolan creased his brows. "So you're saying yes?"

"Maybe. Tonight, I can give you a maybe. I want to talk to my dad first." She peered at him through her eyelashes. "Is that okay?"

"Better than okay. I can take a maybe." This time, Nolan wasn't forcing a smile through his nervousness, because somehow, he was already one hundred percent sure her maybe would turn into a yes.

The diffuser emitted lavender essential oil into the air. The scent filled Serene's nostrils and helped to calm her down as she sat down for dinner with her father, mother, and brother.

"Nolan asked me out last night," Serene announced, before popping a piece of roasted chicken into her mouth.

Jeremy frowned. "You said no, right?"

"I said maybe."

"What does that even mean?" Her brother still had a long way to go before he could get to a point of forgiving Nolan for what he still viewed as Nolan dragging Serene's name through the mud in his reality show, *The New Red*. "You either say yes or no to a date."

"I wanted to talk to Dad about it first. I'm not even sure what's going on with him or why he's suddenly asking me out."

"You invited him to your house blessing, for one thing. Why is Nolan still even a part of our lives after what he did to Serene?"

"Jeremy, that's enough." Mama Aida gave him a pointed look. "Your sister and Nolan have a long history that's precious to them. Nolan has been trying to change. We don't want to rob him of that opportunity."

"Fine. He can change, but dating Serene again? Don't you think that's too much? You're okay with this?"

Their father cleared his throat. Samuel Sinclair seemed to be deep in thought, weighing his words. "I encouraged Nolan to ask you out."

"What?" Jeremy's face contorted with confusion.

Serene was beyond intrigued. "I saw you at a coffee shop with him. Like you were having a Bible study."

Jeremy's face drained of color. What she said made him retreat as he leaned back on his seat.

Serene didn't know what was going on with him, so she brushed it off to focus on her dad. "I said maybe to him, because I wanted to ask you before jumping headfirst into this. Nolan and I don't have a great track record of keeping accountable and seeking out your blessing. And if I'm going to consider a relationship with him, I want it to be different this time."

"Nolan sought me out not long after what happened at his concert. He expressed wanting to change and wanting to seek the Lord. I was skeptical at first, especially after what happened during his youth, but after having regular weekly meetings with him, I believe he is being genuine this time. He wants to make Jesus the Lord of his life, and I respect that. He has been faithfully attending AA meetings and has miraculously overcome his addiction to alcohol. The changes I've seen God do in his life are amazing. As for him wanting to date you, it took him a while to even mention you to me. I guess he felt, for good reason, it would be an awkward topic to bring up. It was hard for me to hear, I'll be honest, but after hearing him speak of his feelings for you, even the regrets he has over how he went about being in a relationship with you, I told him I'd be fine with it if he asks you out. However, whether you agree will be up to you."

Serene tried to process her father's words. When it came to her relationship with Nolan, it had always felt like they were hiding something, like they had been enjoying something forbidden, like they had to lie to stay together. Having everything in the open and out in the light made it feel right — something she had never felt the entire time she and Nolan had been a couple.

Later that night, she made a phone call.

"Hey, Nolan. I had a talk with my dad. I'll go out with you."

He didn't seem all too surprised. "I'm excited to get to know you again, Serene."

Serene had to smile, because though he had a point — that they were both getting to know each other again — she was already falling in love with this new version of Nolan Stone.

twenty — one

THE ONE
WHO DATED
AN EX

ating Serene Sinclair used to be like dating someone he knew like the back of his hand, but that Saturday, Nolan felt like he was dating a complete stranger.

He shuffled his feet on the floor as he waited for Serene to meet him at the lobby of her building.

"Mr. Stone?" the doorman, Charles, moused over to him. "You are Nolan Stone, aren't you?"

Nolan nodded. "That would be me. You're Charles, right?"

Genuine surprise appeared on the older man's face. "How did you know?"

"You spoke with my brother-in-law when we came over this week."

"I didn't think you would notice. You seemed preoccupied."

"I noticed." Nolan smiled. "How can I help you?"

"I meant to ask when you came over with your family, but I was too embarrassed. You see, my daughter is a big fan of yours. She wants to become a singer someday. I was hoping you could give her a video greeting, some advice, and words of encouragement. Just a quick video. She will love it."

Nolan shrugged. "Sure."

"That's great. Thank you so much, Mr. Stone." Right then, he lifted his phone to record.

"Oh." Nolan chuckled. "You mean right now?"

"If that's okay."

"What's your daughter's name?"

"Amelia."

"Pretty name. Are we recording already?"

"Yes, yes." Charles nodded. "We are."

Nolan looked at the camera. "Hello, Amelia. I'm Nolan Stone. Your dad here clearly loves you, and that's amazing." He paused, giving a quick thought to what he wanted to say to this random stranger. "I don't know who you are or what you want from life, but Amelia, I know God knows you and loves you. He will never stop giving you second chances. If you learn to follow Him, you'll see that everything — your hopes and dreams — all of it will fall into place. It may not be what you want or expect, but it will be as it needs to be, and you'll later find it's all for the best."

Someone cleared her throat behind him. He spun around to find Serene standing there. She smiled.

Charles's face lit up. "Miss Serene! This is getting better."

"We're making a video for Charles's daughter," Nolan explained to Serene. "She wants to be a singer someday. Do you have advice for her?"

"Oh wow." Put on the spot, Serene lightly slapped Nolan's shoulder. She faced the camera.

As she spoke, Nolan held his breath as he gave her a look-over. He would never get over how beautiful she was.

"Nolan and I... We were blessed to get to where we are now. It's crazy the many great breaks we got, and we're so grateful for that. Still, just because something seems good, or it feels exhilarating, it doesn't mean that's what God called us to do." Serene glanced over at him. "Take this man, for example. Nolan has always wanted to do music, and he's amazing at it. When we became *Red & Ice*, I jumped in for the ride, because he was my best friend, and I loved being around him. But I realized that though it was an amazing experience and an opportunity not everyone gets, it wasn't for me. I guess my point is— What's her name?"

"Amelia," Charles said.

"Amelia, know your purpose. There's nothing like knowing what God created you for and going after it. To find out what your purpose is, it takes knowing the One Who created you to fulfill it."

"God bless you, Amelia!" Nolan waved at the camera.

When it was all over, Charles dropped the camera. Only then did they realize he was in tears.

"What's wrong?"

"My Amelia." His shoulders slumped. "She walked away from the Lord the moment she turned eighteen. My wife and I pray for her every day. That she would remember the things of God we taught her when she was a child. Thank you for your words. I pray she will listen."

"Amen, amen." Serene nodded as she reached out to the doorman. "Thank you for sharing that, Charles."

"We will pray with you and your wife for Amelia."

"Thank you, thank you." Charles held both their hands in his firm grip. "My wife will be so happy to hear that. Now, you two go now. Don't let me keep you from a beautiful day outside. The weather is perfect for being outdoors."

Nolan and Serene exchanged glances. A smile appeared on her face.

"Shall we go?"

She nodded.

Nolan's initial instinct was to take her hand or place his hand on the small of her back, but he fought the urge to do that. He had promised himself this time, it would be different, and he intended to stay true to that. Charles opened the door for them, and Nolan allowed Serene to step ahead.

The valet was already waiting outside with his car. He opened the door for her before going to the driver's seat.

When Serene saw where he was taking her for a date, she laughed. "Seriously?"

"I'm going for nostalgia," he said.

"Our neighborhood playground?"

"You have to admit—" he shrugged "—we have a lot of memories here."

She smiled. "I remember."

"Come on. I have some stuff in the trunk we need to set up for this date to be perfect."

"Nothing is ever perfect with us, though."

"True, but we've always gotten away with imperfect, haven't we?"

"I guess you can say that."

Ten minutes later, they had a red blanket spread over the grass near the swing set and the sandlot.

Serene seemed perfectly happy with the grilled cheese sandwiches and soda he had brought. He asked her about *Thrive* and her plans for it, and it didn't take long before she couldn't stop gushing about her new endeavor.

"For it to work and make a profit, the talent has to be legit. It's competitive out there, but I feel like we can make it happen. We already have plans for a collaborative Podcast we could use to promote one another's work, and—" Serene straightened the hem of her blue dress "—I was hoping you might help? Between your connections and mine in the music and art world, and Caleb and Nova's in the literary world, we could provide a great launching pad for these artists."

"You believe in them, don't you?"

Serene nodded. "I do."

"I don't get it, Serene. Why not just register Thrive as a non-profit organization? What you're doing is a worthy cause, which can fit the bill."

"Because I don't want to further the starving artist stereotype. If I believe artists can thrive doing what they are great at, then I should be able to back it up and not expect to run *Thrive* on the donations of people, but to run it with what the artists and I earn. *Thrive* is a jump start. I was blessed to have a jump start. Few artists get that."

"You had a jump start?" Nolan quirked a brow up. "I don't remember anyone doing us favors, Serene. We worked hard to get *Red & Ice* to where we were."

Serene laughed. "Nolan, you worked hard. I just rode along with the whole thing, so I could stay with you. Don't you get it? You were my jump start. Even the success of my first art show could be attributed to you."

"Oh no." Nolan flicked his forefinger back and forth. "That was you. Those paintings were beautiful, and it was all you."

"They never would have had the value they had if those paintings weren't somehow tied to *Red & Ice*, to famous rock star, Nolan Stone." She winked at him. "I worked hard, for sure, but many artists work hard, and they're still working hard, but they never got to where we are now. The dream is to help at least some artists get the leg up I got, because you were in my life."

He stared at her and studied the contours of her face, every freckle and every mole. This was a side of Serene he had never seen before. So passionate. So sure of herself. "I'm sorry, Serene."

"For what?"

"For not giving you the space to bloom on your own. My most distinct memory of this playground was me and you in the swing set when Dad died. I made you promise to always be with me. We were so young. We barely knew who we were and what we wanted, and I was already pulling you into my world, just assuming that what I wanted was what you wanted. That was selfish of me."

"I loved it then, even if in the back of my mind, I was always questioning if what we were doing was for the best. I never spoke up, because I loved how you were fighting for us every step of the way. It would be unfair for me to let you take all the blame like you have all these years, Nolan. You shouldn't have had to do what you had to do just so you could get people like Rhoda Petersen off your back."

"Since you mentioned Mrs. P., I still sometimes wonder how she got married to Robert. She was so mean when she was our Sunday School teacher. Is she still a Sunday School teacher?"

"I think so, yeah. Though she's overseeing more now, I'm not sure." Serene sighed. "Mama Aida says she's been changing a lot over the years, but I sometimes feel sorry for her daughter, Rachel. Someone as strict as Mrs. P. can't be easy to have as a mother. Jeremy and Max were so happy when they got transferred to youth group. Jeremy loathes her."

"We're all works in progress. Even the church. We're all learning and growing."

Serene nodded. "That much is true. For all it's worth, I'm glad I grew up with you, Nolan." She reached out to touch his hand, and Nolan's knee-jerk reaction was to withdraw.

He couldn't ignore the hurt in her questioning gaze. His mind flailed about in search for an explanation. "I'm sorry. I just— We should limit physical contact while we're dating."

"Why?" Serene creased her brows and laughed at the same time.

Nolan swallowed hard. The absurdity of it wasn't lost on him. Their first kiss had been when they were fourteen. But, he couldn't risk it with her. Not this time.

"Nolan?" Serene tilted her head to the side.

What was he supposed to say? That he would rather not touch, because he didn't think he could keep himself from wanting to go too far with her? This wasn't something one would normally talk about on a first date, right? "Have you ever been on a first date before? I don't think I have..."

Serene opened her mouth to say something, but instead, to his relief, she made a face and her eyes rolled up. "I don't think I have either. We didn't go on dates as teenagers, or at least I never saw them as dates. Just lunch at school together?"

"So you never dated anyone after leaving Red & Ice?" He narrowed his eyes at her.

She shook her head no.

"Why not? I'm sure it wasn't for the lack of guys going after you."

Serene pulled her legs up, so she was sitting akimbo on the picnic blanket. "It didn't seem fair. I didn't know what I wanted then, and I was still trying to sort through what happened between us. It wasn't easy to get over you."

"And are you?" He tried not to smirk. "Over me?"

She laughed and tapped his cheek several times. "Eat a sandwich, Stone." She grabbed a triangle of grilled cheese sandwich and tried to feed it to him.

"Not until you answer my question!"

"Then you'll starve." She got on her feet and went to the swings. Seeing her at ease and relaxed around him made Nolan want to hug her and kiss her. But all of that had to wait until he could come clean to her about everything.

Not today, Nolan thought, his chest tightening. Not today.

Nolan joined her at the swings and allowed himself to fall right back in love with his ex.

twenty-two

THE ONE WHO NEEDED TO OVERCOME

All his life, Nolan had dreamed of nothing more than to make music and marry Serene, but after their "first" date, his mind morphed into a land mine when it came to how much he wanted Serene. It was one thing to struggle with wanting to be with her when he had never experienced sleeping with someone before, but after having had a taste with Diana, he couldn't seem to stop thinking about sleeping with Serene.

After several dates, he could tell Serene was beginning to notice how he tried to avoid touching her — sometimes even looking at her — for fear his thoughts would stray to forbidden territory. He had tried to avoid the topic and ignore the way unspoken questions appeared in her gaze, in the way she would wince or bite her lip whenever he withdrew from her. One Sunday morning, however, the worship team played a song highlighting God as a father.

Conviction struck Nolan as he bowed his head before the Lord. He couldn't keep doing this to a daughter of the Most High God. With eyes closed, Nolan focused on the God he now served. *Forgive me, Lord. Help me get to the root of this struggle, and give me wisdom to handle this in a way that honors You and in a way that honors Serene and her family.*

By the end of the service, Nolan had a strong sense of determination. He had to find a way to talk to Serene about his relationship with Diana and help her understand what was going through his mind. The moment he saw Serene, however, he balked.

Serene stood by her father and mother, who were greeting church members as they milled out of the church sanctuary. When their eyes locked, he forced a smile.

Pastor Sam waved at Nolan as he approached.

"Nolan!" The way Mama Aida's face lit up with delight and affection every time she saw him comforted Nolan, but that morning, he couldn't look her straight in the eye.

"Pastor Sam." Nolan embraced their pastor and his wife. "Mama Aida." He cleared his throat before daring himself to look at Serene. Her smile assured him. He brushed his thumb against her freckled cheekbone. "Serene."

"When will you both have dinner with us? I want to know how you both are doing." Mama Aida grabbed their hands and squeezed. "We should set a time."

"We'll find time, Mama," Serene said. "Nolan has just been incredibly busy with his music, and *Thrive* has taken up a lot of my time and energy."

"I understand." Mama Aida let go of their hands and gently brushed her fingers against her daughter's hair. "But if you're to have a family soon, you need to prioritize. You can't just let your careers take over. Family comes first."

Serene blushed. Nolan had to grin. Starting a family with Serene had been a lifelong dream of his. He could only hope he would be the kind of father Damien Stone never was.

"Why not have lunch with us now?" Pastor Sam joined the conversation. "Serene said she would join us."

Nolan shuffled on his feet. "I would love to, but my mom has been looking forward to having Sunday lunch with me and Nova's family. They're waiting for me now."

"I was hoping to meet with them after lunch, if that's okay." Serene gave her parents a pleading look.

"We'll make time this week, Mama Aida," Nolan quickly added.

"Sure." Mama Aida smiled. "Enjoy your time with Clara, and let Caleb and Nova know I think they're doing an amazing job with the twins."

"It will be encouraging for them to hear that," Nolan said. "Thank you. As for dinner with the Sinclairs, I'll let Pastor Sam know when the best time is after Serene and I figure out our schedules."

"Sounds great." Pastor Sam clapped him on the back.

"See you later, Serene." He hugged her. Both of them tensed as he did. Nolan hoped her parents didn't notice. Unable to discuss his wayward thoughts about Serene to her own father, Nolan proceeded to the only other figure of authority he trusted fully: his mother.

Clara Ramirez Stone, with her value system rooted in the generally conservative culture of the Philippines, bristled at his confession as they cleared the dishes at Nova's house after lunch. "You take so much after your father, it sometimes scares me, *pero* you are also so different from him. So pure."

Nolan bristled. "Pure isn't how I would describe myself, Ma."

"Trust me." Bitterness laced his mother's laughter. "Compared to your father, you're pure."

"Ma." Nolan sighed. "Come on."

"Nolan, what can I say? You have done what you have done. You can't take it back. What you can do, however, is cut the soul tie you have created with Diana all those times you've slept with her."

"What's a soul tie? How do I do that?"

"Aida explained it to me once, and we prayed about it, but I don't remember."

The blank expression on Clara's face as she scratched her head made him laugh. "You're not much help, Ma. This conversation is awkward."

"I'm just glad you're with Serene now. Diana is lovely and all, but she isn't right for you. Not like Serene is."

Nolan flinched. Why then couldn't he stop thinking about Diana whenever he touched or kissed Serene?

Clara grabbed his hand and squeezed. "Nolan, I pray for you every day — that you will not repeat the same mistakes your father and brother did. That the curse of alcohol and drug addiction would stop with them and will not go on to the next generation — to you and your children. You will be an amazing father someday, my son. Believe that."

Nolan swallowed hard. The words healed a wound so deep within him, he didn't even know it existed. "Thanks, Ma."

"I love you, *anak*."

"I love you too."

"Oh!" Her face lit up. "This is what you should do. You should talk to Caleb. He's your brother, after all. I'm sure he'll help. Aida has tried to explain so much to me, but I know Jesus, and I know how to pray for you, and that's good enough for me. I'm getting too old to remember all the details."

"What are you talking about, Ma? You're not even sixty yet. You're nowhere near too old."

"Details." Clara waved her hand in the air.

"You really think I should talk to Caleb?"

"Yes. He's a good man. Your Ate Nova was smart to marry him."

As if on cue, Caleb appeared in the kitchen, carrying a giggling Claudia in his arms. "Serene just arrived."

Nolan squared his shoulders. Before he could say anything else, however, Clara scooped up her granddaughter from Caleb's arms. "Nolan wants to talk to you. Us ladies can take the twins out."

Caleb's eyes flitted from Clara to Nolan then back to Clara. "Out where?"

"Wherever." Clara walked on without further explanation, leaving the two men in the kitchen, not sure what to do with each other's company.

Caleb cleared his throat, his chin tilting as he regarded Nolan. "Do you want coffee?"

Relieved that Caleb broke the silence, Nolan said, "Yes, please. I'll load the dishwasher."

"Thanks. Glad to know you would be willing to do that despite your rock star status."

Nolan shrugged. "Ma and Nova keep me grounded."

Apart from clinks and bumps caused by them going about their work, both remained silent until they finished what they had set out to do.

Finally, Caleb spoke up. "You wanted to talk?" He placed two mugs of freshly brewed coffee on top of the kitchen counter.

Nolan propped himself up on a barstool and winced. "I'm not sure, exactly. You and me. We barely talk about anything other than Nova and the twins."

Caleb chuckled. "We have little in common, that I can say is true, but you have something on your mind, and you're technically my little brother, so what is it, rock star?"

"How was it with you and Nova when you were dating? Like—" Nolan grimaced "—physically." He shuddered. "Never mind. I don't want details about the nature of your physical relationship with my sister."

"Maybe it's better to go to the living room for this." Caleb took a gulp from his coffee. "This coffee's hot," he croaked out. "That burns."

Nolan had to laugh. "I never once imagined growing up Nova would end up with you."

"What? Why not? How could she resist all this charm?" Caleb feigned surprise, but in a split second, the mockery and fun morphed into this straight-laced seriousness that Nolan had come to expect in Caleb. "Look, Nolan. While we were dating, Nova and I kissed. That's about it. Now, I've observed enough in this family to conclude you and Diana were doing more than just kiss. Am I correct?"

Nolan gulped. "I thought we were being discreet."

"As discreet as a jackhammer. Does Serene know?"

Nolan nodded, a distant memory coming over him. With it, came the guilt and shame. "I kind of rubbed it in her face several Christmases ago."

"The one we celebrated at Ma's house?"

"Yes. That one." Nolan gulped from his mug of coffee. "Wow. This is strong."

"For this conversation, we need it. It's affecting how you relate with Serene now?"

"The images that go through my mind when I'm with her—" Nolan's hands tightened around his mug of coffee, his palms reddened by the heat of the drink. "It's not how I want to view her."

"It's a battle for a lot of men, Nolan. You need to train yourself to take captive every thought and submit it to the will of God. That you want to overcome this is a great first step, but we cannot ignore the fact that you have had sex with Diana. When you slept with her, you created a soul tie with her."

"A soul tie?"

"I am of the conviction that sex should be within the confines of marriage, because it is an act of commitment between two people. A commitment to a future. A commitment to a family. Something spiritual happens when we make love to someone. It's tying souls together to make two people become one. You did that with Diana, and you need to cut that tie with her."

"How do I do that?"

"First, you confess the sin to God and ask for forgiveness. You ask Him for help and direction on the steps you need to do to cut the soul tie. If it is possible, it may require talking to Diana and asking her for forgiveness."

"She will think I'm crazy. She's not a Christian. It's a huge part of why she went crazy on that stage."

"That may be so, but you are a Christian, Nolan. Release her and release yourself, and trust God to take care of her even if you don't understand. Pray about it. Do what God tells you to do."

Nolan stared at his cup of coffee before gulping and asking his brother-in-law for prayer. Caleb graciously obliged. The prayer ended, and after his amen, Nolan wasn't quite sure what to do next, but for the rest of the afternoon, Caleb managed to lighten the atmosphere with video games and a game of billiards. With three brothers and two sisters, Caleb Grant had quite a bit of experience entertaining siblings to distract them from whatever was bothering them. By the time the ladies returned, Nolan had relaxed enough to pull Serene aside to ask her something he never thought he would have to.

"I want to go see Diana tomorrow. I'll have Ramona make an appointment with the rehab center tonight. Is this okay with you?"

Serene stared at him for what felt like an eternity. "Why?"

Nolan took a deep breath. "Serene, it's no secret to you that Diana and I were—" he rubbed the back of his neck with his palm. "We've— We did something we never should have. I didn't treat her right, and I know it. I want to go and ask for her forgiveness."

He had expected her to ask why, to question why he needed to see Diana, so he had a ready answer, but Nolan didn't expect Serene to drop her gaze and say, "I want to go with you."

Alarms went off in his mind. The idea of Serene and Diana being in the same room together while he apologized for his past with Diana made him want to run. "May I ask why?"

Her gaze still lowered, Serene shuffled on her feet. Only then did he realize how uncertain she seemed. A soft blush appeared on her cheekbones.

Nolan put himself in her shoes. How did it make her feel to have her boyfriend tell her he wanted to meet with his ex to ask forgiveness for a physical connection that, as storied, deep, and precious as their history was, they had never shared?

Serene's vulnerability made her beautiful to him. It called out to the part of him that wanted to make her feel safe and protected. Even against himself.

When she finally answered his question, she reminded him of everything he loved about her.

"I won't lie, Nolan. Every time I remember you have been with her that way, it hurts. It brings up so many fears and insecurities in me—"

"Serene, I'm so sorry. I—"

"I'm not done."

Nolan closed his mouth and stared at his feet.

Her gentle voice sent shivers shooting up his spine. "Beyond the hurt, the way you have shown your love to me — how you have fought for our relationship — it takes my breath away. I love you, Nolan, and I thank God for you." Her soft fingers intertwined with his as he leaned his forehead against hers, shutting his eyes to listen to her sweet voice. "I don't ever want to hold your past against you, and I ask God for grace to help us through this. You asked why I want to go with you, and my answer is that I think it would be better for us to do this together. My hope is for us to be able to face the broken parts of our past together, because I believe it's the only way we would be able to forge a Godly future together."

Her words knocked the breath out of him. Choked, all he could say was, "I love you so much."

Nolan hadn't even realized it, but until that moment, he had been terrified he would push too far and Serene would abandon him again. But, with their fingers intertwined and their palms pressed against each other's, transcendent peace came over Nolan when it came to his relationship with Serene. Beyond a shadow of a doubt, he knew their love would last a lifetime.

twenty-three

THE ONE WHO CUT A TIE

Serene drummed her fingers on top of a round glass table as she watched Nolan pace the floor of the rehab center's visiting area, where multiple plush couches, and comfortable tables and chairs were available for those visiting the wards of *Hope's Well*.

She could only imagine what her boyfriend felt about the situation. Then again, she could barely comprehend how she felt about it. Her heart drummed against her ribcage as questions circled her thoughts. What would Nolan tell Diana? How would he go about his apology? How would Diana react upon seeing them both there?

Serene held her breath when Diana walked into the room. A smile was on her face, and a skip was in her step as she scanned the room. She had bunched her wild curls up in a ponytail, and it swayed even when she froze at the sight of her visitors.

Nolan — still pacing — remained unaware of her presence, so Serene cleared her throat to alert him. "Nolan."

He stopped pacing. Serene stood up and took several steps forward so she could hold Nolan's hand. He squeezed tight.

As if trying to figure out if she should approach them, Diana cocked her head to the side, the tips of her curls brushing over her left shoulder blade. She walked toward them, her gait confident, her expression quizzical. "If it isn't Red and Ice. Miss me already, Ice?"

Nolan flinched before nodding slowly. "I actually did miss you," he admitted.

An insidious lie tried to seep into Serene's psyche: *He misses her. Maybe you're not enough for him anymore.* Serene's grip on his hand tightened. What if this was a bad idea? What was she thinking coming here?

"You remember Serene?" Nolan gestured toward her with his free hand.

Diana gave Serene a complete look-over. "Of course."

"Hello, Diana," Serene said.

Diana raised a brow at her before striding forward to brush past them.

Serene exchanged glances with Nolan before they both turned to face Diana, who had plopped herself onto a couch.

"It's only been several months. You haven't even called once." Diana scowled. "Now, you show up here — with her — and then tell me you miss me? Ugh. I need a cigarette for this." She rolled her eyes. "You're not one for mind games, Nolan. Why are you here? What do you want?"

Nolan's hand found the small of Serene's back. Somehow, his touch comforted Serene. He led her to a cushioned bench across from the couch Diana had chosen. He then sat next to her.

Serene gripped his arm. She told herself she was doing it to show him her support, but something she hadn't felt in a long time had begun to take root in her: insecurity. This encounter was proving to be harder than she had anticipated.

Nolan cleared his throat. He seemed to have difficulty looking Diana in the eye. "I came to check on you," he said before a slight smirk appeared on his face. "I would have come earlier, but I didn't want to be at the stabbed end of your drumsticks."

Serene couldn't hold back a small smirk.

Diana grimaced.

Nolan narrowed his eyes at her. "Too soon?"

"You think?" Diana huffed. "What is this, Nolan? Why are you both here? Say what you need to say, and be done with it."

Nolan sighed. "That's fair." His jaw clenched. "I came to apologize."

Confusion marred Diana's pretty round face as her eyes flitted from Nolan to Serene, back to Nolan. "Apologize for what?"

"For everything."

As Serene watched Nolan struggle to find the words to say, something shifted within her. Compassion moved her — not only for him, but for Diana as well. In her silence, she prayed: *God, intervene in this situation. Soften Diana's heart and strengthen Nolan's. Give him wisdom to speak the right words necessary for reconciliation to happen. Be with us, Lord, even as I surrender this moment to You.*

"I'm sorry for using you." A muscle in Nolan's jaw twitched as he gave Diana a resolute nod. "I wasn't over Serene, but I still—" he gulped. "I shouldn't have taken advantage of you the way I did."

Diana creased her brows as she straightened herself and shifted to the edge of her seat. "Did she make you do this?"

"No. I came because I wanted to apologize. She came because she cares."

Serene could barely stand to look at Diana, whose expression morphed from confusion to seeming indignation. Suddenly, as her stare lingered on Nolan, Diana's eyes softened. Her shoulders sagged. "We used each other, Nolan." A bitter smile formed on her lips. "I should have known I would be on the losing end of this whole nightmare, though." She tugged at strands of her hair several times. "I ruined what I had chasing after someone I doubted could ever be mine. I'm so stupid."

"Don't say that." The force by which Nolan said the words surprised even Serene. "Diana, you will get better, and you will pick yourself back up. Serene and I will help you. I'm sure Ramona will too. You're so talented and—"

Diana tensed. "Serene and you." For a moment, a flash of anger sparked in her eyes.

Despite knowing she had done nothing wrong, Serene wanted to apologize. The compassion she felt toward Diana overwhelmed her heart. *Lord, comfort her through the heartbreak. Heal her, heal Nolan, and heal me even as you break the tie connecting them.*

"Did you come here just to flaunt your relationship to me?" Diana's eyes moistened. This time, the anger was gone. She sounded defeated.

"No." Serene shook her head. "That's the last thing we want, Diana. I insisted on coming not to hurt you, but to support Nolan, because I know how hard this is for him."

Diana scoffed. "This is hard for him?!"

"Only because he truly cares about you."

A tear ran down Diana's cheek. She quickly wiped it away and swallowed back the tears.

"This is most likely harder for you than it is for him, Diana," Serene dared to say. "Neither of us take pleasure in your pain. On the contrary, we want you to know you're not alone. We're here for you. We care about you, and we commit to pray for you and support you in whatever way we can."

Diana looked at her like she had gone mad. "Why on earth would you care about me? I did everything I could to take him away from you."

Serene's chest tightened at the admission, but the reason for caring came quickly to her. "Because I know what it feels like to love someone and not have him. I loved and lost once. So did Nolan. We wouldn't wish that agony on anyone."

"That's why I'm sorry," Nolan said. "For hurting you. For all it's worth, we're rooting for you, Diana. We believe in you and your talent. You are a gifted musician and a brilliant songwriter and that voice of yours—" he whistled. "Should you ever decide to pursue a solo career, I will back you up all the way. Serene will too. We have your back."

Diana shifted on her seat. "What if I still want to be with you? Would you and her still back me up? I gave you everything, Nolan. I wanted so badly to be with you."

"Why though? I don't get it, Diana. Why would you want me?"

"Why wouldn't I?" She shrugged. A bitter chuckle escaped her lips. "You're Nolan Stone."

"And you're Diana Rake. Don't you want someone who wants you just as much? Someone who will give as much as he takes, if not more? You deserve someone like that. I didn't deserve for you to be mine, and I knew that, but I took advantage anyway. That's messed up. What I did to you was messed up, and I'm sorry."

Diana stared at him for the longest time before her eyes cleared. She set her eyes on her fingers, which she stretched one-by-one. She nodded slowly. "Can you blame me if I wished for you to be happy with me?" She locked eyes with Serene. "I never understood why you left him in the first place. I had hoped that if I just got him to sleep with me, then maybe he could forget you, but here we are. It didn't work out that way. I'm sorry too. To both of you. I also took advantage of Nolan in his weakness, even though deep inside, I could tell he wouldn't be happy with me. That was selfishness on my part."

The moment Diana stopped talking, Serene exhaled. It felt like a weight had been lifted off her chest and the atmosphere had significantly lightened. The silence that followed almost felt reverent as Serene quietly praised God for the humility everyone in the situation exhibited.

The best, however, was yet to come, because Nolan then asked — with confidence in his voice, "Would you want to pray with us, Diana?"

To Serene's surprise, Diana said, "Sure."

All three of them bowed their heads. Nolan said a prayer of blessing for Diana. By the time they all said amen, Diana was sobbing.

"Just because I'm crying—" she laughed and sniffed at the same time "—doesn't mean I believe in Jesus. I'm not becoming like you two."

Nolan and Serene smiled.

"I wasn't expecting you to," Nolan said, "but I'll keep hoping and praying you eventually find God, like I did." He stood up and gave Diana a hug.

As they bid Diana goodbye, faith came over Serene. The Prince of Peace had triumphed that day.

"She'll come to know Jesus someday," Nolan said as they walked out of *Hope's Well*.

"She will," Serene agreed even as she wondered if everything she and Nolan went through as a couple was part of God's plan to draw a prodigal like Diana into the Father's arms.

twenty – four

THE ONE
WHO WORE
A RING

After having shot another episode of their *Thrive* Podcast at the incubator, Serene found a bouquet of wildflowers waiting by the main door. A red envelope with Serene's full name in Nolan's handwriting came with the lovely floral arrangement. Serene picked up the flowers and walked back to her desk while staring at the envelope.

"From Nolan?" Michiko, who handled most of their tech and also designed dresses, asked.

Serene nodded. She pulled a card out of the envelope and tilted her head to the side as she read his message: *Be my date at the launch party this Saturday. Love you. Nolan*

"Hmm," Serene said. That Saturday, the label and Ramona were throwing Nolan a party to celebrate his new album and release it to the press.

"What is it?" Jon, the graphic artist, swiveled his chair to face Serene, but his eyes were still on his computer screen.

Serene shrugged. "An invite to his party this Saturday."

"Didn't he already invite us?" Michiko asked. "We're all invited, right, Rick?"

Rick, a long-time fan of *Red & Ice*, had recently helped produce one of Nolan's tracks at the incubator. "Yeah. We're invited. Why is he inviting you again?"

"He wants me to be his date," Serene said. She found the request a bit strange. Didn't it go without saying?

"Big move," Michiko said. "You know what this means, right?" Michiko asked.

"No." Serene frowned. "What does it mean?"

"It means he wants to go public." Jon sighed as if Serene was being extra dense. He deadpanned as he gave Serene a pointed look. "It's an announcement that you and him are back together."

Serene drew a short intake of breath. A public announcement? What for?

"You're back together, right? Officially?" Piper, who had just launched her debut novel — successfully — swiveled from side-to-side on her chair as she tapped her temple with her pencil. "This thing seems serious."

"You can't expect a casual dating relationship between Nolan Stone and Serene Sinclair," Rick said. "When they started dating again, I figured it had to be all or nothing. I'm expecting wedding bells."

Serene blushed. "Let's not get ahead of ourselves."

"Rumor is he already proposed to you once." A glint of mischief covered Rick's face as he typed something on his laptop. "And you said no."

"Obviously." Piper rolled her eyes. "If Serene had said yes, they would be married now."

"You don't know that." Michiko sauntered over to Serene. "She could have said yes at first then broken the engagement later. How did it really go, Serene?"

"No way. I'm not going into that. That's just dredging up a lot of history." Serene shook her head and took a deep breath. "I should give Nolan a call. Excuse me."

Ignoring their objections, Serene stepped out of the incubator and dialed Nolan's number.

"Hello?" His voice alone made her heart skip a beat.

"Nolan? Thanks for the flowers. I love them."

"So, you'll be my date, right?"

"You sure you're ready for this? Your fans might not like it. Especially those who ship you and Diana hard."

"It's you who should answer that question. I'll do everything in my power to get them off your back and keep our relationship private, but I can't help it if the press bothers you at least for a time."

Serene gave it some thought. "I'll be honest, Nolan. I don't think I'm ready for this."

A long pause followed from the other side.

"Nolan?"

"Yeah, I'm here." He cleared his throat. "I understand, Serene. Don't worry about it. When you're ready."

"You're not okay with it." Serene leaned back on the wall. "It's not good to lie."

His chuckle gave her a degree of comfort, but the serious tone of his voice yanked her back to the issue at hand. "I'm disappointed, Serene," Nolan said, "but I'm glad we're communicating. I wouldn't want to jump into this if we're not on the same page. This is us being on the same page."

"Thank you for understanding."

"Of course. I love you, Serene."

"Love you too, Nolan. I'll see you on Saturday."

"See you."

The moment he hung up, Serene couldn't calm herself. An insecurity she couldn't shake settled on her chest. Serene returned to the incubator to inform everyone she was going for a walk, hoping to clear her head and figure out why she felt so shaken. Listless, she strolled around the block. She failed to soak in the warmth of the summer day, because a cloud of restlessness followed her as she strolled along. Nolan was the one for her, wasn't he? She had meant it every time she had told him she loved him, hadn't she?

What then was holding her back? What was she afraid of?

Lord, I know we're doing the right thing this time, that we're doing what You want. Why can't I go all in even when I see Nolan giving this relationship everything he's got?

She stopped walking, shut her eyes, and drew in a deep, long breath as she lifted her face to the sun.

A tear ran down her cheek when one of the most painful things Nolan had ever said to her haunted her.

"You really are something, Serene. A bit full of yourself, don't you think? What on earth gave you the idea I would ever want you back?"

Serene pictured Nolan with Diana in his arms and found herself barely able to breathe at the heaviness it caused her heart. She walked forward and grasped the arm of a nearby bench to take a seat.

Was she still afraid to love Nolan, to commit herself fully to a relationship with him, because he had been with Diana?

She bowed her head and stared at her fingers.

Hadn't they already resolved this at *Hope's Well*? Serene swallowed hard. Had she not forgiven both Nolan and Diana? The lie that had visited her at the rehab returned. What if she couldn't be enough for Nolan?

Serene gritted her teeth. *Lord, please help me.*

Suddenly, she remembered the vision of the warrior bride — the one she had painted when they were only six years old. Only this time, she was the one in the dress.

Father, heal me. Lead me. I'm overwhelmed right now, and I'm afraid to make myself vulnerable to Nolan. I know he loves me, and I know I love him, but this time, You are the foundation of our relationship. Lead us both to the Rock that is higher than us. Only You can make this relationship work.

She mouthed her amen.

After several deep breaths, a Voice not her own spoke to her heart: *"You don't need to be enough for Nolan. I AM enough for both of you."* The statement took root within her and blossomed into hope that cleared her mind. She didn't need to be enough for Nolan or even for herself. God was more than enough.

An hour later, she was in the lobby of Nolan's building. The doorman recognized her and made a call to Nolan to ask if she could come up. Minutes later, the elevator swung open to reveal a luxury apartment at least three times larger than hers.

Nolan leaned against a brick wall that separated the living room from the elevator door. A curious smirk appeared on his face as he crossed his arms over his chest. "To what do I owe this surprise visit?"

At first, Nolan captured Serene's attention with how dashing he looked in a black v-neck tee and jeans, but something else drew her eye. The wall behind him had a single piece of decoration: one of her paintings. *Cowgirl.*

"I didn't think it was you who purchased that piece."

"How could I resist?" Nolan lifted a brow. "I used to love seeing you wear that red hat. Do you still have it?"

"I do." Serene nodded, her eyes still fixed on the painting. "I thought Ethan had bought it. I guess he bought Magenta."

Nolan turned and stood beside her to look at the painting. "I gave that one to Nova. She had always been a fan of Magenta. Hey, Serene—" he gulped "—since you still have the hat, I actually have half the mind to ask Ramona to have Saturday's party be a cowboy theme or something. Just to see you wear it."

"Unnecessary. Not to mention strange. You don't sing country music. It wouldn't make sense, but I'll wear the hat if you want me to."

"Don't say it unless you mean it." He stood straight. "What's wrong? You look like you're about to cry."

Serene's vision blurred when her eyes moistened. "Nolan, the things you do. You never fail to take my breath away. It means a lot that you support my art enough to buy those two paintings. You paid so much too!"

"They're worth that and more." He nudged her on the shoulder. "I have to admit I didn't hang it here until after you said yes to our first date."

"Understandable."

"Good. What isn't understandable is why you're suddenly here."

"I wanted to see you, because—" she shuffled on her feet and faced him "—I wanted to meet you halfway."

"What do you mean?"

"It's always been you who's doing something for me, for our relationship, and I've just gone with it. When we hung up earlier, something felt off, and I couldn't quite put my finger on it."

Nolan tensed. "And? Serene, you're not breaking up with me, are you?"

"What? No!" Serene laughed. "How is breaking up with you meeting you halfway? That doesn't even make any sense."

He released a breath of relief. "You're being so serious! Also, showing up like this isn't your usual M.O. More like mine."

"Well, yeah, because I never knew what I wanted, and now, I do. I'm not sure I'm ready for all the media attention, Nolan, but it comes with the package if I want to be with you. What I'm saying is I'm all in. I've been holding back, and that's unfair to you. If you think you're ready on Saturday, then I'm with you all the way."

The grin that spread across Nolan's face made it all worth it. "I adore you." He brushed her hair away from her face, tucking strands behind her ear. "You can't imagine how much it means to me to hear you say that." Nolan stepped forward and leaned his forehead against hers.

Serene trembled at his proximity. He ran his palms over her arms and held her hands in his, and then ever-so-slightly, he brushed his lips against hers. She drew a breath.

He held back. "I can't wait, Serene," he said, his voice raspy.

"For what?" Her heart pounded against her chest. He wouldn't repeat the same mistakes of the past, would he? He wouldn't ask of her something she couldn't give, right?

"I can't wait to live the rest of my life with you," he said.

Serene breathed with relief. The truth was, neither could she.

Upon returning to her apartment after going out to dinner with Nolan, her immediate instinct was to pay a visit to a locked chest in her closet. Inside, she kept some of her most valuable belongings, which included a red hat and a velvet box Nolan had once insisted she keep. She wore the hat and checked herself in the mirror. She smiled. The hat would go perfectly with the dress Michiko had designed for the party. Satisfied with her appearance, Serene opened the violet velvet box and held the diamond ring between her fingers. At that very moment, Serene knew one thing for sure: Nolan was the one for her. Without giving it another moment's hesitation, Serene slipped the ring on her finger.

twenty-five

THE ONE WHO (FINALLY) SAID YES

The spotlight had always loved Nolan Stone, and Nolan loved it back, but the night of the party to celebrate the launch of his solo career, the spotlight shone on no one but Serene Sinclair.

At least as far as Nolan was concerned.

The moment she entered his penthouse, she captured his full attention. Serene had stayed true to her word. She wore the red cowboy hat he had given her so long ago with an evening gown — a blood red, vintage, renaissance bodice and skirt. Satin gloves covered her arm all the way above her elbows.

The red hat, the red hair, the red dress.

Serene was the embodiment of the title of his new album: Ablaze.

Knowing she had worn the "costume" for him made his heart race, and so did pretty much everything she did that night.

"Congratulations!" Serene exuded excitement when she arrived. She threw her arms around him and whispered in his ear, "I'm so proud of you. You're so handsome in that suit." She playfully tugged on his sleeve.

Her proximity made his pulse quicken. He stepped back and said, "Let me have a good look at you." The dress flattered her form in just the right ways. "I love it. How did you pull this dress off on such short notice?"

"I had a lot of help from the crew at the incubator. There are definite perks to having a group of talented artists around."

The artists of *Thrive* were right with her, donning their own twists on creative costumes that could pass for any black-tie event.

"You all are definitely dominating the scene." Nolan grinned at them, but his gaze kept flipping back to Serene.

Michiko smiled at him. "I'm sure you can share the spotlight for a few minutes, Mr. Stone."

"I'm never one to hog a spotlight." He gently brushed his fingers against Serene's soft hair. "Hard to do that with this beauty around."

"We can tell. You can barely stop looking at her."

"Nolan, there you are." Ramona approached, linking her arms with his. Upon seeing Serene, a smile lit her face. "That dress is gorgeous, Serene. You have to tell me where you got it after this, but first, are you both ready?" Ramona linked arms with her as well.

Serene's eyes widened. "Ready for what?"

"Nolan told me you're okay with going public with your relationship."

"Uh, yeah, but I assumed we would pose for a few photos, and then just let the press speculate?"

Ramona sighed, grabbed their arms, and pulled them both to the side, away from the rest of the people. "That's one way to do it, Serene, but I've discussed it with Nolan, and I recommend you let the press ask their questions right here and now. If we give them answers, then there's less of a chance you'll have them hounding you when you're out in public, trying to get a statement or a photo. If he had been in a relationship with anyone other than you, then it wouldn't matter, but what happened to Diana is still fresh in the memories of everyone. We need to address that."

Nolan could see the wheels in Serene's brain spinning.

"I wouldn't know what to say, Nolan." She was the picture of a deer caught in the headlights.

How had she gotten through those years being in Red & Ice with him? How had he not noticed how uncomfortable she had been? His heart swelled at the realization of everything she had put up with just to be with him.

"All you have to say is the truth, Serene." Ramona shrugged. "He will do most of the talking, anyway. If they ask you, tell them what happened: Nolan asked you out again. You said yes, because it's hard to say no to that kind of history. What else is there to say? Don't worry about it."

Without thinking it through, Nolan took her hand and squeezed it tight. "We'll get through this together."

And there it was. That smile of hers. The smile that made him feel like a hero so many times before. The smile that made him feel like he could conquer anything.

Serene nodded. "Let's do this."

They showed up to the party, hands clasped together. Immediately, the press took notice. Ramona announced the couple would like to make a few statements and answer a few questions, but after, Nolan and Serene would like to enjoy the rest of the party and would appreciate that the reporters not hound them for the rest of the evening.

Just like old times, Nolan took the lead, and Serene was right there with him, exchanging witty banter and brilliantly answering questions directed at her. Until someone asked a question that gave them both pause.

"It's sweet to see you together again, but let's be realistic. The dynamic isn't the same as it was before. With Miss Sinclair going after her own interests, how will the relationship work with Nolan's schedule getting busier from here on out?"

They exchanged glances. To that, Nolan didn't know what to say. He had tried not to dwell on it, because he had feared how Serene would respond. To his relief, Serene answered the reporter.

"One reason I left *Red & Ice* was because I needed to find myself, to figure out what I wanted. My art played into that, and now, supporting artists through *Thrive*. I didn't think Nolan could ever be a part of my life again, but now that he is, I can only be grateful. We'll be honest when we say we're still figuring things out, but this time around, we have a deeper knowledge of who we are as individuals and as a couple. I support Nolan, and I know he will support me, too."

Nolan couldn't keep the grin from his face. It meant the world to him to hear what she had to say, but something else had to be said. "More importantly," he said as his hand rested on the small of Serene's back, "we are both more rooted in our faith in Christ. It's God Whom we put our trust in to help us make it as a couple. He is more than enough to keep us together."

The way her eyes lit up at what he had said made his heart soar.

Another reporter was about to ask a question, but Ramona butted in to stop the interview.

Nolan took a deep breath.

"Did you really mean everything you said?" she asked when they were able to break away from the reporters and spend a moment to themselves.

"I do. This time, I do. I promise, Serene, should you one day decide to marry me, it is God Who will lead our family."

She smiled. And then she laughed. And then tears began to brim her eyes.

Had he said or done something wrong? "Serene?"

Before he could make sense of why she seemed like she was about to go into hysterics, Serene's hands cupped his face. Her satin gloves felt cool against his skin. Serene leaned forward, and then, ever-so-slightly, she brushed her lips against his. He drew a breath.

Serene held back. "I can't wait, Nolan," she said, her voice raspy.

"For what?" he asked, a smirk forming on his face as he recalled the pleasant surprise of her showing up in his apartment and him doing the exact same thing to her. Only this time, he couldn't stand just a brush on the lips.

"I can't wait—" Serene pulled off the glove from her right hand and placed it on his hands "—to spend the rest of my life with you." She then pulled off the glove from her left hand and lifted her hand for him to see a familiar diamond ring from the proposal she had once rejected.

At the sight of the ring, Nolan took a short intake of breath. He sought her gaze and found her eyes lowered, her cheeks flushed.

"Only if you still want me," she said.

At her words, his past, present, and future seemed to converge into this one moment — this one tiny speck of eternity that had Nolan convinced God had a purpose for everything, and part of Nolan's life purpose was to be the man for Serene Sinclair.

"I don't think I'll ever stop wanting you, Serene," he gasped out. Unable to hold himself back, he cupped her face with his hands and claimed her lips with his. Some of Thrive's artists, as well as other guests, took notice, and cheers and applause exploded across the penthouse.

"Finally!" someone yelled out.

Nolan gathered his self-control and pulled back. He panted for breath and found her doing the same. He leaned forward to whisper in her ear, "I should probably wait until we're married to do more of that." He took a step back, winked at her, and grinned. "I can't wait. Then again, I will, because you're worth waiting for."

Serene laughed, joy flowing from her. He brushed his thumb under her eye to wipe a stray tear away. This time, he felt like he wasn't fighting a losing battle against his own impulses. He would be able to wait. Heart full, Nolan lifted her hat to get a better look at her face. "Thank you for the second chance, Serene."

"Thank God for giving us both more chances than we deserve," she said.

"Amen." He made a face at her. "So, we're engaged now, right?"

"I guess."

"Is it a big secret?"

She shrugged. "I guess not."

"Magnificent." Nolan clapped his hands loudly to get the attention of whoever else wasn't looking at them. "Serene and I have an announcement to make!"

Ramona sighed and drank from her glass of wine. Nolan doubted anything would surprise her when it came to him, so he went on to celebrate the love of his life with some of their closest friends.

"Serene finally said yes!" he exclaimed.

Serene lifted her hand to show everyone the ring.

"You proposed?" someone asked.

"I did." Nolan nodded as he exchanged glances with Serene. "Six years ago at our high school graduation."

As expected, the story was far too interesting to be ignored by the press, so the questions came flying his way. His immediate concern was Serene, but to his relief, she clasped hands with his and stood by him, assuring him that this time, she wasn't going anywhere. They were in this together.

The night they got engaged was a glimpse of the Nolan of their youth. The guy who made her perform at the cafeteria on their first day of high school. The guy who proposed to her on their graduation day. The guy who disrupted her class to sing her a song that would shoot him to fame. Reckless, daring, confident Nolan.

And yet, in so many ways, different than the Nolan she had loved in her youth.

Serene didn't know if it was the change in him or the change in her that gave her the confidence to take the leap toward a lifetime commitment with Nolan, but she had no regrets. Perhaps it was the change in them both. Or maybe it was just God delighting that they had finally discovered they belonged together. In His perfect time.

Whatever it was, that night, Serene reached a place of secure faith that despite whatever obstacles awaited them, they would make it as a couple, and this time, she didn't have to lose herself to be the right woman for Nolan Stone.

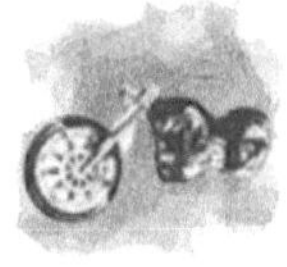

THE END

THE ONE
WHO WROTE
YOU A NOTE

Thank you for reading **The One Who Rocked Away**!

I wrote this story at a time I felt like I had to choose between my writing and what God is calling me to do. I've always believed that God is the Original Artist, the Great Dreamgiver, but He is also the God Who calls us out of our comfort zones, the God Who can swallow kingdoms and kings, nations and oceans. The God Who is good, but not safe. This story turned from a short, fun love story I wanted to write to something more—at least for me.

It will forever be a reminder to me that God deserves wholeheartedness. He is a jealous God. I dare even say He demands all of us. So to the God Who is constant, kind, and just—my relentless Prince of Peace—A.F.T.L.

May His dreams be our dreams.

May you always be blessed! Shalom and Mabuhay!

-JOANNA-

Nolan Stone - main male protagonist
Serene Sinclair - main female protagonist

NOLAN'S FAMILY
Damien Stone - Nolan's father
Clara Stone - Nolan's mother
Nate Stone - Nolan's older brother
Nova Grant - Nolan's older sister
Caleb Grant - Nova's husband; Nolan's brother-in-law
Nate & Claudia Grant - twins; Nova & Caleb's children

SERENE'S FAMILY
Samuel Sinclair - Serene's father; Pastor of Connect Church
Aida Sinclair - Serene's mother; "Mama Aida"
Jeremy Sinclair - Serene's brother

NOLAN'S CIRCLE
Ramona - Nolan's manager
Diana Rake - Nolan's co-star

SERENE'S CIRCLE
Drew Oliver - Serene's manager
Laila - Serene's roommate
Ethan Caine - Serene's suitor; Caleb & Nova's boss
Jon Abraham, Piper Lacey, Michiko, Rick - Thrive artists; respectively: graphic artist, writer, techie & fashion designer, music producer

FRIENDS FROM CONNECT CHURCH
Max Owens - Jeremy's best friend
Rhoda Petersen - Lady from church; doesn't like Nolan
Rachel Petersen - Rhoda's daughter
Jake Harris - Worship leader who taught Nolan to play the guitar
Vic - Worship leader Nolan & Serene taught

OTHERS
Brad Maxwell, Mick Raymond, Claudine Schafer, Trent - Nolan & Serene's school friends

THE ONE
WHO WROTE
THIS BOOK

Joanna Alonzo is an author of Christian fiction novels with grit, grace, and wonder. She has a Bachelor's Degree in Information Technology from St. Louis University, but her creative leanings drew her away from software development to a career in faith and uncertainty. Her homebase is La Trinidad Valley in the Philippines, but she wanders around too much to have a permanent residence. She is a fascinated apprentice to the Greatest Storyteller of all and loves to highlight His supernatural grace in her stories. She loves having coffee chats with people, but isn't a fan of them hugging her too much.

www.ingramcontent.com/pod-product-compliance
Lightning Source LLC
LaVergne TN
LVHW041507170726
843492LV00005B/1396